I0654277

# Lead Us Not into Temptation

## by
## Richard Davidson

*This book is a work of fiction. Any resemblance to actual events or persons, living or dead, is entirely coincidental.*

"Lead Us Not into Temptation," by Richard Davidson. ISBN 978-0-9976381-0-3.

Second Edition June, 2016
Published 2016 by RADMAR Publishing Group, P.O. Box 425, Northbrook, IL 60065, USA. ©2016, Richard Davidson. All rights reserved. No part of this publication may be reproduced, stored in a retrieval system, or transmitted in any form or by any means, electronic, mechanical, recording or otherwise, without the prior written permission of Richard Davidson.

Manufactured in the United States of America.

*This book is dedicated to my wife, Jean, and her identical twin sister, Joan, in recognition of their mysterious ability to simultaneously and independently decide to do the same thing at the same time in two entirely different places. Some mysteries will never be solved.*

# CHAPTER 1
## ARTHUR BLAKE

T he hymn straggled to its raggedy conclusion as Arthur Blake loosened his tie and took his first hesitant step toward the pulpit. He could feel his sweat kicking in. He noted disapproving glances as he lowered his hand from his tie, but he knew that he would be self-conscious preaching with that noose tightened around his neck. He pushed a lock of curly brown hair back from his right eye. They would have to accept him as he was. The droning of the portable fans in the aisles affirmed that he had every right to seek at least a pretense of comfort. The church was only about one quarter full, but people sat in widely scattered locations including filling the very last pew. Many had been conversing in low tones, but all talking ceased as Arthur stepped forward. Every adult eye was on him. The few children in the congregation played and fidgeted as though he wasn't even there. Six older women in the first two pews greeted him with defiant stares.

Arthur had arrived late for his first Sunday as pastor at Parkville United Methodist Church, and he was both nervous and fatigued because of it. He had mistakenly driven first to Villa Park instead of Parkville. Illinois had a habit of naming villages from various combinations of picturesque and natural features, and it was always "Newcomer, beware!" when navigating the Chicago suburbs because of the name similarities. He also had a strong sense of "Beware!" because he was replacing an older minister who had died suddenly two weeks earlier. He   hadn't even had the chance to meet any of the church members prior to this service.

Arthur had looked forward to starting his first full-term appointment as the pastor of the United Methodist Church in Rochelle, Illinois, but once again he would not have a normal assignment. The District Superintendent had given Arthur an emergency change of appointment to replace the deceased pastor in Parkville, and she had told him that he had better improve member unhappiness at Parkville if he wanted a full-term appointment anywhere. Even from a distance he had heard rumors that both the deceased minister and his death were unusual.

Most Methodist pastors serve in a different post every five to seven years. Arthur had been ordained only three years ago. Because of temporary replacement assignments, this was his third church already. His seniority was low because he had entered the ministry as his second career, having first worked fifteen years as a NASA engineer, an occupation that had taken so much of his time that his wife Cindy had left him for a TV weatherman with a more stay-at-home job. Despite the long hours Arthur had devoted to work, he had barely avoided being laid off during two NASA budgetary squeezes and had been terminated when his job was eliminated in a third one. After leaving NASA, he had decided that it would be much more fulfilling to raise his eyes toward heaven instead of toward the stars. Faith had always been a basic part of Arthur's life, and his decision for the ministry had felt right. The ironic part of his new career was that now he would have even more home time than that weatherman.

Arthur was amazed by the stream of thoughts assaulting him during those few steps before his sermon.

*Yea, though I walk through the valley of the shadow of death...*

*...I hope I get to stay here for a while. I think I can help this church grow if they'll accept me...and if the District Superintendent will cut me some slack...*

*...The first Russian Cosmonaut, Yuri Gagarin had looked around in orbit and said, "I don't see any god up here," but Yuri had been just a little bit too literal about that...*

*...Why had the District Superintendent said that old Pastor Middlemiss had been more than a bit strange and that some members had been afraid of him?...*

*...How did he die?*

Arthur finally reached the pulpit with a carefully controlled expression on his face. He gripped the edges of its slanted desktop as he watched people in the pews tense in anticipation of his words. His eyes scanned the high sanctuary space, the organ and choir loft above the rear entrances, and the surrounding balconies on both sides.

"I am pleased to be joining you here in your impressive sanctuary. I appreciate the opportunity to become part of the Parkville Church family, even as I join you in mourning the passing of Pastor Middlemiss. I look forward to learning more about him from you during my service here.

"And now, gracious God, I pray that the words of my mouth and the meditations of all our hearts will be acceptable to you, our Rock and our Redeemer.

"My message today is about stories and their heroes. The history of humanity from the very beginning is God's story. The English language was so right in using the word, 'history,' and I am sure that in its original form it would have been capitalized, for the story of the world is His story, God's story. *A red-haired lady halfway back on the left side of the sanctuary stiffened, and he realized that he had not succeeded in slipping that*

3

*capitalization remark past the English teacher.* From the very beginning, God was there, shepherding our waywardness through all of our past, as He will on into our future. God's story is not just the progress of the world. *We* are God's story, and history is our context. *Arthur saw a white-haired man in a brown suit starting to nod off halfway back on the right side, so he noticeably raised his voice and increased the tempo of his words.*

"As the history of the world is God's story, so also your life is your story. The value of your life increases to the extent that you become the hero of that story. You may say that there is no heroism in you, but I say that if God made man (and hence you) in his image, then you must have what it takes to be a hero. *Brown Suit abruptly woke up to see the preacher's eyes focused directly on him.* If you have bad times, aggravations, and conflicts in your life and you overcome them, then you are a hero. Overcoming conflict is what a hero does.

"If you will at least temporarily grant my argument that you are the hero of your life story, then we should ask whether you see yourself as a hero in your imagination. Heroes tend to take action when circumstances require it, whether they encounter those situations through their own initiative or through unexpected events. *Surprise! The children were now concentrating on him and his words after hearing about heroes and imagination.*

"Jesus had another measure of an exceptional hero. In the Lord's Prayer he said that we should pray, "...lead us not into temptation." This line is in the prayer because Jesus believed that most people cannot resist temptation when they face it. The Bible has many examples of people failing this test, from Adam and Eve, to King David, to Judas. However, Jesus was able to turn his back on the temptations of Satan and of everyday life. We have to learn to be

4

good heroes by following the example of Jesus and resisting temptation. *In several parts of the congregation, people were shifting nervously, and Arthur suspected that they had personal experiences of wrestling with temptation.* I will discuss techniques for resisting temptation in the future. For now, I ask that you spend this week in prayerful contemplation of your situation as hero of your life. In closing let me assure you that I look forward to meeting and sharing with you individually in the weeks to come. With that prospect in mind, let us all say Amen."

Arthur followed the sermon with pastoral prayers. He then announced the offertory collection and sat down. The ushers began their ritual of promenading up and down the aisles as they passed the collection plates from one end of each pew to the other. Arthur noticed how few of the people added to the plates as they passed them along. At the conclusion of the organ music, the ushers marched forward with the proceeds for his blessing and dedication as the people rose and joined in singing the Doxology.

In keeping with his hero theme while trying to appear traditional, Arthur had chosen *Onward, Christian Soldiers* as the closing hymn. He followed that hymn with the final blessing and took his place in the narthex to greet members of his new flock as they left the sanctuary. Most of them appeared to be uncomfortable with his "hero" talk and with their new younger, taller pastor. They approached him uncertainly and failed to make eye contact as they mumbled their way back into the outer world.

# CHAPTER 2
## BISHOP'S OFFICE

D istrict Superintendent Angela King knocked on the office door and was surprised by how tentative her knock sounded. She sensed that the Bishop was not exactly happy with her. Rumors had started to spread that she would be a candidate for Bishop when the next slot opened up due to someone's retirement. She had the qualifications on paper, but friction between her and Bishop Chandler would not help her cause. Bishops were members of an exclusive club and they could assert subtle influence on the process of choosing an Episcopal successor. She opened the door slowly, with a subservient expression on her face.

Bishop Howard Chandler rose from behind his desk and motioned her to one of the two wingback chairs near the decorative but nonfunctional fireplace.

"Good morning, Angela. Thank you for rearranging your schedule to meet with me. I wanted to discuss this business about the death of Middlemiss at the Parkville Church, and what you are doing about it. I see you have installed Blake there. Why did you move him from his planned appointment, and do you think he is the right person for that church?"

"I always had the feeling that Middlemiss had his own agenda. He was a loner and never volunteered his opinions at conferences. I had to drag information out of him, almost through an interrogation procedure. Blake has an engineering

6

background. He'll probably do as good a job as anyone at finding out what Middlemiss was up to at Parkville. Then we can replace Blake with a more qualified pastor for the long run."

"What do you mean by more qualified, Angela? Blake's engineering background gives him a modern outlook, and he's personable enough. Are you bothered that he has only a few years of experience in the ministry?"

"Bishop, he's an engineer, and they look at theology differently. They tend to be too precise and argumentative. We need people who will adhere to traditional approaches without quibbling. Besides, I was married to an engineer once, and I know they are apt to get interested in a career change whenever something interests them more. Blake is my responsibility, and I plan on watching him closely to be sure he doesn't further degrade that church or make trouble for the Conference in some way."

"You know your responsibilities, Angela. I won't interfere. However, allow me to remind you that at the time of Jesus' ministry, one of the closest professions we had to engineering was being a carpenter. You are right that when Jesus changed from being a carpenter to starting his ministry he was not traditional nor accepted by religious authorities; but you wouldn't be here if he hadn't done pretty well."

# CHAPTER 3
## PARKVILLE UMC

Parkville United Methodist Church had a long and unremarkable history. It had its origins 140 years earlier. The name of the village then was Bemis, the same as its founding family. The village trustees renamed it Parkville after World War II, in the hope that it would soon be part of Chicago's expanding suburbs and that newcomers would be attracted by the bucolic sound of the village's name. The first white wooden church building had been constructed upon the foundation and basement of an even older church that had burned and been abandoned some years earlier. The building's triangular lot was located at the X-shaped intersection of Main and Jeffers Streets.

The unusually shaped intersection found itself sandwiched between Swanson Hill, the neighborhood of the few rich people in the village, and Mallard Lake, to which residents turned for fishing and swimming in the summer, and ice-skating in the winter.

The entrance to the original building was at the point of the triangle, convenient for early residents who walked to church from any of the clustered dwellings within the small village. Farmers and others who came from a distance could hitch their horses and rigs to railings in the ample space at the rear of the triangular lot. As time passed, a gravel parking lot took the place of the field with the hitching rails, and much later a small white, purely decorative, steeple adorned the peak of the roof. Not long after the village changed its name from Bemis to Parkville, the Methodist Church congregation had embarked on a fundraising drive in expectation of a population boom as people moved outward from the city of Chicago. The result was a new red brick church building attached to the rear of the original structure and filling most of the available space behind it. Because of the lot's triangular shape, its location on the lower slope of Swanson Hill, and the large size of the new building, there were two parking lots. One lot served the entrance to the upper level and the sanctuary on Main Street, and a second lot served the entrance to the lower level and Sunday school rooms on Jeffers Street. For simplicity, people referred to the two areas as the upper and lower parking lots. Passage from the new building to the old building was possible only on the upper level. The attic and the basement of the old building were completely separate from those of the new building due to architectural considerations. After completing the new structure, the contractors had modified the old church building for its new functions. They converted the old sanctuary to be a multi-purpose room for fund-raising events, meetings, and basketball. They combined the single Sunday school room and the old church office to be the pastor's study and office. This arrangement kept the pastor very distant from the main church office and meeting rooms, an arrangement that pleased most of the subsequent pastors.

The addition of the new building and the reworking of the old building had been examples of excellent planning except for one thing, the migration of Chicago people to Parkville had never happened.

# CHAPTER 4
## PASTOR'S STUDY

T he first time Arthur walked into his combined office and study, he felt that he had entered a garage sale or the debris from an avalanche. The room was big and bright enough, with its two windows on each of the corner walls. The paneling on all of the walls was oak, which kept the place from being too dark. He thought that he saw brown carpeting on the floor through tiny gaps among the many piles of stuff and miscellany that filled the room, touching every wall and reaching depths of two to four feet.

The anarchy of Pastor Middlemiss' study reminded Arthur of the time he had helped investigate a test rocket crash for NASA. In that case, the errant missile had disintegrated upon impact with the side of a thickly wooded mountain. The only hope of determining the cause of the accident had been to find every piece of the vehicle, map its current location and condition, and then reconstruct its original configuration in a large hangar. It had been a jigsaw puzzle effort, required to determine whether they had found all of the parts, the way the missile had fractured, and the cause of the guidance error. He knew that he would have to apply the same principles to taking inventory of this room.

Arthur needed to learn as much as possible about his deceased predecessor. He had to discover what had happened to drive off members and discourage those who remained. He wanted to identify church leaders and learn how to improve their procedures for working together. His first job would be to determine the relative values of the many books, documents, and objects that filled the room. His engineering background prodded him toward being very careful to avoid discarding something important.

Arthur had decided to tackle this mess as his first major project. He started the cleanup after an early supper on his first Monday, his normal day off. He felt that he had to grasp the existing structure of relationships in this church before ongoing matters and congregational crises kept him from setting his own agenda and schedule. He also knew that he would have trouble concentrating on anything new and major while he sat in the midst of chaos and disorder. He had always been unable to do his best work while loose ends of old projects pulled his thoughts in multiple directions.

To be fair to the late pastor, part of the mess in the study resulted from Middlemiss having lived in a small rental apartment in the basement of a house on the other side of the lower parking lot. The old pastor had set up this living arrangement because he lived alone and did not need nor want to dwell in the large, two-story white parsonage four blocks down Jeffers. His choice of living quarters had been a windfall for the church, allowing it to gain substantial income by renting out the vacant parsonage. Following the memorial service for Pastor Middlemiss, the trustees had moved all of the former pastor's personal belongings from his apartment to his study at the church. They had put his furniture into an unused room on the Sunday school level to await the next rummage sale. Now Arthur Blake faced two problems. He had to analyze the bloated and haphazard contents of the study; he also had to negotiate his way into the parsonage. Those living quarters had been included in his contract, despite the existence of current temporary tenants. Until the end of the month, Arthur would live in a small office at the rear of the church's Sunday school level. Then he would be able to move to the parsonage, assuming the tenants departed as scheduled.

Arthur rolled back his sleeves with double cuffs and cleared a small space in the far left corner of the study by adding the stuff there to the adjacent pile. He figured that the logical approach to sorting the overall mess would be to proceed in the manner of solving a magic square puzzle, moving items he had checked from their original location into the small open space. This would empty their original space so that he could transfer items from another area into it. If he worked his way back and forth in strips of small areas, he would know where to resume the task after any break by locating the single empty space.

He decided to start with the books in each pile because they would be the easiest things to examine and put away. There were shelves on one wall of the study filled with stacks of papers and old church mail, most of it unopened. He decided that he would exchange books for batches of papers on the shelves so that the books would end up neatly shelved. He would defer the papers for later study.

As he sorted through the first bunch of books, Arthur realized that Pastor Middlemiss had not been a reader of fiction. He looked at fifteen books and saw that they were all nonfiction and usually serious in nature. There were books on interpretation of the Bible, a few on the subject of counseling people with problems or a death in the family, and some on the history and geography of the United States and Britain. There were also several books on the history of World War II. Arthur wanted to learn more about the WWII period, so he set those books aside for future examination.

After he sorted through the books in his first section of the floor, Arthur gathered the papers in that section into a neat stack and scanned through them, flipping them with his thumb. Most of them appeared to be drafts of sermons, but he also saw meeting notes, receipts, mail, sales brochures, museum catalogs, and lists of things to do. He could tell that these papers would take a long time to review, so he separated out the mail and brochures as most likely to be unimportant and then set the remainder aside for future study. Removal of the books and papers from the first examination area left a small pile of miscellaneous items. There were odd pieces of hardware, a pair of slippers, eyeglasses with one lens missing, a single bookend, ninety-seven cents in change, a cross on a chain, and several unlabeled keys, two of which looked very old. Being a good engineer, Arthur gathered the miscellaneous bits of hardware into a small junk box. He had always found such collections to have at least one valuable item. He put the other items into a carton that had contained only a water glass. Then he moved on to the second section of floor and repeated his sorting and scanning procedure.

The second pile of objects was similar to the first, except for its inclusion of several items of clothing. He uncovered an old spy-style raincoat, a red scarf, three brown sweaters, and a red-and-yellow striped necktie. Arthur sorted the books and papers as he had with the first pile, put the clothing into a laundry bag that he had spotted across the room, and reviewed the miscellaneous items. These included a long steel bar with a pair of wheels attached to it at one end. He set the steel bar aside, put the hardware into his junk box, added the small miscellaneous items to the carton he had started for them, and moved on to the next pile on the third section of floor.

Arthur worked his way around the room, floor section by floor section, pile by pile, until he had covered the entire study. This took him about five hours. It was getting to be a lot later than he had intended. He realized that it would take several more sessions in the future to complete his examination of the room's contents. When he had finished what he could handle for one evening, he sorted through the boxes of miscellaneous items and set aside those that were the most interesting. The resulting *treasure box* contained a pair of binoculars, an old camera with a half-finished roll of film, a wedding ring, two old keys, a family picture of a young man with his pregnant wife, and a prosthetic left leg. He had definitely found something unexpected in the latter item. Arthur hoped that his review of the papers would reveal the story behind the artificial leg, but he realized that he had a huge mass of papers to examine. Even after perusing them, would he know anything significant about the old pastor? At least he had made a start, and he had about half of the study emptied enough for him to use it.

# CHAPTER 5
## ATTIC

O ne state west of Parkville someone else was sorting through old papers and miscellaneous objects, this time in the attic of an old two-story house. Bob Caspar, a forty-nine year old woodworker, was helping his Aunt Bertha decide what furniture and belongings she would want to keep when she moved in with him and his wife. Bertha was getting to be a bit unsteady due to her recent minor stroke, and Bob wanted her to settle in with him and Paula so that Bertha would have family nearby and aware of her activities. Bob and Paula lived in a big old farmhouse, and there was plenty of space available, especially with both Kevin and Michelle off at the University of Wisconsin at Platteville. Bertha preferred to live in Iowa City, the former state capital and current college town, but Bob had argued that she would still have adequate access to Iowa City from his home in Monticello, Iowa, only forty-eight miles away. Bertha hadn't liked the idea of moving and imposing on them, but he had finally convinced her. Now they were looking into every nook and cranny of the attic for treasured items that would accompany her.

Aunt Bertha had done her best to keep her attic clean, but every day that she remained downstairs had been another day for the spiders to spin webs and the field mice to nibble on old books and Christmas decorations. The slanted roof above the attic was high enough for Bertha and Bob to stand in most places. That made the search easier, but sorting through the older items required sweeping mouse droppings and spider webs out of the way.

"Aunt Bertha, here are three old cartons that look as though they date back to World War II. I had to blow off a thick layer of dust before opening them. They contain some old Army insignias plus papers and pictures and even a few German items." Bertha bristled at the dust remark, but responded calmly, "They must be some of Dad's souvenirs and other things he brought back from the war. He had a whole bunch of wartime cartons. I thought Mother had sorted through them and had discarded almost everything a long time ago. I was just ten years old when he came back from the war, and I was so happy to see him that I never got into looking through his souvenirs. I spent many hours talking with him about his experiences, but I wasn't interested in the attic cartons. They held boy stuff, and I was his one and only sweet little girl. I was four and a half years old when he left for Europe, so he was away for most of my growing-up years."

"Was your dad in a lot of the fighting? What part of the Army was he in?"

Aunt Bertha laughed. "He was about as far from the fighting as he could get. Dad was based in some small English town, and he was a Captain in the Quartermaster Corps. He referred to himself as the grocer for the troops. He was even able to get favors and special things from the local folks because he could trade supplies like cigarettes and nylon stockings for them."

Bob's face showed surprise. "You mean he was a wheeler-dealer and hustler?"

"Dad was only one of many people who traded things for favors. Bartering wasn't official policy, but most high-level officers knew that they had to use it to get cooperation. The British often resented

American soldiers. They knew they needed our help, but sometimes the Americans behaved as though they were superior. The common British expression was that American soldiers were *overpaid, oversexed, and over here.* The Americans had much better supplies, and they frequently forgot that they were guests in someone else's country. When that happened, it took a generous supply of scarce items to straighten out tense situations. Officers suggested that a U.S. soldier who was invited to dinner by a family should bring along some extra provisions as gifts because his hosts were probably using up all of their rations to entertain him."

"Was this Great-Uncle William's main job in the army?"

"Heavens, no, Bob. His primary duty was to work out the logistics so that every encampment had enough food and the correct menu items on a scheduled ongoing basis. They didn't have computers then, so they had to work out the distribution details using adding machines and slide rules. There were hundreds of large and small U.S. bases all across Great Britain. Dad told me that during the buildup in 1944, there were about seven hundred and fifty thousand American military troops there at the beginning of the year and more than one and a half million just before the D-Day invasion. How would you like to tackle the job of making sure that they all had enough food and that the food was in the right place at the right time? Obviously, Dad didn't do it alone; there were many food planners all working together, but it was a huge job. It was even more difficult because the military wanted to keep the Germans from realizing just how big the buildup was. Dad said that it had been an amazing challenge and that his team was both very proud and worn out after

D-Day. Their job had been so immense that Dad and many of his people had to remain in England for two years after the end of the war in order to dispose of unused supplies and return bases to the British in good condition."

"OK, Aunt Bertha, I didn't mean to minimize the importance of your father's work. It's obvious that you're proud of his achievements, and I'm impressed by them too. Let's get back to looking at the items in these boxes."

Bob started to spread out some of the items he had found in the boxes. "Most of the papers are very brittle after all of this time, so we have to handle them carefully. Let's leave the papers for study later in neater, brighter surroundings. For now let's look at the photographs and the miscellaneous odds and ends."

He put insignias and uniform items in the right-hand pile, medals and unusual items in the center pile, and photographs in the left-hand pile. Bob placed the stacks of papers into empty carton number one. Although each of the three cartons had contained an assortment of items, he thought it would be more efficient to put only one type into each carton for further examination later. He had extra empty cartons, so his sorting would work out no matter how many categories they chose to use. Bob was in the middle of sorting and separating the various items when he heard a gasp from Aunt Bertha.

"Oh, my!"

"What is it, Aunt Bertha? Did you cut yourself on something?"

"No, Bob, it's worse than that. I found some very disturbing photographs. There are at least a dozen photos here of Dad with his arm around a blonde woman who is holding a child. Here's one where the child is an infant. Here's another where it is   older, and I have one where the child is beginning to walk. From that one I can see that the child is a boy. It looks as though Dad was paying attention to other things besides his work during all of that time he spent in England."

"Do you mean that you think the child is his?"

The look of shock faded from Bertha's face. "Well, Bob, I have to at least consider that possibility. Dad was over there longer than most, staying two years after the war's end. He was in a position where he had access to all of the supplies that a family might need, and he didn't have to travel to do his work. Those circumstances would certainly make it easy for him to have a second family."

"Aunt Bertha, when you say family, are you suggesting that he might have married that woman, even though he was already married to your mother?"

"Don't get me wrong, Bob. I loved my father very much, but he was a little different after the war. Everyone who came back had changed to some extent. We all assumed it was due to wartime stress and didn't speak about it. He talked with us about his wartime duties, but he didn't open up about his feelings. Sometimes we would say things during casual conversations that would make him upset and uncommunicative. Given everything that was going on over there, it's conceivable that he married her and that the boy was their son. Stranger things than that happened during the war. Don't forget, Dad knew how to work both the British and American supply systems to get whatever he needed to the right place at the right time. Everyone depended on him and his outfit, and they trusted him. In the hectic times prior to D-Day, he might very well have given people the impression that he was single. Lots of GI's took off their wedding rings when they had a chance for a date, and lots of lonely wives and girlfriends back home would occasionally cheat on their warriors. It was kept quiet because in those days nobody wanted a hint of impropriety, but it happened more frequently than most people will admit."

"OK, Aunt Bertha, people strayed a bit in wartime, but what makes you think your father might have actually married this girl?"

"Well, this picture of the two of them kissing in the center of a crowd in front of a church might have something to do with my suspicion."

Bob stared at the picture in disbelief. There was no doubt that it looked like a wedding picture.

The door opened and Bob's wife joined them with a tray of iced tea. He turned to her to gain time before responding to Bertha.

"Paula, we've just found some photos that suggest that Great-Uncle William married an English woman during the war and had a son with her."

"Bob, he couldn't have done that. He was already married."

Bertha took a glass from Paula's tray and turned to her.

"It is hard to believe, but Dad did some strange things after the war. Mother got very upset with him. They argued at different times. When I was eleven, they had a real shouting match. Mother said that she wouldn't have married him if she had known that he made up his own rules for behavior and business. He said that circumstances determine behavior and that there are no rules for all situations. When I heard them shouting like that, I was sure that they were going to get divorced and abandon me. I was scared. I also learned from that argument that Dad had wanted me to be a boy instead of a girl. I guess I was originally   supposed to have been Albert, and they changed it to Bertha when they saw I was female. It took a week after that argument before they started to talk to each other again. During that period, I hid in my room and tried to stay out of sight. I felt that I must have been a disappointment to Dad all my life."

Bob rose and began to pace back and forth in the attic, dodging cobwebs when he went beyond the main open area. Paula wiped her hands on her jeans and asked, "Your mother talked about your father's rules for business. Did he do anything unusual here in Iowa City? What happened? Did your parents continue to fight?"

"Bob, Paula, this is not for publication or even for discussion within the family. We moved here from Indianapolis after the war. Dad started and built up a successful insurance agency, and for a while family friction disappeared because he was away at work most of the time. The agency grew steadily until it collapsed under scandalous circumstances in 1974. The police arrested one of Dad's employees, Jennifer Borowski. They accused her of laundering money for a drug ring. She supposedly did it by writing phony insurance policies for the ring members, pocketing the premiums, and then paying off frequent claims with money that she had received from the policyholders. They gave her large amounts of money received from drug sales, and she disguised it as insurance claim benefits and gave it right back to them. The drug dealers would have had difficulty coming up with a legitimate explanation for all of their cash, but when they could show that they had received large insurance pay-offs, nobody questioned it.

"After Jennifer was arrested, there were questions about whether Dad and his agency were involved, but it all died down after Jennifer committed suicide while she was out on bail. Business at the agency deteriorated after that, and Dad stopped giving the business his full attention. Jennifer's arrest and suicide bothered him and made him tense all the time. His health went downhill, and he died about a year later in 1975. Nobody proved that he had done anything illegal, but I still have a tiny cloud of doubt in the back of my mind."

Bob still felt confused. "So that's why you can consider it possible that your dad had a bigamous marriage? Lots of people with good personal morality get involved in dubious business situations."

"If I had known about a second marriage when Dad came home, I wouldn't have believed it. If Mother had known, it would have killed her. Only the fact that it happened so long ago lets me consider the possibility now. Dad and Mother are both dead, and I have been living alone since your Uncle Tom died in a car accident in 1977. If that other marriage really happened, I may have a half-brother somewhere in the world. Dad may have fathered his preferred boy after all. I've never had a sister or brother. If he exists, it would make me feel less alone. How would you feel, Bob?"

"I'd be worried about what kind of person that half-brother turned out to be. I'm already bothered about having to tell my kids that they have a very strange family tree."

Paula looked thoughtful and said, "You know, when I was a child I had recurring dreams about having a long-lost twin sister. This is almost the same thing, Aunt Bertha. You may have a long-lost brother."

Bertha looked at one of the pictures again. "He would be six or seven years younger than me. I wonder if we could ever track him down."

Bob returned his empty glass to the tray. "I think the probability of finding him would be less than comparing the one drop left in that glass to the amount of tea in a full pitcher."

Paula turned to Bob. "It may not be absolutely inconceivable. We may know some people who could help us try to find him. What about Penny and Joe Gonzalez?"

"They do have the right background and connections. Joe and I were in the Army together during the Gulf War. He and his wife work for the government now. I'll call them in the morning to see if they would be willing to try. Even if they are, you shouldn't get your hopes too high. Finding what happened to that child will be virtually impossible."

# CHAPTER 6
## CHURCH COUNCIL

They sat around a conference table that had definitely seen better days. Even though there were *NO SMOKING* signs throughout the church, Arthur could count six cigarette burn marks on the edges of the table without rising from his chair. Long straight scratches suggested that from time to time, something had been cut on the table, and he could even see some carved graffiti like *SJ LOVES KL*. The table was a little too big for the room, causing the meeting participants to sit close to the table to allow enough space for someone to squeeze behind them. The others who sat with Arthur were taking things very seriously, and he knew that they had spent a week preparing for this first Council meeting with their new pastor.

The Council Chairperson, Ed Jensen, a tall lanky man with sparse gray hair and a thin mustache, called the meeting to order with two left-handed knocks of his gavel. "I want to welcome you all, and especially Pastor Blake. Pastor, would you like to get the meeting started by giving the Council your overall impressions of our church or your plans for the future?"

Arthur responded with a serious look on his face, to acknowledge that this was an important gathering, "Ed, why don't you just conduct business as usual, and leave the Pastor's comments for the end of the meeting if the schedule allows." He took this approach because he had learned that it tended to make meetings shorter. Long meetings were one of Arthur's least favorite things. He continued, "I would appreciate each speaker giving me a brief personal introduction. I would also like to open the meeting with a prayer, and I would like to make it standard practice that all church meetings start with an opening prayer." He could tell from their expressions that such prayers had not been typical in the past.

Bowing his head, Arthur requested a moment of silence in memory of Pastor Middlemiss. Then he continued, "Lord, bless our words and our deliberations, that we may welcome your Holy Spirit into our midst during this meeting and at all times. Teach us to be good and faithful servants in all that we do. We ask these things in Jesus' name. Amen"

Everyone echoed the "Amen." Then Ed Jensen introduced himself, "I'm a recently retired pharmacist. I sold my drugstore, Parkville Apothecary, so that I would have the time to take my wife, Martha, traveling during our senior years. In fact, we've just returned from a driving trip to the Grand Canyon. It felt great. We even took a tour down into the bottom of the Canyon, just to prove that we aren't too old for it. Druggists hardly ever get a block of time off because people get sick at inconvenient times, and we have to be there to serve them.

"Getting on to Council business, this church has a perennial problem. We have too large a facility and too few members. The membership problem got a lot worse during the last year as more people became unhappy with Pastor Middlemiss and his standoffishness. Because of this, we cut corners on maintenance and new equipment in order to be able to pay utilities and salaries. Every budget is difficult to balance. Pastor Blake, I suggest that you listen to all of the committee reports with these background problems in mind."

Sue Willoughby took the floor as chair of the Finance Committee. Her stylish yellow business suit and her tightly set dark hair were overly formal for a Council meeting. She carried herself as though she was addressing a very important corporate board, but she was a little nervous right now. Sue had been divorced for six years, and at the age of forty-eight, she wanted to make a good impression on the new unmarried pastor. Her problem was that she knew her opening statement wouldn't win any points with him. "I want to point out that Parkville UMC has been having extra income because we rented out the parsonage while Pastor Middlemiss lived in his small apartment. We will soon be losing this income when Pastor Blake moves into the parsonage after the current tenants leave. The budget is tight now, and we don't have any alternate revenue sources to replace the money we now receive from the parsonage rent." Her look implied that she thought that Blake had no need for the parsonage since he had no family, and that his insistence on his contractual benefit was a frontal assault on her budget. By way of introduction Sue added, "I work as an administrative aide at the Illinois Bureau of Tourism. My goal is to use that position to help attract more people to live in Parkville."

Education chairperson and Sunday school superintendent, Stephanie Lim, was the next to report to the council. At age twenty-nine, she was the youngest participant. She had her hair in a long blond ponytail that made her look even younger. She had been born Stephanie Cappisch and had married Alan Lim three years earlier. "It would be easier to run a proper Sunday school if I had more than two volunteer teachers working with me. I understand that I can't expect to have a fully staffed school with only twenty-five children    in classes, but their age range is five to seventeen, and it is difficult to provide enough different levels of teaching. I want to request another volunteer to assist me. If we do get more children, I will want to add more classes.

"Pastor Blake, I teach second grade at U. S. Grant Elementary School. Over there I have large classes and enough budget for occasional field trips. I think that the children learn a tremendous amount from trips, and I would like to have some here as soon as the budget allows it."

Gloria Martinez, the chairperson of the Staff/Parish Committee stood to get attention and to compensate for her small stature. She indicated in a soft slightly accented voice, "I am the Vice President for Commercial Loans at Lakeview Bank. On an ongoing basis, I coordinate with Sue Willoughby and Sue's boss, Sarah Sanders, at the Illinois Bureau of Tourism. We try to attract new businesses to Parkville. We have not yet succeeded, but Sarah has some promising new programs in development. Pastor, I am glad that you are here with us. We have yet to complete the usual forms and procedures, but I will schedule a meeting with you to tie up any loose ends. I look forward to coordinating staff matters with you. We will definitely benefit from your younger viewpoint and your interesting past experiences. Pastor Middlemiss would only try to attract new members by having additional Bible Study classes. We have to do more than that to attract the younger generation. Many younger people were turned off by those classes and by his pedantic teaching style."

Bill Martin, tall and redheaded, was the next speaker as chair of the Trustees Committee. "I'm an independent carpenter. I've always felt attracted to carpentry because it puts me in the same trade group as Jesus. I also think that they nominated me to head the Trustees Committee because people hoped that I would give the church free carpentry work. I suggest that Pastor Middlemiss might not have had his fatal accident if the Church Council had approved my suggestion of installing a connecting door from the upper level of the new building to the old church's attic instead of requiring a very tall ladder for attic access."

Ed Jensen responded after Bill Martin finished his introductory comments. "Bill, you know that we were sympathetic to your suggestion of that connecting door. The problem was that it would be quite expensive and we would have to get a waiver of the building code to make the change. The village has given our old building historic landmark status, and we can't make any modifications to it without going through a special approval procedure. Besides, Pastor Middlemiss said that he thought it was a waste of church money. I promise to put it on the agenda of our next meeting so that we can discuss it in detail. Is that OK with you?"

Bill nodded and gave a thumbs-up sign.

Ed continued, "Pastor Blake, there are two additional committee chairpersons who were unable to make this meeting. Anna Santini heads the Worship Committee. I'm sure that she will be approaching you with suggestions for improving the services. She comes from a Catholic background, and she would like to see more liturgical elements in our worship. She would even like to replace the grape juice with wine in the communion service. Wally Sanborn heads up our Missions Committee. He's a retired career army officer and a former Peace Corps volunteer. He'll have more than a few suggestions about mission trips for you. I'm sure that we can arrange for you to meet informally with both of them so that we'll have all of the introductions behind us before the next meeting.

"I have deliberately limited discussion topics for this meeting because of the importance of devoting time to introductions and setting up formats for working together. I suggest that with Pastor Blake here, we try to have a formal agenda instead of just discussing things that come to mind while we are sitting in the meeting. Please give me a written note with your agenda requests at least three days before each scheduled meeting. Now let's give Pastor Blake a chance to speak."

Arthur looked down at the notes he had taken and then began his response, "First of all, I want to indicate that I feel that this Council appears to be made up of members who are all sincere about their jobs and who are dedicated to improving this church in every way possible. You have run the meeting well, and I appreciate the fact that you all value your time and mine so that we can look forward to well-planned and purposeful meetings in the future. I noticed that you have tended to address me using my title, and I feel that this is not necessary within our church family, so I would appreciate your simply calling me Arthur when we're not in formal situations.

"I had not been aware that Pastor Middlemiss had died due to an accidental fall from a ladder. I had been told that he had died suddenly, but I haven't heard anything about the details or circumstances. Undoubtedly, the abruptness of his demise must have made his passing even more shocking to you. I don't want to take up additional group time, but I'd like to speak with you, Ed, following the meeting to learn the details of his death and the subsequent events." Ed Jensen nodded, and Arthur continued.

"You all have expressed or implied a proper concern for the fact that Parkville UMC has a larger-than-necessary building and a smaller-than-desirable membership. I completely appreciate your feelings, but having recently come from a church with small and extremely limited facilities, I want you to realize how fortunate you are to have this fine building. I have several ideas for using the building as an asset that will help us to generate income and also possibly attract new members. I also feel that if we are good and faithful servants we will soon find ourselves fully using the building.

"You have all been helpful by combining your presentations with your personal introductions. I will attempt to do the same. I'm originally from Richmond, Illinois, where my father, Peter Blake, still lives and operates an antiques shop. My mother, Janice, is a retired art history teacher. Their love of events and things from the past brought my parents together. I have relatives in various places across northern and central Illinois, so I am definitely a product of this area.

"With regard to using the building to raise money for the church, let me tell you that when I was a teenager, I would accompany my dad on trips to long-established villages like this one. We would go to garage and yard sales looking for older items that had been in the family for a long time. My dad re-supplied his antiques shop on those trips. Many people in older villages have no feeling for the value of their household items. I'll bet that members of our church and the village as a whole have more than enough interesting items for an Antiques Fair fundraiser, and our building has plenty of room for it. I might even be able to get my dad to appraise the items for pricing purposes."

Sue Willoughby smiled for the first time since the meeting had started. Now she had something positive to say to the new pastor. "I could get the Illinois Bureau of Tourism to put the Antiques Fair on its schedule. That would attract people from other parts of Illinois and even from other states."

Gloria Martinez added, "I could get Parkville National Bank to sponsor the judging of different classes of antiques. That might attract collectors. If an Antiques Fair were to work and become an annual event, it would make Parkville more of a tourist destination. I think you have a good idea, Arthur." Gloria thought that Arthur wasn't as boring as most ministers she had known, and he was a lot better looking than some with his blue eyes and dimples.

Discussions of the Antiques Fair possibility continued around the table until Ed Jensen called for order. He said that he would add the Fair to the agenda for the next meeting, and he adjourned the Church Council until then.

After everyone else had left the room, Arthur approached Ed.

"Give me more of the details concerning the death of Pastor Middlemiss. Who found the body, and how much time passed before they found him?" Ed thought about it for a few seconds and then said, "I think it was Shirley Hadley, the church secretary, who found his body. Middlemiss had left a message that she found when she first came in, telling her that he would be away from his phone for the whole morning, so she was bringing him his messages just before noon. The old pastor was not into computers and answering machines, so Shirley put everything down on paper for him. At first, she didn't care for the extra work, but she used a duplicating book of message forms so that she could have a record of it all, and she liked the improved organization of that approach. Pastor Middlemiss would look at his messages and then throw them on a big pile of papers or just discard them. You couldn't count on him for record-keeping."

Arthur murmured, "I know about that after trying to sort out his office paperwork."

Ed Jensen continued, "Shirley found him in the middle of the multi-purpose room which was the old sanctuary. He was lying at the bottom of a twenty-four-foot ladder that was poked into the recess below the attic hatchway. The hatch was closed when they found him. It appeared that he had been climbing up to the attic when he lost his balance and fell. Shirley called 911 from the pastor's office phone, and the paramedics and police arrived quickly after that. The Medical Examiner said that she thought that Middlemiss must have been dead for about twelve hours before Shirley found him."

"That means that he would have had to leave the message for Shirley sometime during the previous evening. You said they thought that he fell while going up to the attic. There wouldn't be any way to know whether he was on his way up, or on his way down after being up there and closing the hatch behind him. Did anyone go up to the attic to see whether he might have been doing anything unusual up there?"

"Arthur, I don't see that it makes much difference which way he was going on the ladder when he fell off. We assumed that he was on his way up because there was nothing on the floor near him that he might have been bringing down from the attic. The authorities didn't see any need to enter the attic and take a chance on someone else falling off of the ladder."

"Ed, what is kept in that attic anyway?"

"I really don't know. Frankly, I had forgotten all about the old attic until Bill Martin came up with the idea of opening up a passageway to it from   the new building. I assume that it contains old items from the original church plus some church records from past years. We've had no need to use it at all because the new building has so much storage space that is easier to access. That's why I've been only lukewarm to Bill's connecting door idea. Almost all of the church activities take place in the new building. The old church building has become the private realm of the pastors except for those few times when the multi-purpose room is used."

Arthur digested this information thoughtfully. After a long pause, he turned to Ed and asked, "Is the door of the old church ever unlocked?"

"No, Arthur, it requires a key to open it from the outside, but it has been upgraded with panic hardware on the inside so that people can escape if there is a fire. Just in case you were going to ask about the key, it has been lost. Nobody has seen the key for at least four years."

Arthur nodded and walked toward the exit to the upper parking lot with Ed. He wanted to talk to Shirley before he dropped the matter of the accident from his mind. He turned to enter the church office while Ed continued to the front door carrying his folder of Council meeting notes. Arthur left a note for Shirley saying he would be in at 8:30 the next morning to talk with her.

# CHAPTER 7
## SHIRLEY HADLEY

S hirley looked up from her computer as he entered, "Good morning, Pastor. I found  your note, and I've cleared my desk for action. Is there something new to discuss?"

Arthur laughed. "I didn't mean to make this sound like a personnel review or a major project. I'm just guilty of rushing from one thing to another without taking enough time to sit and talk and get to know the other staff people."

"Well, Pastor, you picked the right day because Walter had a bunch of day-olds at the bakery, and he brought home enough for me to set up  this whole tray. Help yourself."

Arthur scanned the pastry array and inhaled the mixture of bakery scents. He selected a cinnamon bun and enjoyed a hearty first bite. He helped himself to coffee from the pot on the corner shelf and sat down with a relaxed posture. There were definite advantages to having a secretary whose husband owned a bakery.

Shirley was a medium height brunette who tended to wear flowery blouses and dark slacks. Her personnel file said she was forty-three years old, but she told everyone that she was thirty-nine. She was efficient at organizing her work and excellent at office computer tasks. He was learning that she was also adept at keeping him informed about most of the activities and nearly all the problems of members of the congregation. He knew that she would be a great help in pinpointing  those who would need visits from him for prayers and counseling.

Arthur leaned forward in his chair and began in a confiding manner. "Shirley, I wanted to thank you for keeping me up-to-date on the needs of church members. I also appreciate your running interference for me to minimize interruptions while I am working on sermons and planning efforts. Most pastors won't admit that a good secretary runs the church while we get most of the credit for it. We also know to turn to the secretary to find out what is really happening around us while we tend to our own duties. As I've already told the Council members, please call me Arthur instead of Pastor in informal situations.

"How is your son Jeremy doing lately? I heard that he had some difficulties."

Shirley was just getting to know Arthur so she didn't know how much she should discuss, but he was her pastor. "Jeremy's a great kid, but sometimes he hangs around with questionable  types, and three months ago it got him into trouble. The police brought him home from a party where he was involved in underage drinking. A neighbor had called in a complaint because of rowdiness and cars parked on his lawn. Jeremy arrived home drunk and more than a little sick. After we had a long discussion the next morning, Jeremy agreed to keep away from that crowd. Since then he tried out for the high school basketball team and made it. Hopefully, basketball will fill enough of his spare time to keep him out of trouble."

"Basketball is a good tool for straightening him out, Shirley. If he wants to practice when the school gym isn't open, he can use the multi-purpose room in the old church building. It's set up for basketball, but I understand that it hasn't been used for that in a long time."

"The church kids liked to use it, but Pastor Middlemiss was disturbed by the dribbling and shouting near his study, so he vetoed that use of the room."

"Well, tell Jeremy and the others that basketball in that room is fine with me. My only special rule is that they may have to play with me if I'm available.

"I've just learned how Pastor Middlemiss died, and that you were the one who found his body. That must have been a terrible moment for you."

"It was a shock, Arthur. I don't like going to the old church building when there's nobody else around because it is so quiet and lonely over there. On a dark, cloudy, or rainy day, it's absolutely creepy being there all alone. To be a little tense about that and then to see someone lying on the floor next to a tall ladder was almost more than I could take. I'll never forget his face; it scared me. I never saw him look as angry in life as he did in death."

"Did he look as though his arms or legs were broken? Was there a lot of blood?"

"That was the part that seemed strange to me. The only wound I saw was on his forehead, and there wasn't much bleeding from that. The Medical Examiner decided that Pastor Middlemiss must have fallen from the ladder and twisted around before he hit the floor so that the front of his head hit first. He was on his side facing the entrance to the new building when I found him."

"One other question, and then we can go on to more comfortable subjects. Where was the ladder normally kept?"

"That's a good question, Arthur. I've been working for Parkville UMC for fifteen years, and I know more than most people about this church. To the best of my knowledge, the church doesn't own an extension ladder like that. It would have had to be brought in from somewhere else."

# CHAPTER 8
## ONE ON ONE

A rthur felt just a little outclassed as he dribbled the ball toward Jeremy. He also realized that his old basketball shorts were unexpectedly tight. The multi-purpose room had a pretty solid floor, and the ball returned to his hand with a true and lively bounce. Jeremy was taller than he was and in better shape, so he would have to try to fake him into moving the wrong way in order to score. Jeremy was leading nineteen to thirteen in a game of twenty-one. Arthur knew that he didn't have much of a chance, but he dribbled once and stepped hard right, halted, and scored with an easy jump shot over the space Jeremy had vacated when he moved to counter Arthur's first stride.

"Good shot, Pastor, but that kind of move is good only once per game. Now it's my turn." Jeremy took the ball out to mid-court, turned, and dribbled toward the right of the backboard, using his height to thwart Arthur's defense with a fade-away hook over Arthur's outstretched hands. The ball ricocheted from the backboard into the hoop. "That's twenty-one and game. Final score is twenty-one to fifteen. Do you want to try again, Pastor?"

"Sure, but not today. I need more solo practice before I take you on again. I'll let you know when I think I'm ready.

"Jeremy, while I have you here I'd like to tap your memory. How did the youth and the younger children react to Pastor Middlemiss?"

"The older youth took him in stride, the way they would respond to a strict teacher in school.

The kids were almost afraid of him and didn't want to be alone with him without parents present. Most of the time it wasn't a problem because Pastor Middlemiss didn't want to be alone with the kids either. For the most part he only talked with my mom or the people on the Church Council."

"Thanks for that information, Jeremy. It helps me form a mental picture of church life before I arrived." They shook hands, and Jeremy left the room. Arthur removed his sweaty NASA tee shirt, wiped his face, back, and chest with a towel, and then headed back toward his office with the towel and shirt draped over his shoulder. He was glad that there was a small bathroom next to his office so that he could wash up. As he left the multipurpose room, he almost bumped into Sue Willoughby who brightened at the sight of Arthur in shorts.

"I brought you the latest budget report. If you would like, I could sit down with you and explain the various entries in the tables."

"That's generous of you, Sue, but I'd rather look it over myself. I'll get back to you if I have questions that won't wait for the next meeting."

"OK, Arthur. By the way, I jog around Mallard Lake on Saturday mornings. You're welcome to join me if you'd like. I see that you like to keep yourself physically fit."

"Thanks for the invitation, Sue, but I'm usually running way behind schedule. Saturday mornings find me struggling to finish my sermon preparation. If I do find a convenient gap in my Saturday schedule, I'll let you know."

Sue turned and walked back toward the new church building, disappointed and unsure whether she had made any progress toward her fantasy goal. At least she knew that she had overestimated the amount of hair on his chest and back.

# CHAPTER 9
## BILL MARTIN

"**B**ill, this is Arthur Blake calling. Would you have some time available to come over to the church to discuss a few things in an hour or so? Great. I'll be waiting for you in my study."

Arthur put down the telephone and started to make some notes on a yellow legal pad:

- *Bill would know whether the ladder belonged to the church, and if not he might recognize it.*
- *Ask Bill what is in the attic. His plan to make an easy access entry from the new building suggests that he knows what's in there.*
- *Ask Bill about the costs and procedures for making the attic entrance. How long would it take?*
- *Ask Bill whether Pastor Middlemiss had requested any special projects from the trustees.*

Arthur settled back in his desk chair to drink his coffee. He had taken his coffee black ever since he had worked at a stock car racetrack when he was in the eighth grade. His friend Roger's father ran the concessions at Lake Geneva Raceway, just over the state line in Wisconsin, and Roger had frequently asked him to go along with him to sell programs, food, and drinks during the nighttime races. It had been cold, and black coffee had been abundant. The coffee had provided just the right degree of warmth. Ever since those nights, he had felt resuscitated by black coffee. This preference also made it easier whenever he visited a restaurant where they keep refilling your cup. The refill tastes the same as the original if the coffee is black, but the taste changes when they give you a refill if you have cream or sugar in your brew.

He heard a knock on the doorpost and looked up to see Bill Martin entering. His curly hair looked even brighter red than Arthur had noticed before..

Jumping up, Arthur cleared the other chair for Bill. "Would you like some coffee from my brand new pot? I even have powdered creamer and sugar if you want them. Now I don't have to go all the way to Shirley's office for coffee."

"No thanks, Arthur. I'm coffeed up for the day; I've had it at every stop I've made. I see that you've cleared some space and created a blue monster. I hope it doesn't attack you."

Arthur laughed at Bill's interpretation of the blue plastic tarp he had thrown over the remainder of the stuff he had inherited from Pastor Middlemiss. It did look like a crouching critter of some type. "I think I've tamed it. Before long I'll teach it to do tricks. That's my very quick version of neatening up. There's a lot more sorting and analysis to be done before I can find permanent homes for everything. I cleared my mind by covering the clutter so that I couldn't see it.

"Thanks for coming over so quickly, Bill. I have a few questions that might give me some insights into the way things work around the church and the type of person Pastor Middlemiss was."

"Fire away, Pastor."

"First, I'm curious about a couple of aspects of the death of Pastor Middlemiss in the multi-purpose room. I understand that he died at the foot of a ladder set up to climb to the attic. The police concluded that he had fallen from the ladder while climbing up. I'm curious about the ladder itself. Shirley tells me that she had never seen that ladder in the church before. Can you confirm that it isn't ours, and if so, do you have any idea where it came from? The ladder is in the back of the multi-purpose room now if you want to look at it."

Bill hesitated and looked thoughtful; then he shrugged his shoulders. "Actually, Arthur, I can answer both parts of your question without looking at it. The ladder doesn't belong to the church; it belongs to me. Somebody stole it from behind my garage a few weeks ago, just about the time when Pastor Middlemiss died. I live just a block and a half from here, so when I saw the ladder after the Pastor's death, I wondered if someone from the church had borrowed it for use here without telling me. I didn't say anything about it at the time, because I get nervous around police, and I didn't want to draw any official attention to myself. You see, I got into trouble for stealing a car when I was a teenager out east. I saw that it was unlocked and had the key in the ignition, so I decided to enjoy a springtime drive. I spent a year in reform school for it. That's where I learned to be a carpenter. After Pastor Middlemiss died, I debated whether I should take the ladder back home, but I decided that I'd be smarter to leave it here because of its having been part of the death scene. Besides, if it belonged to the church, I could always borrow it when I needed it."

Arthur smiled. "I understand your situation, Bill. There's no need to draw attention to your connection to the ladder at this time. I was surprised that we didn't have a ladder that long at the church, given the height to the attic here in the old building and the even higher sanctuary ceiling in the new building. Have you ever been up in the attic? What's up there?"

"I've never been up there, but I think that Pastor Middlemiss was in the attic at least once. We rented portable scaffolding a couple of years ago for changing light bulbs and installing the banner-hanging system in the new building sanctuary. Before we returned the scaffolding, he asked me to reassemble it in the multi-purpose room so that he could get into the attic. He didn't say what he found when he was up there, but I think he was looking at the attic as a possible secure storage location for church records."

"Bill, did Pastor Middlemiss ask the trustees for any special projects while he was here?"

"Not really, Arthur. He requested the wall-to-wall carpeting here in your study, but that was just maintenance. It also helped keep down the noise from traffic at the intersection outside. This old church building was constructed long before traffic was an issue, and it's not very soundproof."

"I agree that the carpet does help reduce the noise. It also helped my knees when I was sorting through all of the stuff on the floor. From what you said, you never saw what was in the attic. Why did you propose a connecting passage to the old building attic from the new building?"

"I guess I just like neatness and efficiency. When Pastor Middlemiss wanted to go up there, I had to set up the special scaffolding. When I looked at the drawings of the buildings, it looked as though the architect must have planned for an eventual connection. The new sanctuary balcony level is at exactly the same height as the floor of the attic. There is even a logical location for a door in the wall at the altar end of the balcony. That's in an area that was designed for occasions when we might want to have the choir or musicians perform above and behind the altar."

"Have you figured out how much the connecting entry would cost, Bill? How long would it take, and would you do the work, or would you get an outside contractor?"

"Well, Pastor, if we received an OK from the village building department, I could do it myself with two assistants for about five thousand dollars. I don't charge the church the same rates I charge to others. There might be additional costs if the village makes us put sprinklers into the old building attic. We might want to improve the attic floor if we are going to make significant use of that space, and for safety reasons we should seal the existing hatch so that it couldn't be opened by someone up there."

"OK, Bill, if you and Ed Jensen get together and come up with some good uses for the attic space, I'll back your proposal at the next Council meeting. However, you'll also have to develop plans for using the existing space in the new building. All of the available extra space including the attic has to fit into a long-range usage plan.

"Now, let's go to the multi-purpose room and set up that ladder. If you'll hold it for me, I'll take a quick look at what's in the attic. Ever since I learned how Pastor Middlemiss died, I've wanted to find out whether there's something valuable or important up there."

# CHAPTER 10
## TELEPHONE CALL

"Hello, Boss, it's Barry. I'm just checking in to see if you want me to do anything else on your project. I've been staying out of Parkville for a while just in case anyone is suspicious about the old minister's death. That evening was a shocker. I went to the church with the ladder per his instructions, and the minister let me in when I knocked. I thought that he was being unusually cooperative, but it must have been because of what I told him when I called him with the message you wrote out for me. I asked him where he wanted me to put the ladder, and he led me to a big room with a basketball court in it. The old man said he had to get tools because what I wanted was in the attic, and he needed the tools to unfasten the hatch. When he came back, I set up the ladder against the wood-framed recess below the hatch. I held the ladder while he climbed up with the pliers and the screwdriver. He climbed slowly, which was natural for an old guy, and I took my eyes off of him and looked around the big room. He was almost halfway up when I felt the ladder shake. I looked up, and I saw that he had turned on the step and was jumping down at me. He had the pliers and screwdriver clutched in his hands like weapons. I managed to keep him from stabbing me with the screwdriver by fending off his arm while I stepped backward, but he hit me on the head and the knee with the pliers as he bounced from my shoulder to the floor. If I hadn't looked up and stepped backward he would have killed me, coming down that fast from so high. As it was, I ended up dizzy with a big bump on my head, and I was barely able to walk because of my knee hurting so much. The minister had the worst of it though. His forehead hit the floor and gashed open. When he landed, he just laid there. I decided the best thing for me to do was to get away before anyone else who might be in the church came along. I did take the tools with me in case they had any of my blood or fingerprints on them, but I left the ladder. It was a wooden one, and they never show fingerprints. I was too beat up to take it, and I stole it locally. I'm sure nobody would be able to connect it to me.

"What's that? No, I'm certain that nobody saw me entering or leaving the church. When I arrived, I made sure the street was clear before I approached the door with the ladder, and when I left, I peeked out with the door open only a crack to be sure the street was empty. At least I wasn't hurt badly enough to leave a trail of blood. I was surprised to read the next day that the minister had died. He must have broken his neck when he hit the floor. I thought that he would wake up after an hour or two. I wasn't worried about him talking to anyone because of his fear of the threat you had me give him.

"OK, I'll stick around for another few weeks in case you need me again; but then I'm going to spend some time in a totally different part of the country, just in case. Call me if you need me during that time. Goodbye."

# CHAPTER 11
## PENNY AND JOE GONZALEZ

B ob Caspar burst from the front door of his farmhouse in Monticello to welcome the couple who were emerging from their red Ford Explorer. "Hello, Penny. Buenos dias, Joe. It was great of you guys to come and help us solve our little mystery."

"Bob, when you threw in the all-expenses-paid vacation in the Iowa countryside, Penny and I couldn't refuse. Besides, I owe you a lot more than this effort for getting that sniper just in time in Iraq. He was ready to pull the trigger on me when you nailed him. Anyway, we've been chained to our desks in Washington for too long. As they say, it's time for us to get outside the Beltway. We both wore our blue jeans and checkered shirts so that we would look like Iowans."

"I'm afraid you won't find many folks around here in your stereotype attire. Look at me; I favor loud Hawaiian shirts. Come on in. I want you to meet my Aunt Bertha. It's her mystery that we're going to try to solve. We're in the process of moving Aunt Bertha in with us to help fill this rambling old place and to give her some nearby family as she grows older. Paula has a big spread of snacks on the family room table, so we'll gather in there as soon as you two are settled."

"Don't worry about us, Bob" chirped Penny. "We need social interaction after being cooped up with each other all the way here; bring on the people and the food."

They all greeted each other and dove into the piles of lunchmeat, cheese slices, veggies, and dips that Paula had arranged on the table. "Good vittles, Paula, and where did you get this homemade bread?"

"That's what Iowa is famous for, Penny—locally produced and homemade foods. If you check out that metal tub on the floor you'll find some Iowa beer and root beer from the Amana Colonies."

Bertha added, "And save a little room for the Dutch apple pie that I made. It's still in the kitchen."

The conversation ebbed as they began to attack the food. Dessert followed, washed down by a variety of drinks. Eventually, they ensconced themselves in the circle of comfortable chairs that surrounded a large rough-hewn oak coffee table that Bob had designed and built. On that table was a pile of the pictures and papers they had rescued from Aunt Bertha's attic.

Bob led off the discussion, "Now that we're all fat and happy, let me explain the situation. When Aunt Bertha and I were rummaging through her attic to decide what items she would bring when she moved here, we came across some surprising pictures, papers, and relics from her father. They suggest that he had a bigamous marriage while he was in the Army, stationed in England during and after World War II. Aunt Bertha is both shocked and intrigued by this possibility, because it suggests that she has a half-brother somewhere. She would like to track him down."

Penny exchanged smiles with Joe and flipped her blond ponytail as she quickly turned to Bertha. "Joe and I have solved missing person problems that have had less to go on than this one. Here we have a good starting point. England has had a civil registration system for births, marriages, and deaths since the middle of the nineteenth century. It's a lot easier to find the details of a marriage over there than it is in the U.S. We'll get our computers out of the car and start working on it as soon as we finish our background discussion. What do you have in the documents on the table?"

Bertha replied, "I'll summarize them if you don't mind, Bob. You can chime in whenever I miss something.

"First, we have a stack of family photographs, including a couple that appear to be wedding pictures taken with a very unusual old church in the background. Second, we have some newspaper clippings of ads for clothes for young boys along with ration points required. We also have a flyer inviting American soldiers to the Columbia RC (Red Cross) Club, an article from *The Quartermaster Review* titled "The Food Situation in the European Theatre of Operations," and a photograph of a sentry guarding a gate to a residential neighborhood. The caption on the picture with the sentry reads: *A suburban housing estate is transformed into a US Army Base.*"

Bob added, "I also found some fragmentary handwritten notes about talking with the chaplain. It didn't specifically say the subject matter was a wedding, but it sounds as though it might have been. If this was a case of bigamy I would think that Aunt Bertha's father would have avoided involving the military because his records would show the existing marriage."

Joe rose and went to look at the items on the table. "Bob, you're looking at this situation through twenty-first century eyes. The records weren't in computers then with instant access via a search engine. Personnel records were papers in file folders, especially at overseas posts. For all we know, he may have been planning to see his chaplain friend to convince him to help by changing the records to show him as single. He might also have convinced the chaplain to leave the existing records but to avoid adding the new marriage record. However, I think it was more likely that Bertha's father just wanted to talk to the chaplain about procedures for marriages between military personnel and British civilians, without telling the chaplain who would be involved."

Penny added, "We also don't know whether the chaplain might have performed the wedding ceremony or if it was performed in a church or before a civil registrar. That picture you have in front of the church shows a couple surrounded by a crowd, but it doesn't prove that the wedding was performed there. They may have just announced their wedding after the fact to friends who are congratulating them. I think that we'll be able to discover the facts, but they may not be what you assume from the initial evidence.

"If you folks will excuse Joe and me, we'll get the rest of our stuff out of the car and get set up to take a preliminary look at this problem. Bob, do you have a wireless network setup so that both Joe and I can work online at the same time?"

"We sure do, Penny. You can work in any room, or even out on the patio."

"If it's OK with everyone, we'll set up right here. Then Joe and I can call you back in to ask questions and to show you our progress."

Bob, Paula, and Bertha cleared the family room of snacks and rubbish. Then they headed for the basement to get Bertha's old drop-front desk that she wanted in her room so that she would feel more at home. Joe and Penny returned with their computers as Bob and Paula were carrying the desk upstairs.

"Joe, why don't you get into the Army record archives to see if the marriage was performed by a chaplain, while I check the General Registrar Office online files in case the record is in the civil registration database. We know that his name was William Perkins and that the marriage probably took place in 1944 or early 1945 because he came home in late 1947, and the boy in the picture looks about two years old."

"OK, I'll also see if I can figure out the name of the chaplain he would have contacted and whether that chaplain is still alive. Perkins was Protestant, wasn't he?"

"Bertha said he was Methodist. She also said his home was in Indianapolis, so that gives us a couple of additional facts to use. She thinks that her father was 20 when he married her mother in 1935, so William would have been 29 years old in 1944. That fits with him having a responsible position in the Quartermaster Corps. He was older than most. His father had owned a small town grocery store, and he had grown up working there."

"Penny, you realize that any records we find may be incomplete, especially if the wedding occurred in London or if the records were stored there. London was being bombed all the time, and I'd be surprised if some of the records weren't destroyed or misplaced during cleanup operations."

The conversation trailed off as they became serious about the data-mining process. Joe used his government agency passwords to get into the Army archives, and soon had access to huge amounts of data on personnel based in London. His task was difficult because 1944 was the year of D-Day. The city of London and its surrounding areas were the temporary home for the largest concentration of troops in history. Nevertheless, he was able to find the file for Captain William Perkins.

He checked marital status and found that the file clearly listed William as being married to Sophie Perkins of Indianapolis, Indiana and as being the father of Bertha Perkins who had been born in 1937. There was absolutely nothing in the file that indicated a marriage while he was stationed in England. After satisfying himself of these facts, he called out, "Penny, I'm not sure what happened back then, but as far as the Army was concerned William had a clean record and was married to his wife Sophie in Indianapolis. Have you found any evidence of a civil marriage or registration of marriage?"

"Not so far. Does the Quartermaster Corps file show his address or addresses while he was there?"

"Not much luck there, Penny. In order to keep from having to update papers every time they moved him around, they gave him the official address of the Quartermaster headquarters and General Littlejohn: Number 1, Great Cumberland. Actually, there were more than thirty different Quartermaster units spread out all over the country, but for simplicity and security as to actual locations, they listed the single headquarters address in his file. They may have changed procedures later, but that's how they handled his case. Officers weren't required to live on base, and many had quarters with civilians who welcomed the extra revenue from renting out rooms. I'll try to track down the chaplain next. Was there any name or initials in Perkins' notes?"

"The handwriting's pretty bad, Joe, but I think it may say *S.E.* It's alongside the note that reminds him to see the chaplain. Those might be the chaplain's initials. At least that would give you something to chew into. I'm getting nowhere with these civil registration checks. I think I'll have to try working from that picture of the church to try to find a location. It's always possible that he was just living with a family and had his picture taken with their son."

"I considered that, Penny, and I might believe it if there had been just one picture with the boy, but there must be a dozen pictures with the boy at different ages starting at birth. There definitely had to be something going on. You work on the church, and I'll work on the chaplain."

"I've already made a bit of a start at that. Because the churches in England tend to be so old, they have become tourist destinations, and you can find photographs of many of them online. I'm going to compare the church in the wedding celebration picture with the old churches that are shown on the tourism sites. If I don't find the same church, I might at least find a similar one. That would suggest the area in which the other church is located."

"Good start, Penny. I've found an organization called the Military Chaplains Association—USA, and I'm hoping to find the chaplain with the initials S.E. through them. I might find something through their directory or past issues of their newsletter."

The staccato clicking of their keyboards became the sporadic background music for the pleasant afternoon as it passed into early evening. Joe added punctuation to the mix of sounds by popping his bubble gum periodically, a habit that dated back to his childhood in Los Angeles and the gum that came with baseball trading cards.

The others had gone out of their way to spend as much time as possible in the back yard so that Penny and Joe could concentrate in the family room. As the shadows started to lengthen, Paula turned to Bob and said, "I think it's time to start thinking about one of those famous Caspar family barbecues. The kids are staying over tonight, partying with friends in Iowa City. They have a couple of weeks before they have to go back to UW Platteville for the fall term, and they're trying to fit in as many special events as possible. We'll just have the five of us for dinner. If you start thinking about the meat, Aunt Bertha and I will make some salad and get some biscuits ready. By the time your meat fragrance wafts in through the family room windows, Joe and Penny should be ready for a break. And yes, Bob, you can show off the chef's hat you won in that barbecue contest."

When the food was almost ready, Bob went into the family room and found Penny and Joe looking perplexed. He tried to sound cheerful. "Are you two ready for a country barbecue? It looks as though you might need some nourishment and a little relaxation too."

Penny responded, "You don't have to revive us, Bob. We're just surprised that we haven't made more progress. We've both agreed that something significant happened and that a child was involved, but we haven't been able to find any record of a marriage. Joe thought he had a line on the chaplain that William Perkins had consulted, but the S.E. on Williams notes about the meeting turned out not to be initials but a reminder that the chaplain's office was in the southeast wing of the headquarters building."

Joe added, "We concluded that S.E. meant southeast after I contacted the Executive Director of the Chaplains Association, and his records ruled out any chaplain from WWII London with those initials. He said that he would do a search for a Protestant Quartermaster chaplain of that vintage and that he would call me back if he found the record to tell me whether that person is still alive. The ranks of World War II vets are rapidly thinning because of their age, and it's a long shot that he will find that chaplain. I'll be getting a call from him within the next hour if he finds anything at all."

Bob looked impressed by all of the ground Penny and Joe had covered. "Well, it looks as though you two have done all the searching you can for a while, so take a break, and join the rest of us for some food and a cold drink. Come out to the patio while there's still some sunshine."

Several beers plus a few helpings of ribs later Joe's cell phone erupted with a lively rendition of *La Cucaracha* to announce a call. He grabbed it and rushed back into the family room. He was gone for almost forty-five minutes, and when he returned he had a strange expression on his face.

"Listen up, people, I have good news, and I have bad news. The good news is that our chaplain is still alive. His name is Fred Timmerman. I called him at his retirement home in Florida, and he actually remembered William Perkins. When I mentioned the name, Timmerman said that Perkins might have been the most manipulative but saintliest guy he had met while serving in London. At first, he didn't want to discuss Perkins' personal matters, but when I told him that Perkins was deceased and that I was calling at his daughter's request, Fred agreed and told me all about it.

"Actually, I have wanted to tell someone this story for years, but I've never felt that I could ethically share it before.

"William Perkins came to me in 1944, just after D-Day and told me that he had a problem. He said that he had gotten an English girl pregnant and that he really loved her and wanted to do right by her but that he couldn't marry her because he already had a wife and family back home. Neither Perkins nor the girl believed in abortion, and it was pretty risky in those days anyway. He was afraid that the neighbors and her family would    ostracize the girl and her baby if they learned about the illegitimacy of the birth. To protect the girl he came up with a harebrained scheme. Perkins persuaded me to say nothing to deny his made up story that I had performed their wedding ceremony. I just avoided situations where somebody might have asked me about it. Perkins planned to live with the girl in an area pretty far from our military operations, and he would raise the child as his own for as long as he was in England. When he went home, he would leave the girl with enough money to move to America, but she would be on her own when she got there, because he would have gone back to his own family. The girl would then tell her family that they had been divorced, and she would raise the child as an American. Perkins had lots of connections, and he was sure that he could arrange for the immigration paperwork. He didn't tell me, and I didn't want to know, but I thought he would probably set her up as being the wife of a GI who died during the invasion. There was so much going on that it was difficult to get every record straight, and he knew the people who kept the records. I never knew the girl's name or what happened after Perkins started his fictional adventure, but he sure looked to me like the kind of guy who could pull it off."

Joe continued his report on the telephone conversation. "Like I said, finding the chaplain and learning his story was the good news. It's also good news for Bertha that her father did not exactly have a bigamous marriage. The bad news is that because nothing was official, there are no records to track the girl or the child. That is why we kept hitting dead ends in our search. Our only remaining chance of learning more is to work on finding the church in that photograph and people who knew them in that area."

# CHAPTER 12
## JOHN HENDRIX

John Hendrix smiled as he put down the telephone. The report from his man Barry in Parkville had been astonishing. What an unexpected scene at that church! The arrogant and unholy minister had ended his own life through an act of vengeful folly. Too bad that shepherd's flock hadn't been there to see the big event. He wondered how forgiving God would be to his irreverent Reverend in the afterlife. John sat back in his big red chair and sipped his drink. He had to make new plans now that the hypocrite minister was gone. How to proceed and with what chance of success? He had thought the object of his long quest was about to be achieved, but now he knew that it might even be lost forever. He also knew that forever might be a relatively short time for him at eighty-five years of life. Better men than he had gone long before his age. He would have to stay strong to complete an extended quest before he yielded to inevitability.

John suspected that he might find his answer or a key clue in or near that church in Parkville, Illinois. Middlemiss played his cards too close to his vest to be far away from his treasure. The hard part would be finding a reason to hang around there and ask questions. He would have to work out his most promising strategy. Hendrix felt the completion of his effort was approaching, but would it be successful?

# CHAPTER 13
# EVENT PLANNING

A rthur completed his prayer, opened his notebook, and then addressed the group that had gathered in the sanctuary following the Sunday service. "Thank you all for staying to discuss our Antiques Fair that we have scheduled for a little more than two months from now. The Church Council has approved the event, and Wally Sanborn will head the planning committee, assisted by Anna Santini and Stephanie Lim. My father, Peter Blake, who is an antiques dealer in Richmond, Illinois, will judge the best antiques on display, and he also will run the appraisals booth. Wally Sanborn will now tell you more about the scope of the event and its rules."

Wally pushed back his graying hair from his forehead and began, "Thanks, Pastor. We plan to take advantage of the size of our new building by having as much as possible indoors. This will help our exhibitors by protecting their valuables from possible inclement weather and by our being able to lock up the exhibit halls overnight for security of their items. The main exhibit will be in Fellowship Hall, and special exhibits about which you will hear later, will be in smaller rooms on the lower level of the building. Local and out-of-town exhibitors will rent table spaces and booths from us, and the displayed items will fall into two categories, those that will be judged and those that will be for sale at the booths and tables. Thanks to Sue Willoughby, the Illinois Bureau of Tourism is publicizing our event, and we hope that it will become an annual fund-raising project. Gloria Martinez has arranged for the Parkville National Bank to offer cash prizes to go with the awarded ribbons. As Arthur mentioned, his father, Peter Blake, is a professional and will do the judging. Peter will also charge for his appraisal services, which will be available to individuals as well as to exhibitors. He has generously offered to give all of the proceeds from appraisals to the church. Exhibitors will have to designate which antiques are for judging and which are for sale. Those listed in the judging category will not be for sale over the counter. They will only be sold in an auction that will take place during the last two hours of the Fair. The church will receive ten percent of the proceeds of this auction. This will guarantee that there will be quality items for people to see throughout the event, and interest in the auction will keep people here until the end of the Fair. We feel that this event will attract many local people as well as tourists who don't go to our church. We want all of you to be prepared to welcome them and to extol the virtues of Parkville UMC to them so that they might want to visit us in the future. Next, Anna Santini will tell you about her special display."

"Thank you, Wally. On the lower level, I will have a display of religious artifacts on loan from all of the churches in town and a few distant churches as well. This will be a mini-museum, and nothing will be for sale. Peter Blake has offered to appraise these items without charge so that the cooperating churches will know the value of their items. I hope to set up this display in a way that will show both similarities and differences among the various denominations. There will be a second special display, and Stephanie Lim is going to tell you about that now."

"Thanks, Anna. As most of you know, I teach second grade at the U.S. Grant Elementary School. My display will encourage children to come to the event. I am hoping to gather antique toys from various townspeople as well as other sources. As in the case of the religious items, we will appraise these toys without charge. In some cases, with the owner's permission, we will let the children play with them. Gloria Martinez has already offered to display the Parkville National Bank's collection of antique coin banks."

Wally Sanborn got up again. "We are going to need everyone's help to make the Antiques Fair successful. We have a short time to put it all together, but we wanted to get it going this year before it starts to get cold. We'll give you more details as we go along, but at this time are there any questions?"

Jason Fielding got up. He was an elderly man who had recently lost his wife. "What if we have just a few old things we'd like to sell? Nobody is going to rent a table with just a few things."

Wally responded, "Thanks for bringing that up, Jason. That's a special situation where it pays to be a member. Church members and others who have come a few times and expressed an interest in joining the church can display at a joint venture table. At these tables, people will be allowed to sell one or a few things without a rental charge. We hope that by publicizing this feature of the Fair, we will attract at least a few people to start worshipping with us right away. The Antiques Fair has many objectives. We want to make money for the church. We want to increase appreciation of antiques and raise some money for people who own them. We want to get more members. We also want to attract some outsiders to consider moving to Parkville. I hope that we will achieve some of each.

"Now if there aren't any more questions, we would like you to go home and make lists of items you would like to show, sell, or get appraised. Start bringing your lists in next Sunday. Tell your neighbors we would like to have them also make lists and bring them here. Any lady, member or not, who brings a list to church next week will receive a free bouquet of flowers. This will be a great time to go treasure hunting in your closets, attics, cellars, and garages. Just remember that we want antiques and not junk. This isn't a rummage sale."

# CHAPTER 14
## CHURCHES

P enny showed Joe the online sites where she had found pictures of English churches. Most of the churches were old enough to have been there during World War II, so she had lots of photographs to examine. Many of the sites were set up to publicize a particular area, but some had churches from all over the country. In many cases, tourists had taken their own photographs and had posted them as an addition to an existing site. After looking at several pages of church photographs Joe grumbled, "There certainly are a lot of old churches in England. Let's try to simplify our job by only looking for Protestant churches. We know that William Perkins was a Methodist. We don't know anything about the woman, but in those days families raised children to date people from their own denominations whenever possible. Let's assume that she wasn't a Roman Catholic. She would probably have been Anglican, Methodist, Presbyterian, or in one of a few other Protestant denominations."

"Let's try that, Joe, but keep in mind that many of these pictures aren't captioned with the denomination. At least the church in the old photograph with the congratulatory crowd is unusual. It's larger than most and white or light colored. It's hard to get a good feeling for color from a black and white photo. It's also hard to get a feeling for the architecture of the church because the view we have seems to be the side of the building. There are large doors, but the high parts of the church are either located elsewhere or are obscured by the trees."

"Well, Penny, that's why they call this sort of search a challenge. You start at the beginning of your list of sites, and I'll start at the end. We'll meet in the middle if we don't branch off and get lost because of some new clue." As he worked with his computer he whistled, *Get Me to the Church on Time.*

Once again mouse clicks, keyboard clicks, and pops from Joe's bubble gum provided intermittent rhythm for the dances of images across their laptop computer screens. Just over an hour later, Penny started to whistle, and Joe knew this meant that she thought she was getting close to her goal. A few minutes later, she exclaimed, "Yes!" and followed that up with, "Centenary Methodist Church, Boston, Lincolnshire, England. That's the town the Pilgrims sailed from. The population is about thirtyfive thousand today. It would have been less during World War II except for possible military installations. OK. We have a church, and we have a place they might have lived, but we have no records because they were faking their marriage. What do we do now?"

# CHAPTER 15
## MEMORIES

H e had been Captain John Hendrix then, stationed in Salzburg, Austria in 1946 following the war. His job as liaison to the United Nations had been to assist the UN to reunite displaced persons with other surviving members of their families. His work involved cross-tabulating all available census records for the different camps. This job put him into contact with those who were trying to reunite art treasures and valuables stolen by the Nazis with their original owners. He had become especially friendly with some of the enlisted men and officers of the 5th Infantry Regiment. Their duties included guarding the huge Property Control Warehouse in Salzburg.

The Property Control Warehouse contained all manner of valuable items accumulated by the German Army from the homes of Jewish families, museums in conquered territories, and executed prisoners in the concentration camps. It also contained property confiscated by the American Army from Nazi leaders and German aristocrats at the end of the war. By far the biggest source of the treasure in the warehouse was the Hungarian Gold Train. The advancing American forces captured this train in Werfen, Austria on May 16, 1945. The train had been loaded with gold, jewelry, art and other valuables seized from the Hungarian Jewish population as well as some museum treasures. The pro-Nazi Hungarian government had developed the treasure train project in an attempt to keep their confiscated riches and museum treasures away from the rapidly advancing

Soviet forces. They were attempting to reach neutral Switzerland after months of gathering additional voluntary and compulsory contributions and fighting off robbery attempts by both German SS and Nazi-Hungarian troops. The advancing American Army discovered the train partially concealed in the Tauern Tunnel south of Salzburg, Austria. It had been stopped there in an attempt to evade allied bombers. The Americans took the captured train to Werfen where its contents were unloaded and then transferred to the Property Control Warehouse in Salzburg.

The Property Control Warehouse had tight security, but it soon became apparent that many of the valuables were going right out the front door. Generals and others of high rank were requisitioning unique and irreplaceable items to furnish their offices and those of headquarters associates. This became obvious to the troops assigned to guard the warehouse, and before long there were frequent clandestine visits to the warehouse by enlisted personnel who removed items and sometimes shared them with the guards.

Captain John Hendrix found himself in the position of having accumulated priceless valuables both through high-level associates who had simply requisitioned them for his use and through friends in the security regiment who had *liberated* them. These acquisitions of priceless items had seemed so unreal to him that he had little trouble reacting to them as being outside the realm of right versus wrong. He and his friends had simply convinced themselves that they were entitled to them because of all that they had suffered during their wartime service.

Being young, single, and now very wealthy in a foreign land, Hendrix had felt the need for a social attachment. He soon found himself in a   serious relationship with Helga Schmidt, a ruggedly beautiful clerk in the local office of UNRRA, the United Nations Relief and Rehabilitation Administration. UNRRA was the primary international agency for repatriation of Displaced Persons (DP's). John moved into Helga's apartment, and the two of them enjoyed a life of subdued luxury thanks to John's warehouse loot. Less than a year later, Helga gave birth to Maria by cesarean section following a period of painful labor. The cesarean operation was required due to the baby being oriented in breech presentation rather than being ready for a head first birth. There had been complications in the delivery, and Helga had been slow to recover. John had been ordered back to the United States before she was capable of traveling. He shipped out as scheduled and used his high-level connections to transport his Property Control Warehouse acquisitions as classified material which would not be inspected. Within two months of his arrival in the United States, he received his discharge. Once Hendrix returned to America, and especially after he became a civilian, he realized that he wanted to put all aspects of the war behind him, including Helga. He felt an ongoing responsibility for Maria, but he did not want to marry her mother and settle down. Helga may have fit his army situation, but he felt that she wouldn't fit into his expected lifestyle back home. This realization led to a big telephone argument with Helga as she recuperated from her childbirth ordeal.

"Helga, life is different for me now. I'm out of the Army, and I want to get back to things that were my objectives before the war. Those goals won't fit with my being married."

"What do you mean? You weren't talking like that when we were living together, and I was pregnant. I was good enough for you then. Whether you like it or not, you have a daughter."

"I want to do right by you and Maria. I just can't be married right now. I'll send money toward her support."

"You bet you will, John. I have lots of information about some of your unusual belongings. Are you sure you don't just have a new girl that you like better than me?"

"I swear there's no one else. I just have to be on my own for at least a few years. Don't worry about support, Helga. I'll send you money to help out for now, and when Maria gets older she can come here and get her share of those belongings. By that time any search for them will have died down."

"John, some of those things are unique. The search will never stop. I'll go along with support for Maria, but some of those items will have to stay hidden for a very long time. You can't just hand them to Maria and have her worry about them. You have to find a way to give them to her so that she knows she has something valuable but without knowing what it is. The best thing would be for her to get income without knowing what it came from."

"OK, I think we're starting to find some common ground. Maria won't be coming here for quite a few years; she's still an infant, after all. I'll work on a means of handling her property so that it appears to be conventional when the time comes. In the meantime, if you need money for medical care or anything let me know. We've had something special together, but it was during the transition from an insane war to a more normal peace. Now that I'm home, I feel that I'm on the other side of that transition, and my outlook has changed. You'll always be a special part of my life, but from a period that is now behind me."

"You're a bastard, John; but at least you've been my bastard for a while. You'd better make good on your promise to take care of Maria when she's older, and you'd better keep in touch with us along the way, or I'll cause you a lot of grief with the authorities. You're still her father, and I may need your support when I have problems."

"You'll get it, Helga. I just have to be on my own for a while. I have to see what I can do with my life. I wish you nothing but the best."

"Nothing is certainly the right word. You can count on my keeping in touch with you, John, every step of the way. *Auf Wiedersehen.*"

# CHAPTER 16
## SOMETHING OLD

"Bill, hold the ladder tightly while I hit the old latch on the attic access panel to jar it loose."

"OK, Arthur, I have it firmly. Bang away."

After three hits with the hammer, the sliding bar moved, and Arthur pushed the panel upward into the attic. "Wow, something smells strange in there. Hold tight again; I'm going up."

Arthur hoisted himself upward, aware that he had done himself a big favor by keeping up his exercise routine. He searched the attic with his flashlight and found a string dangling from a bare light bulb on the ceiling. "This place hasn't been visited for a while. This light bulb still works, but it's an older larger type that's clear rather than frosted. There's a layer of black particles all over the floor from stripping off the old roof before putting on new shingles. There aren't many things up here. There are some boxes of old papers, probably church records. I'll take some of them down for Shirley to look through. There's a pile of very old lumber scraps. Underneath the lumber I see the side of some kind of metal box. I'll bring that down, and we can look at it later. That smell that greeted me when I opened the hatch seems to be coming from a chair and a pile of old rags in the corner. I'll bring down the metal box and two cartons of papers, and then I'll come back up to look at that chair."

Arthur climbed halfway down the ladder with each carton, stretched to pass it to Bill, and then climbed back up to get the next one. After transferring the metal box he climbed back up into the attic and walked over toward the chair. As he approached the chair, he looked at it and the pile of rags next to it very intently. Then he turned, went back to the hatch, and called down to Bill.

"What's up, Arthur, did you find anything interesting?

"You might say that I did, Bill, but before I move anything, I think we had better call the police. I found a rat nest in the chair, several recently and anciently deceased rats, and one very human skeleton." As he talked with Bill, his memory returned to his cleanup of the pastor's study and to that prosthetic left leg that matched the missing limb on the inhabitant of the old church attic. Any charitable thoughts of Middlemiss having been an innocent person who had died in an accident, had just become past tense. Arthur knew he had to work toward getting these deaths resolved before he could have a stable and positive relationship with his congregation. This was his new mission.

# CHAPTER 17
## LEGITIMIZATION

H endrix thought back to the few instances when he had    spent time with his daughter. The first few months after her birth had been special, but then they had ordered him home and discharged him into a life free of war but tainted by his war experiences. When he had first returned to civilian status, he had felt unable to trust anyone and anxious to accomplish some of his childhood goals before something evil could catch up to him. John felt anxiety and the need to be prepared for anything including an abbreviated lifespan. The war had taught him that life was a fragile thing. These feelings were ingredients in his decision that he could not settle down with Helga. She had meant a lot to him, more than he had been willing to admit to himself, but she had been part of another world and another lifetime. He wanted to put all of the trauma and memories of war into a locked compartment that he would never again have to visit. The flip side of his wanting to live a normal peacetime life had been that he could no longer ignore the ethical implications of his treasures. He found himself having nightmares about con- centration camps and raids by the Nazi Gestapo. He had misgivings and regrets about his treasures, but not nearly enough regrets to make him willing to give them up.

In order to give himself a reason for handling valuable and unusual objects, John had set up a small import-export and antiques business which he had operated with diligence while living  frugally.

This business was supposed to have been his sideline while he studied and practiced law, but his legal career withered before blossoming. He soon realized that the centers of his whole life were his illegal possessions and the business that he had created to dispose of them.

He had known that he could not sell his acquired property, nor could he hide it in plain sight by loaning it to a museum or a university. Government and international agencies would be questioning everyone associated with the art and jewelry fields. They would be circulating descriptions of known items and generic classifications of objects and artifacts that would henceforth require proof of ownership for sale.

To avoid these potential problems John had come up with a scheme to obtain valid ownership documents for a large portion of his treasure. He had purchased similar but inexpensive versions of many pieces of jewelry and art from his collection. He would study the obituary listings, and spot a listing for a European-born person who might have been expected to own a particular piece of jewelry or art. Then he would contact the estate and say that he had been hired to recondition the item, and would offer the estate more than its apparent value for its purchase. In most cases, the attorneys for the estate had jumped at this "found money," and they had furnished Hendrix very impressive bills of sale and other legal documents per his instructions. If the family had refused to sell, he had substituted an inexpensive copy of the item and had "returned" it to them. Over the course of the years, he had in this way accumulated legal documentation for many valuable items and then been free to sell them. Any subsequent investigation would lead back to deceased persons and estate attorneys who would vouch for the validity of the transaction. Through this technique, Hendrix had converted a significant portion of the jewelry collection to cash that he invested in mutual funds. These supported him, while giving him clear ownership of liquid assets that he would pass on to Maria when she grew up and moved to America. He had processed a few of the paintings by relatively unknown artists through this *estate documentation* system and then sold them, but he did not dare to do so with works by better-known artists. He would have to figure out what to do with those paintings later.

John had been pleased with the slow and steady way he had legitimized a good portion of his collection until that Friday morning when it proved to be all for naught.

# CHAPTER 18
## MARIA

H endrix thought back to that strange morning many years ago and the telephone call that had altered the course of his life.

"Good morning, Dad. Did I wake you?" She remembered seeing him in person only once, on a rainy day in Paris when she had been ten years old. He had been there for a conference on international trade procedures, and Helga had taken Maria to Paris to see the Louvre at the same time. John and Maria had corresponded infrequently, but Maria had kept and treasured every one of his letters. Maria had always thought of Hendrix as "Dad," and she had visualized several alternate versions of the scene that would transpire when she would finally become part of his world. She was now twenty-one years old, and she would soon learn which of those fantasies had been closest to reality.

"Maria? Where are you? Is everything alright?"

"I'm fine. I'm here in Boston, and I have special news for you. I got married last week in London to William Middlemiss. He's a minister who was born in England and whose father was also an American soldier. We became interested in each other after we met in London and realized that we both had similar backgrounds. He was born in England, but after his father died in the war, his mother moved from England to America. He grew up in West Virginia with his mother and her second husband who adopted him. We'll visit his family next week, but I wanted you two to meet first."

"Why didn't you write that you were serious about someone? Did your mother approve? Was she at the ceremony?"

"Dad, you know that we have rarely written to each other, and lately it has become harder. I didn't want to tell you right away, but Mother hasn't been at her best for a while. She has been talking as though she is still in the time after the war when you were with her, and she has been forgetting many recent things. They think she is getting Alzheimer's disease. She may have to move into a special home they have for people with that disease. When William and I got married we just had two friends for witnesses. It was very small."

"Maria, how could you get married and move away when she is unable to cope with things?"

"I guess I'm your daughter, Dad, because that's what you did to her when I was small. It's not as harsh as it sounds. Before she got this bad, Mother had a long talk with me and made me promise to go off on my own. She said it would be much better for me. She also said that if she didn't have any family members at home she could get into a special government home without cost to her. Mother said that you had been putting aside savings to help me when I came over."

"She was right. I have been preparing for your arrival. All of this is too much for the telephone. Come over with your new husband, and we'll get into everything at length. It's wonderful to hear your voice. Give me an hour to get things cleaned up before you come."

Hendrix finished his breakfast and did a quick cleanup in bachelor fashion. His cleaning lady would not be here for two more days, so his version of neatness would have to do. There were many questions that needed answering during this visit. He was just finishing the neatening process when the bell rang. With mixed emotions, he trudged to the door.

"Dad, it's great to see you." Maria followed this greeting with a big hug. "This is William. I'm now a preacher's wife."

Hendrix's smile showed his appreciation for Maria's appearance and style. She had grown to be a tall and beautiful woman with sandy hair and a very vigorous demeanor. She appeared to him to be ready to tackle the challenges of any career she chose, and he expected that she would be the moving force in this new family. The minister husband did not impress him very much. He was somewhat shorter than Maria and very skinny. He appeared to be more hesitant than most ministers Hendrix had known. Perhaps that was because he was so young or because he was intimidated by meeting Maria's father for the first time.

"Hello, William. Having Maria appear so suddenly is a big surprise for me, and having her show up married to you is even more of a shock. Pardon me if I take a little while to get used to the situation. I'm sure we will all get along well enough, given a period of adjustment.

"Maria, you have become a beautiful woman. I am very proud of you. You definitely remind me of your mother at your age, but you have some other traits that must come from my side. Tell me more about Helga's health situation."

"As I said on the phone, she has been diagnosed as being in the early stages of dementia or Alzheimer's disease. Her long-term memory is much better than her short-term memory. Possibly because of that and because of long-suppressed emotions, she sometimes thinks that she is back in the period she spent with you following the war. When I introduced William to her, she thought he was you for a while and started talking to him as though you were still together, and I was still an infant. It was probably a case of wishful thinking for her. Anyway, we straightened her out, but when she came back to the present she was not as relaxed and talkative as she had been before. As I indicated on the phone, they have a strong state treatment program, and she will be living in a residence with others who have similar conditions."

"How do you feel about that, Maria? Won't it bother you to be living over here while she is in that residential treatment center? You realize that her condition is not curable and can only get worse."

"Of course I'm concerned, but Mother and I had a long talk about this during the earliest stage of the disease. She said that it had been rough for us during my childhood and that if I stayed with her it would only get rougher. She wanted me to take my opportunity to have a new life in America where you could assist me. Mother knew that she could no longer help me, and she also pointed out that if I stayed home and had a job she wouldn't be eligible for the state residential treatment plan. I argued, but she finally convinced me that she had had her opportunities and that now it was important that I have mine. I don't know if you two were together long enough for you to realize it, but she was particularly well-suited to be a great mother. That is success enough for many women. I love her very much, and I know how much she sacrificed for me." The room grew quiet as a tear rolled down Maria's face, and John found himself surprised to find moisture in his eyes also. He knew that his selfishness had put a huge burden upon Helga. Maria's leaving her in the same way would make it even harder for her, even though this time she would not be able to understand everything. A spark of his old feeling for Helga flickered as these thoughts crossed his mind. It was time to change the subject.

"William, I understand that you are originally from England and that an American soldier was your father. You don't have an English accent. What was your father's name?"

"My accent is gone because Mother brought me over here when I was just three years old, and I really don't know my father's name. Mother remarried when I was five, and my new father adopted me. By the time I was old enough to consider asking my biological father's name, I was well established as William Middlemiss. I really didn't want to rock the boat by starting to think about a different family. Besides, my original father had been killed in the war before I was old enough to even remember him. I'm quite satisfied with my new family, and I hope that you, sir, will be satisfied with me as Maria's husband."

"I'm sure I will be, William. You can call me John or Dad, whichever is easier for you. Tell me why you decided to become a minister, and what is your denomination?"

"I think I'll use John until we get to know each other better, if Maria doesn't mind. I'm a Methodist minister, or I should say United Methodist. We recently merged with the Evangelical United Brethren, and now I have to get used to saying that I'm a United Methodist pastor. I've just been ordained, and have not yet been given my first church assignment, although I expect it very soon. It will probably be in Illinois because that is where I went to seminary, but my parents live in West Virginia. I decided on the ministry as a career because when I was a child, church seemed to be the only place where I felt that I truly fit in with others, and because I have been a follower all of my life, and now I want to become a leader."

John involuntarily raised an eyebrow at this explanation and turned his attention to Maria. "I had hoped that when you came over here you would live in Boston and possibly get involved in my business. I hope that we will at least be able to keep in touch while you are off in Illinois."

"Well, Dad, our relationship has to improve compared to what it was in the past. Illinois is a lot closer than Austria. Once we're settled out there, I may just want to learn more about your business. Who knows? You might want to open a midwest branch."

John laughed as he realized how compatible Maria's personality was with his own. Maybe this marriage development would not be too much of a problem after all. "OK, I give you two my blessing. Now let's all go out to eat and to have a celebration. This place is not set up for feeding you."

Everything was jolly as they left, until William said, "Later I'd like to have a long talk with you, John, about what Helga said to me while she thought I was you, about those postwar days."

# CHAPTER 19
## BOSTON

T he old world Boston had been a small town during World War II, and the older members of its population might be expected to have some recollection of individuals who had grown up there, assuming that William Perkins and his lady friend had indeed set up their living quarters in her home town rather than in a completely neutral area. The question would be how to find the right people to contact.

"Penny, I think I have an idea that has a good probability of finding someone who knew William Perkins and his supposed wife. Even though they were only pretending to be married and therefore had no marriage record, they were probably friends with others at the church who were properly married and who thought they were also. All we have to do is get a list of young couples who were married at the church during the correct time period and try to find a couple still living in Boston, England who knew *Captain and Mrs. William Perkins* during or after the war."

"That's a possibility, Joe. Of course, they would be elderly by now, and there might not be any such couples."

"All we need is one couple to give us the woman's name and, if possible, some information about the boy. We can get contact information from the Centenary Methodist Church website. I don't want to cause any trouble in the girl's family by letting them know that she wasn't really married, but I'll have to be very diplomatic to get information on all of the young couples who were married there between 1943 and 1945."

"You could you say that you're doing a genealogy study of your family, and that you've learned that your maternal grandmother attended that church as a youth and that she may have been married there. Say that you don't know your grandmother's maiden name or even her first name. The only way you could find information about her would be to contact her friends and contemporaries. It's a little convoluted, but an avid genealogist would do such a thing to try to track a family member."

"That sounds like a reasonable approach, Penny, but it would probably be more successful if you made the contact. In that period they were pretty traditional, and they might raise an eyebrow if one of their young English Methodists had ended up in the Gonzales family."

"Joe, you're either very weird or very forgetful. I was a Methodist who ended up being a Gonzales. Anyway, I think I've known you long enough to act on what you mean rather than what you say. I'll make the contact."

Penny turned to her computer and found the e-mail address for Centenary Methodist Church. Then she composed her request for information to them, signing her message as Penny Greene, her maiden name. Then she looked at her watch. "We're lucky that it's still early in the morning. We have a chance of receiving a response today. They are six or seven hours later than we are; I'm always uncertain of the time difference with Daylight Savings Time.

"Shall we play cards while we wait for a response, or do you want to play Latin Lover?"

Joe laughed. "That is really tempting, Ms. Greene, but I was trying to plan ahead a little bit. Let's assume that we manage to get a name for the

81

woman and possibly even for her son. We still have to determine when and how they came to the U.S., which was Perkins' plan according to the Chaplain. He also suspected that Perkins might have had her come over as the wife of a dead U.S. soldier, which would mean that her records would be under a different name. If that were the case, the searches we're now doing would be pretty meaningless."

"You just took one step backward, Joe, but I have an idea which may be one step forward. Up to this point, we have been looking for records of a marriage or for marriage records of people who might have known them. There may be a better and easier approach. If the girl had been a member of that church as a single person, they would have changed her church membership record after she supposedly got married, to read *Mrs. William Perkins* and indicate her first name. They might even have a Baptism record for her son under the Perkins name. That would at least get us her first name. If William was as slick at manipulating things as Aunt Bertha indicated, I'll bet he had her come to America as the wife of a deceased soldier *named Perkins*. That way she would be able to use her same name and church records as long as she avoided mentioning her husband's first name or his mortality status."

"That's perfect. Sometimes I forget just how brilliant my wife is. Fortunately, when that happens you're usually quick to remind me. Of course, William Perkins would have had a sneaky plan like that. He could even claim to be a cousin of her deceased husband in order to get her clearance to come to America under the War Brides Act provision where the husband's family was supposed to state that they would support her when she first arrived."

"I found their website and e-mail address. Even as we speak, Brilliant Wife is asking them about church membership records for our family's genealogy project. I told them I am looking for information about Captain and/or Mrs. William Perkins during and after WW2. Hopefully we will get a response back from them before they go home for the day."

"While you wait for them to get back to you, I'm going to check the passenger lists of the ships that were used to take war brides back to America. Some were passenger liners, and some were specially outfitted military ships. There were so many voyages that it will take some industrious computer work to find and scan the entire passenger lists in detail. There couldn't have been too many brides named Perkins. If William managed to get her over that way, he would have had to have a marriage certificate for her. I wonder what connections he would have used to manage that. I just did a quick check of the National Graves Locator site, and I see that there were fewer than a dozen soldiers named Perkins who were stationed in Europe and were killed during the final years of World War II, in 1944 or 1945. That should make the ship passenger list search a straightforward operation for the computer.

Penny's computer signaled the arrival of new e-mail. She hastened across the room, put her drink on the table, and sat down to open it. She read aloud, "Thank you for your request. All of our records dating back to the war are now in the Lincolnshire Archive Offices in Lincoln. I will pass your enquiry to our district archivist." The message was from one of the ministers at Centenary Methodist Church.

Penny sent a quick reply thanking the minister for making efforts to search the archives for her.

A few minutes later, a response arrived indicating that the archives would be checked within the next day or two.

Joe suggested that they break for lunch, following which he would start checking passenger lists on the War Bride ships.

# CHAPTER 20
## JANE DOE

T he Parkville Police arrived within five minutes of receiving Bill's phone call. Arthur had climbed down the ladder and was giving Bill more details of what he had seen when the police came in through the propped-open front door to the old church. Chief Bobby Andrews approached with military bearing and a toothpick clenched between his teeth. He shook hands with both of them. "I guess we blew it when we came to investigate the old pastor's death. We felt the contents of the attic were not important because of the locked hatch. It appeared to us that he had fallen while going up the ladder. We even saw cobwebs across the hatch recess, so we figured that he'd never gotten up there."

"Don't criticize yourself too much, Chief. From the looks of the remains, they predate the death of Middlemiss by quite a bit. Your Medical Examiner will have to put a date on the death, but my guess is that the body had been in the attic for a very long time. I do have a feeling that there was a connection to Middlemiss because shortly after I arrived, while I was cleaning the Pastor's Study, I found a prosthetic leg that appears to match a missing limb on this body in the attic."

Chief Andrews stared at Arthur in disbelief. "I guess that means that the old pastor may have been more complex than the impression he gave. We all considered him a little unusual, but I thought that his problem was just a lack of social skills. This new body and the artificial leg  you found suggest that we should reopen the investigation of his death. Maybe it wasn't an accident after all. The County Medical Examiner is on her way in now. She'll have to determine some facts for us to use in investigating this new body."

Irma Custis came under the yellow "Crime Scene" tape across the steps and through the open door. Her long face featured high cheekbones, and she had sand-colored hair piled tightly on top of her head. She was wearing pale green coveralls with a big black *CME* on the back. "Hi, Bobby. What do you have for me today?"

"We may have a strange one, Irma. First, let me introduce Pastor Blake who found the body. Arthur, this is Dr. Irma Custis. She's probably the most intuitive Medical Examiner I've ever met. During a death investigation, when she gets a hunch about what happened, it almost always turns out to be correct." Arthur and Irma shook hands while Irma looked at the ladder and the open attic hatch.

"Bobby, why is it that every time you call me to investigate something at this church, I see that ladder? Is it the stairway to Paradise?"

"Unfortunately, that ladder seems to be deeply involved with the transition from this world to the next. This time you're going to have to climb it to meet your client. I haven't had the chance to view the remains yet, so I'll be joining you. Pastor, you can stay down here for now. Just give a detailed statement of how you found the body to Sergeant Gomez. Irma and I will form our own impressions when we go up, and then we'll compare them with yours when we get down."

Bobby Andrews, Irma, and Fred Adams, Irma's assistant, took turns climbing the ladder carrying portable lights, cameras, examination kits, and plastic bags for the body and other evidence. When they arrived at the top of the ladder, Fred started taking pictures of all corners of the attic plus the body. Arthur had been very emphatic in saying that he hadn't moved anything once he had realized the presence of the body, so each tried to approach the scene as though he or she were the first to see it. Later they would compare their initial impressions.

Irma was the first to speak. "The individual is female, and she has been dead for at least six months, but it would be difficult without a thorough autopsy and laboratory analysis to say how much longer it has been since the time of death. We are well past the point of dry decay, which would say several months, probably longer in this semi-sealed attic environment. There is virtually no skin or hair left, which would indicate additional feeding on the body by the rats whose bodies are also present. There are very few signs of insects around the body, so they apparently ran out of food and left through the many cracks between the boards in this old building. The bodies of the rats are in earlier stages of decay, so it looks as though they ate the remaining skin and hair and then had to look elsewhere for food. I see just a few shreds of material that may be leather on and around the body. We can test the material in the lab to determine what it is for sure. The rats then began eating the rags and the chair. The fact that there are several dead rats suggests that the rags, chair and other items up here may have something on them or in them that is highly toxic. Fred, we should take samples of all the items here for further analysis as soon as Bobby has completed his initial investigation concerning the significance and location of everything. What's your first impression, Bobby?"

"You haven't said anything about cause of death, Irma, but I can see an indentation on the skull that suggests blunt force trauma to me. If that does turn out to be the cause of death, I don't think it happened here because there is no staining of the floor from blood. I'm pretty sure that she was killed elsewhere and that the body was placed here to hide it. That also would say that we are talking homicide or at least a cover-up of a suspicious death. The missing leg is particularly interesting, especially since Pastor Blake says that he earlier found a prosthesis that matches it among the belongings of Pastor Middlemiss. That tells me that we should reopen the investigation of the death of Middlemiss. We should also try to determine the relationship of the old pastor to this poor individual. Let's keep a lid on the details of this crime for as long as possible, both to give us an advantage in questioning possible suspects and to minimize emotional problems for members of this church. They haven't known that they've been worshipping here for a long time with a body in the attic. It'll take us a while to determine the significance of the old papers and artifacts up here. We'll have to work closely with Pastor Blake on that one."

Irma nodded her agreement. "Fred, finish photographing all the details of the attic and its contents. Then take the remains to the morgue in a body bag so that no specifics of the individual or her condition are obvious to anyone who sees you. If anyone from the press shows up, say that we will not issue any statements until after we perform the autopsy. That should be a reasonable statement, and it should give us time to compare notes and determine how much information we want to give to the public."

By way of agreement, Bobby said, "Let's go down and talk with Blake, Irma. I'll have Sergeant Gomez give Fred a hand with the body."

Arthur was waiting near the foot of the ladder as they climbed down. "I gave your sergeant my statement, but I'll add to it if I think of anything else. Bill Martin, who held the ladder for me when I found the body, gave the sergeant his statement also."

"That's great, Pastor, but for now could we go into your office and see this artificial leg you found? I'll have to take it for evidence, but first I want Irma to examine it to give an expert opinion on whether it would fit as the missing limb of the corpse."

The three of them went into Arthur's office. Arthur delicately lifted the blue plastic tarp that was covering the stacks of sorted items, wondering as he did so whether he would set off an avalanche of the hidden miscellany and junk that lay beneath it. He was proud of himself when he located the leg after having only an alarm clock and a coffee can full of checkers tumble down as he probed the pile. "Here it is. I was really surprised when I found it in the middle of this stack of odds and ends. I had a feeling that there had to be a story that went along with it." He handed the leg to Irma.

"It's just about the right length, and it's capped with a woman's left shoe, a penny loafer, so I think that I have to agree with Arthur that it belonged to our new friend. The loafer may help with your identification job, Bobby. I'll also be able to give you DNA information plus x-rays of her teeth. None of this will help until we get close to a final identification, but at that point we might get absolute confirmation."

"Thanks, Irma. I think the first step is going to be to search all of the missing person reports for a female with an artificial left leg. I have a hunch that it will be a very short search. She has to be someone in Pastor Middlemiss' past who was important enough to him that he wanted to keep her prosthesis as a remembrance."

# CHAPTER 21
## TELEPHONE MESSAGE

"Hi, it's Barry again. When I called before, I said that I would stick around a bit in case something else happened. Well, it has. The police were at that old church building again, and I saw them carrying a body bag out. I had to gossip with a lot of people before I finally found someone who knew anything at all. After I bought him three beers he confided that they had found a body in the attic of the old church building. That's about all he knew, but my guess is that if I hadn't dodged that crazy preacher's attack from the ladder, I would have ended up being a second body in the attic. After I learned that, I continued to try to get information without being too conspicuous, and I finally did get one more detail. I found out that the body was female. They're keeping things very quiet, but I'll try to get a little more information before I leave. I don't know whether any of this is important to you, but it has me spooked because I don't like the idea of ending up in a bag like that. That's all for now."

# CHAPTER 22
## ARRIVAL

T he bell tone on the computer signaled the receipt of a message. Penny stopped doing her aerobic exercises and scurried over to her desk chair to view it. She gave a sigh of relief when she saw that it was from Centenary Church. Penny read the message quickly and then shook Joe awake from his nap on the couch.

"We have the missing link. Mrs. Ralph Perkins, first name Carolyn was a member of Centenary Methodist Church between July of 1944 and March of 1947. Their records show that her brother-in-law, William Perkins was also a member during most of that period. Carolyn is listed as the widow of US Army Sergeant Ralph Perkins who died in 1945 during the final offensive of the war in Europe. In March of 1947 she sailed with her son to America on the Cunard Line's *Aquitania*. The church apologizes because they have this information on Carolyn, but they have no record of her son's first name or her maiden name. They said that many of the old records had been damaged in a flood and that some were missing and others were just not legible anymore. The other interesting thing about this message is that William Perkins must have arranged to change the records after the fact. They show Carolyn as the wife of Sergeant Ralph Perkins before he was killed. They must have selected his name and created this relationship after his death. That's another indication that William Perkins was a pretty slick operator."

Joe jumped up from the couch and activated his computer from its standby mode. "I had started to scan the data on the War Brides Ships, but your information saves me a lot of work. It says here that the *RMS Aquitania* was one of the main ships of the Cunard Line. It was built before World War I, and ferried troops across the Atlantic in both World Wars. It also says that it was used to transport war brides and military family members to Canada, usually landing in Halifax, Nova Scotia. It looks as though Carolyn had an easier passage than most. Some of the wives were in tight quarters on troop ships that had very few amenities and they sometimes had outbreaks of serious diseases. It also appears that she must have had a second leg of her trip from Halifax to her U.S. destination. I think this routing to the U.S. was due to the fact that fewer ships were transporting war brides by March of 1947. If she took a second ship, she probably would have landed in Boston which is the closest major U.S. port, or New York which was the biggest processing center. If William Perkins had made the arrangements, and he knew that someone might question Carolyn's status as a war widow, he probably would have had her enter the country in Boston thinking that fewer questions would be asked there. In either case, we have a whole new problem figuring out where she went and what became of her in America. Let's give Bertha, Bob, and Paula the new information before we tackle what happened to Carolyn and her son after they landed."

# CHAPTER 23
## IRMA

B obby, the other police personnel, and Fred Adams had all left the church along with their equipment and the body of Jane Doe, but Irma had remained behind in Arthur's office, ostensibly to learn more about his finding of the body, but actually to learn more about him.

"Why did you decide to explore that old attic at this time anyway?"

"It was a combination of things. First, I was bothered that the police hadn't looked up there when the body of Pastor Middlemiss was found. That happened before I arrived here, but the engineer in me kept saying that it was an obvious thing to check. They found his body at the foot of a ladder set up to go to the attic, but they never went there. Second, Bill Martin who heads our Trustees Committee has been wanting to build a walk-in entrance to that attic from the new church building, and I wanted to see what he would find if he did that. I also wanted to satisfy myself that the old attic would be structurally sound enough that it wouldn't be hazardous to have that walk-in entrance."

"Well, Arthur, you are a lot more practical than a lot of preachers I've known. I think your engineering background is going to continue to help you here. I'm sure that you'll have fun with some sermons on alternate views of creation of the world and the relative importance of the Bible and science."

94

"I probably will, once I feel that the congregation and I know each other well enough to explore that subject. Right now, I'm sticking to preaching on biblical texts to make the older members feel more comfortable with me. Pastor Middlemiss scared people off by being distant and pedantic. I don't want to change things too soon. I might scare them away by being too chummy and modern.

"I sense a kindred spirit in you, Irma. I have the feeling that you have a thriving belief system even though you scientifically explore the transition between life and death. Are you a member of a church?"

"Your senses work well, Arthur. I knew that you had a good feeling for analysis. Yes, I'm a member of the Episcopal Church, St. Mark's in Evanston. Now that I live and work in this county, I need to find a new spiritual home. Maybe I'll give your church a try sometime. The travel time's a little long, but it's a possibility."

"That sounds great. I need to bring in some new people, and if they share my views on the relationship between science and religion, so much the better. Now it's my turn to ask about your background. How did you come to specialize in pathology, and how do you determine the time between death and the discovery of a body?"

"Well, believe it or not, I first found myself interested in pathology when I studied biology in high school, and they had us dissect a frog. They also did dissections of the mouth parts of a grasshopper and a few other interesting specimens. Most of the kids found these experiments to be grizzly and boring, but I found them to be exciting. I wanted to learn how a frog's muscles could twitch long after it was dead and why different animals had developed in so many unique ways.

"After I finished medical school, it just seemed natural to pursue this specialty. Besides, I don't have to try to impress my patients or argue with them about a course of treatment that they found on the Internet or the amounts of their bills. As far as judging the time since death of a body, it's complex, but there are definite clues. If you're interested, I'll give you a longer lesson later. Briefly, during the time shortly after death, you can judge timing based on things like temperature and flexibility of the body. Later, there are five stages of decomposition as insects and other creatures are attracted to the body and feed on it. When I was studying the action of insects and animals on dead bodies, I became so enthusiastic that my classmates gave me the nickname of *Irma the Wormer*. Many people see beauty in the way a fertilized egg becomes a fetus and then a living being. I have learned to see the hand of God in the way a being after death becomes part of the environment again through the action of other living creatures. It's not a popular way of looking at things, but it satisfies me."

"Wow, that's an interesting viewpoint. I definitely want to talk more with you about outlooks and viewpoints. I'd like to see you here at Parkville United Methodist Church, but I certainly hope that it won't happen again in the context of your professional work. We've had enough bodies around here for a while. Come join us in worship. If you'll pardon the expression, our church could use some fresh blood."

# CHAPTER 24
## HOUSE OF CARDS

John Hendrix ricocheted from his daydreams, memories, and musings into present-day uncertainties with a suddenness which belied his age. He had little time left to undo the damage that Middlemiss had done to his painstaking long-term plans, assuming that anything could be undone.

Ever since he had come into his fortune via the Salzburg Property Control Warehouse so many years ago, he had worked to build a new world in which he and his adult daughter, Maria would do special things and live among the richest people in America as equals. It was partly because of these grandiose plans that he had left Helga. She had been the woman he needed at that time right after the war, but she wouldn't fit in with the sophistication of his planned life among the elite. Nevertheless, she had raised Maria in such a way that Maria would fit his vision perfectly—at least she would have fit his vision if she had never met William Middlemiss. That slimy creature had fragmented his dreams, and he couldn't have been good for his church either. He had become a minister for all the wrong reasons.

Beautiful, vibrant Maria had settled down with Middlemiss thinking that she would be a preacher's wife who would love him and serve as the matriarch of his church family. At the same time, she would use her education and the shrewdness gained from her experiences during the tough times of postwar Europe to assist her father in his business. But it was not to be.

After the night when Maria and William had first visited him in his apartment, John knew that something was wrong. William had implied that Helga had talked to him about the art and jewelry acquired from the Property Control Warehouse because in her state of dementia she had thought that she was talking with John. Helga had kept secret from Maria the source of the wealth that she and John had shared. Now Maria would learn about it from William who would be looking to acquire and control as much of it as possible.

It later turned out to be even worse than Hendrix had anticipated. Middlemiss had confronted him about giving the couple Maria's share of the treasures, not just proceeds from mutual funds but works of art and jewelry. After some vigorous discussions John had agreed and had given William a portion of the collection.

Maria had grown up to be idealistic. She remained so despite her hard postwar background as Europe recovered. Her move to America and her marriage had given her feelings of self-sufficiency and determination as well. Maria wanted no part of the art or the money from the funds once she had learned about their origin. She and William had violent fights over his claims that he and she deserved this wealth. Within six months, Maria walked out on William and filed for an Order of Protection to keep him away from her.

Maria told her father that she wanted no part of his fortune, both because of its source and because it had caused the rift between him and her mother. She said that she felt he loved his treasure more than he loved her or other people. Maria said that she was going to go away to be her own person. If he wanted to ever have the possibility of earning her renewed respect, he would let her go and agree not to track her location or call her. She would contact him at some time in the distant future if she felt that they could again be a family. She also stated that she had filed for a divorce from William on the basis of mental cruelty.

John had lost his relationship with his daughter, and he had also lost the portion of the treasure that he had reluctantly given to Middlemiss. William had retained and hidden it when Maria walked out, and when Hendrix asked that it be returned to him, Middlemiss had refused and tried to blackmail John for even more of his booty. John had responded with a threat to get William blacklisted from any clergy job in any church in the world, and after an exchange of several punches which left William with a bloody nose and a missing tooth, the two had parted ways as sworn enemies.

Shortly afterward, John had hired people to keep track of William in all of his clergy appointments and to monitor his activities in detail. John analyzed all of the periodic reports he received in the hope that he would be able to find an appropriate time and place for revenge. His agents also tried to locate the hiding place of William's portion of the treasure, but in this they had been unsuccessful. Although he had people tracking Middlemiss, John loved his daughter enough to give her the freedom and anonymity that she wanted. He kept his word and refrained from checking on any aspect of her current status. If and when she wanted to come back, he would welcome her, but he would not interfere with Maria's life again.

# CHAPTER 25
## JEREMY

A rthur was reviewing his notes for his next sermon when he heard a knock on the doorpost. He looked up to see Jeremy Hadley standing there. His close-cropped blond hair suggested that he had come directly from the barber shop.

"Hi, Jeremy. Looking for a basketball practice partner?"

"Not this time, Pastor. My guidance counselor says that I have to interview someone about his or her occupation or profession. If you don't mind, I'd like to talk with you."

"Sure, Jeremy, come in, and sit down." Jeremy folded his six foot three inch frame into Arthur's wooden arm-chair rocker and slid it closer to the desk.

"Well, it's certainly great that you're considering the ministry for your career. What can I tell you about it?"

"Sorry, Pastor, I might talk about the ministry some other time, but right now I'm more interested in becoming a NASA engineer or an astronaut."

"Fair enough, I felt the same way at your age, and I actually followed through and did it. You realize, of course, that you have a much greater chance of becoming a NASA engineer than an astronaut. There just aren't that many openings for astronauts, and given the limited space exploration budget, some of them never even get to fly in space at all, even though they spend many years training for it."

"Yeah, but I'd feel a lot of glamour and status in just being accepted for training."

"Is that what you're looking for, glamour and status? It's far from easy to get to that point, Jeremy. First you have to become highly qualified, either through engineering or science or through military service. In addition to academic preparation, you have to have several years of work experience in your field, and you have to pass a very rigorous physical exam. If you want to be an astronaut with pilot status, you have to have at least 1,000 hours of flying experience in appropriate aircraft. It's not an easy career, and there are no shortcuts. Some of the astronaut candidates who are accepted only get the glamour and status of representing NASA in an exhibit booth at a convention or air show. You're looking at four or five years of education to earn a Bachelor's degree, probably another couple of years for a Master's degree, two to three years of work experience, and about three years of astronaut training if you're accepted into the program. That's a total of about twelve or thirteen years. By the time you finish that, you won't be thinking about glamour and status. You'll just hope that you'll actually get to fly on a space mission of any kind whatsoever. There's less glamour and more chances to use your skills on the engineering side, but even there you can't count on career stability. When the government decides that the budget has to be cut, or when a program ends, they eliminate the jobs of many well-qualified people. Then when they fund a new program, the qualified people are gone, and they have to train new ones."

"Is that what happened to you, Pastor?"

"Yes, Jeremy, after making it through two rounds of cutbacks, I got caught in the third. Then I re-evaluated my life and chose new training for the ministry, not because of increased stability, but because I felt pulled toward it by the way I had sensed the presence of God in my life up to that point. It wasn't an easy decision, and it required more years of training on top of all the background I had before. If you remember my first sermon after I arrived here, I talked about each of us being the hero of his or her life story and of the need to fight temptation in our lives. There are no easy ways to be a hero. Life requires commitment, perseverance in whatever you do, and avoidance of the traps that look like easy success.

"Well, now you have me talking like a preacher instead of a guidance counselor. You know from experience how easy it is to get drawn into a situation that looks glamorous but messes up your life for a while. You've worked your way back from that through hard work and commitment. I'm proud of you for that."

"Thanks, Pastor, I feel as though I accomplished something since that time. I do hope to get somewhere special, even if it isn't glamorous."

"Good attitude, Jeremy. If you're interested, I'll speak with Wally Sanborn about adding your name to the list for the next mission trip. We're scheduled to help repair hurricane-damaged homes in the south, and I might be able to set up a side trip to see NASA engineers at work at Cape Canaveral."

"Thanks, Pastor, that would be great. Let me know if you need a couple of extra hands to work on something around the church. I can put aside some time. By the way, Mom wanted me to let you know that Lisa Paulson, the Choir Director, is quitting. She said the deaths occurring in this church have made her too nervous to do her job. She also said that you're supposed to call the District Superintendent right away."

# CHAPTER 26
## CAROLYN

J oe and Penny were taking a break from their computer searches by walking along the unpaved road that led down to the Maquoketa River. It was cool beneath the trees and a welcome relief from the hotter-than-normal day. They reached the river at a point where it was snaking back and forth so aggressively that only a short segment of its length was visible. Penny turned away from the river to face Joe. "You know, this river is like our quest for Carolyn and her son. We find a new fact and think we are on our way to a solution, and then a new twist points us in a different direction. It's one twist after another, just like this river."

"Penny, our twisting river of leads is starting to dry up. We're running out of leads on Carolyn and her son after they landed in the United States at either Boston or New York. William Perkins probably sent her enough money to get started over here, but then broke off contact to protect his own family relationships. What do you think happened to them after that?"

"Well, Joe, if I had been in her shoes, I would have looked for a job to get some income on my own and an apartment. Those steps would have been easier in a big city than in a rural area. I also would have felt psychologically more at home getting started in Boston, because I would have lived in a city with the same name in England. I would guess that she would have wanted some breathing time of at least a year to feel at home in this country, but that after that she would have been open to moving on to a different area and perhaps to a new relationship with a man who might become the father her son needed."

"Good analysis, Penny, but do we have any information regarding where she might have gone after Boston? The only thing I know is that she would have avoided Indianapolis because that's where William Perkins lived. From what we learned from Bertha, her dad had the same separation idea. It was just about this time when William and the rest of the Perkins family moved to Iowa City. I'm sure that he didn't tell Carolyn about that move. She was part of his past, and he wanted to build a new future with his own family."

"Try this, Joe. Carolyn had a job, and maybe even the start of a career. She was in a new country, but she kept her ties to her family and friends in England. They were satisfied with the story that she was a war widow, and they were probably encouraging her to get remarried, both for the sake of her son and for economic security. They may have even tried to get her socially involved with contacts they had over here. However, we don't know any of those contacts, or the people with whom Carolyn became involved through them. My guess is that if she arrived here in 1947, she would have remarried by 1950. We could do a search for anyone named Carolyn or Carolyn Perkins who got married anywhere in the U.S.A. between 1947 and 1950. We'd end up with a fairly long list of people to check out, but it would be a lot easier than trying to trace her moves from Boston to any other part of the country."

"That's a good approach, but your search wouldn't yield anything like a complete list of marriages. At that time virtually all of the records were on paper. There were few computers, and those were large and assigned to high-priority projects. Even today many marriage and other personal records of that period are missing from public databases. The genealogy folks frequently have to visit local libraries and copy records by hand. We can't even do that without knowing what local area to visit. We'll have to do more than computer searching from this point forward, because her information probably exists only on paper in some unknown location."

# CHAPTER 27
## ANGELA KING

A rthur sat at his desk holding the telephone while the District Superintendent's secretary went to find her. Finally, he heard, "Hello, Blake, thank you for getting back to me. I've just learned about your new dead body and the resignation of your Choir Director. It sounds as though things are going from bad to worse over there. I hope we're not going to see a lot of bad publicity for the United Methodist Church because of it."

"Hello, Superintendent, you appear to have instant information with whatever happens over here. No, we don't have a new body. We have an extremely old body that I discovered in the attic of the old church building while I was investigating how Pastor William Middlemiss met his death. I have already requested and been assured minimum publicity while the police investigate this additional death. These acts of violence occurred before you assigned me to this post. How did you learn about events here?"

"Your departing Choir Director, Lisa Paulson, inquired about the status of her pension benefits. I issued standing instructions that I am to be contacted when district personnel with pension benefits leave. I've just had a long conversation with Lisa. She had been there for seventeen years and had taken reduced pay, in exchange for pension. Did you know that?"

"No, I didn't have those details, and she left before I had the chance to discuss her situation and outlook."

"Well, you had better get on top of things, Blake. It appears that events are moving faster than you are. I'll want a weekly report from you on your progress starting next Monday. Goodbye, and I hope to see better progress from you."

# CHAPTER 28
## BOBBY

C hief Bobby Andrews flicked his toothpick back and forth with the end of his tongue and tapped his foot to the music from an old B. B. King tape. He was sitting at his desktop computer searching through data and images on missing persons. Bobby remembered when he had been seventeen years old and had run away from his home in one of the poorer sections of Louisville, Kentucky. He had been on the missing persons list for two weeks before he gave up on living in the streets and hitchhiked home to his lumpy bed. His parents had made him agree to do extra chores for a year to offset his brief brush with independence. At that stage of his life he had thought that he would never even get away from his neighborhood. He had thought he would end up like most of the other black kids, hanging around the corners except for the occasional periods when temporary jobs were available.

Thank God for the U.S. Army. Given his height and athletic build, they had selected him for Military Police duty right away. He had received good training, outstanding crowd-control experience, and excellent references. He had returned from his duty in Kosovo far better prepared to run a small-town police department than any of the college-educated or academy-trained applicants. In Kosovo they had been charged with both maintaining order and learning how to keep opposing sectors in the neighborhoods from killing each other. Most of the time they had succeeded.

Bobby was thankful for Internet databases so that he didn't have to shuffle through huge stacks of paper missing persons bulletins any more. It sometimes amazed him how many children and adults were in the listings. He turned to the adult section and sorted for females only. He wished that he at least had some information about the age of "Jane Doe," but he wouldn't get that until Irma completed her autopsy. There were several thousand women in his listings, so he knew he needed some additional information to narrow things down. Bobby typed in "Female, Missing part of left leg" and leaned back to await the results.

A few seconds later, Bobby saw the results of his search on the screen and stared at them in disbelief.

# CHAPTER 29
## WALLY

Arthur had remained behind after Wally Sanborn adjourned the Missions Committee meeting. "Wally, if you can spare the time, would you join me for a cup of coffee and a chat?"

"Sure thing, Arthur; are you going to give me an assessment of my running of the meeting?"

"You handled things very well, but I just wanted to have an off-the-record conversation with you and learn more about your outlook."

Arthur poured two cups of coffee from the carafe on the meeting table. He took his black, but he pushed the creamer and sweetener packets toward Wally, who shook his head and sat back with his own cup of black coffee. "No thanks, Arthur. I was in the Peace Corps when I was young, and I quickly learned that niceties such as cream and sugar are no-no's when you're out in rural developing areas of the world. Besides, once you start drinking your coffee black you appreciate the taste of the coffee more. It's not masked by the tastes of other things you put into it."

"I agree. When you're working long hours getting ready for a space launch or re-entry, there is nothing like the taste of just plain coffee. Some people might say that I drink too much of the stuff, but over the years coffee has become almost a personal friend.

"I wanted to discuss something without the other committee members around. It's a proposed change to your itinerary when you take the youth mission group to rebuild hurricane-damaged houses. I've been talking with Jeremy Hadley, and he talked about having an interest in education and training to be an astronaut or an engineer in the space program. I thought that some of our other youth might have similar interests. With my background and contacts at NASA, I could arrange for a tour of Cape Canaveral and some discussions with technical people there about their current and planned space projects. It would be good experience for our youth and good public relations for NASA. How does this suggestion strike you?"

"It sounds great to me so long as we have enough time in New Orleans at the worksite to finish the upgrade of our assigned house and enough money to cover the additional travel. Let me try your proposal out on the youth who have signed up. They would have to commit to a very tight work schedule in order to earn the bonus trip. On the other hand, if they spread the word about the trip to the Cape, we might have more youth wanting to go, and we could get our work done in a shorter period of time."

Arthur shifted in his seat a bit and removed a yellow legal pad of paper from his fat file folder. Wally could tell from his body language that Arthur was going to change to a subject of greater interest to him.

"On another topic, Wally, I'd appreciate your comments and observations regarding Pastor Middlemiss. Whatever you tell me would be treated as confidential. Pastors usually refrain from discussing their predecessors as a matter of professional courtesy. However, the recent events and discoveries around here have led me to the conclusion that I won't be able to do my job properly until I understand William Middlemiss and the way he interacted with the congregation."

Wally scratched his head and smiled. "I have no qualms about giving you information, but the fact is that I never understood Middlemiss. He was a modern man who acted like a literary character from an earlier century. He reminded me of an unrepentant Ebenezer Scrooge. He kept to himself, and he seemed to have too much love for some of his possessions, both the ones we knew about and others to which he alluded but which none of us ever saw. He was pedantic in his sermons, and while he appealed for donations to meet the budget, he never showed signs of charity in his own life. I believe that he was married at one time, but that was long before he came here, and the scuttlebutt is that his wife left him. Middlemiss was good at administration, but he rarely gave me the feeling that he had deep faith. He did away with prayers before meetings to save time on the grounds that no meeting should last longer than an hour. If you were in a conversation with him like this one, you usually had the feeling that he wasn't really listening to what you were saying. After a while, most of us avoided contact with the man beyond what occurred during formal church services. While Middlemiss was here, the only informal and fellowship activities we had were those which were arranged by the laity without consulting him. He seemed to prefer it that way. He kept to himself in the old church building and only visited the new church building for services and special events. Middlemiss led the services well enough, but he didn't go out of his way to help people with their personal problems. We've been fortunate to have enough concerned lay people to fill the void and provide a good level of mutual assistance and support. I don't want this to go to your head, but we've felt much more relaxed and welcomed at church since you took over. We've even managed to convince a few of our friends who had left the church because of Middlemiss to return and rejoin the family."

"Wow, Wally, I didn't expect a pat on the back like that. Thank you very much. I really hadn't had much feedback as to how I'm doing so far, and I've been a little bit worried that questions about the way Middlemiss died and that other police business were scaring people away. The District Superintendent even called me to caution me about the amount of controversy and negative publicity our church was getting. I told her that we had tried to keep it out of the press, and that I could hardly be held responsible for things that had happened before I arrived here, but she said that this church was getting a reputation for being controversial. She actually sounded as though she was more bothered by the publicity than by the dead person."

"I'm not sure if it's a Christian characteristic, Arthur, but in a small town, you attract more people to church when there's a scandal or other sinister event than when things are going smoothly. People want to observe what's going on at close range so that they can gossip about it. A few years back we had our greatest attendance ever during the period when Mrs. Jasper was in a nasty divorce case with her husband. He contended in court that he shouldn't have to pay alimony because he had married her before the divorce from her previous husband had been finalized, and that consequently, they weren't legally married in the first place. I think the judge agreed with him because Mrs.Jasper left town shortly after the case was concluded."

"Getting back to Pastor Middlemiss, I felt when I first arrived that many people, especially older women, had felt more comfortable with him than they were with me."

"It was a question of the known versus the unknown, Arthur. They knew what they would get from him, but you were younger and more dynamic. They didn't know what you would expect of them. Folks here are anxious to please, but they don't want too big a change from whatever has become normal for them."

"So William Middlemiss was distant and kept to himself. He was probably looking forward to his approaching retirement. I don't suppose that anyone was close enough to him to know what he wanted to do in retirement and where he planned to go?"

"That was one of the reasons why I said that I couldn't understand him, Arthur. He was planning to stay right here in town despite the fact that he had no real friends. He made it apparent that he had savings which would be sufficient to take him anywhere, but he didn't want to leave Parkville."

# CHAPTER 30
## CHANGES

H endrix leaned back in his red leather chair. Its padding was so thick and soft that it practically sucked him into its folds. He had been sitting there for three hours feeling sorry for himself because of the way his plans and dreams had evaporated. Now it was time to get back onto the world before it spun away from him. John could hardly believe that thirty-nine years had passed since Maria had walked out of his life. He had to decide on new goals that would still be attainable at his advanced age. If Maria was not going to share in his hidden treasure there was no point in continuing to convert it to cash. He knew his life expectancy was dwindling. He would be much better off returning the remaining valuables under the pretext that he had obtained them from someone else. This would give him positive publicity that Maria might see, and it might hasten their reconciliation. At this point in his life family relationships were more important than wealth anyway. If he died, and the authorities then found his collection, he would be remembered as a villain. If he "discovered" the same items and turned them in for return to their rightful owners, he would be remembered as a kind of hero.

He would become an even bigger hero if he followed up this initial "discovery" by finding where William Middlemiss had hidden the portion of the collection that he had forced John to give him. Then he could return that treasure too. That would give John the sweet revenge of making sure that the world remembered Middlemiss as a scoundrel masquerading as a saint.

These thoughts so resonated with John's inner being that he climbed out of his sensuous chair and started pacing with new energy. He was surprised to hear himself exclaiming, "I think I've found my new crusade, and I'm really going to enjoy it!"

# CHAPTER 31
## CONFERENCE

B obby Andrews sat across the police station conference table from Pastor Arthur Blake, Irma Custis, and a scholarly looking man with thick glasses and a pronounced bald spot. The newcomer had long blonde hair wrapped in a tight band and dangling down the back of his brown tweed sport coat. The stranger's extremely pale face with its stubble beard contrasted sharply with Bobby's dark face and Irma's very noticeable tan. She had always pursued a deep tan because she was so frequently confronted by the extreme pallor of her deceased clients. Irma wasn't exactly superstitious, but she used her tan to make it very clear that she was *just visiting* in the morgue. Bobby opened the meeting by making introductions.

"I'm Bobby Andrews, Chief of the Parkville Police. On my left is Arthur Blake, Pastor of the Parkville United Methodist Church. To his left is Irma Custis, our County Medical Examiner. Arthur and Irma, I'd like you to meet Edward Middlemiss, Professor of Political Science at the University of Wisconsin at Platteville. Professor Middlemiss is the younger half-brother of Pastor William Middlemiss, now deceased. Edward's father married William's mother, and Edward was born five years later."

Edward nodded his head toward the others and added, "William and I were never close because of the difference of eleven years between us and because we disagreed on almost everything. It was more than sibling rivalry. I tend to be logical and methodical in discussing any matter. William would always make up his mind in advance and would not listen to any counterarguments. He also wanted to control everyone around him, and I would not be manipulated by him. We had a long series of fights and wrestling matches over disagreements, and sometimes I won despite his big age advantage. Then our parents intervened and made us solve things without fighting. After that it got to the point where William and I hardly talked to each other at all because we knew it would be a waste of time. We were practically next door to each other when I was in Platteville, Wisconsin and he was here in Parkville, Illinois, and I didn't even know he was here. Chief Andrews contacted me last week to tell me about William's death and to invite me to join you for this gathering."

Arthur leaned forward with obvious interest. "Thank you for joining us, Professor. I have been trying to learn more about my predecessor indirectly, through those who knew him in the church, but with only fragmentary results. William was not considered conventional in church circles. Our church's District Superintendent who supervised his service in Parkville felt that William was a maverick and a bit of a trouble-maker. I would appreciate the opportunity to talk with you further about William after the conclusion of this meeting."

Irma cleared her throat to attract attention. "Arthur, if I'm not mistaken you won't have to wait until after the meeting to learn more about William Middlemiss.

I have the feeling that he is to be the subject of this meeting. Edward, I will be happy to go over the autopsy report on William with you, but I suspect that Chief Andrews had an additional reason for wanting the County Medical Examiner to be here."

"Your instincts and perceptions are on target again, Irma." Bobby hesitated slightly as though searching for the correct words. "Before I go into the other reasons for this meeting, Edward, I would appreciate your telling us more about your family. Were you and William the only children?"

"No, Chief, there were four of us, and it was a bit of a mixture. My oldest sister, Susan, is the daughter of my father and his first wife who died ten years before I was born. She is twenty-one years older than me, and because of that age difference, she has seemed more like an aunt than a sister. As I mentioned, William was the son of my father's second wife. He was born in England, and his father was an American soldier who died in World War II. William was eleven years older than me. My sister Cathryn is the only one younger than me, and the only one who has both parents the same as mine. She is three years younger than me."

"Tell me something about your sisters. Are they living nearby? Are they raising families? Are they healthy?"

Edward was a little curious about the depth of Bobby's curiosity, but he provided the requested information. "Susan moved to Australia many years ago when she was forty and I was nineteen. She had met an Australian businessman while on a cruise, and they discovered mutual attraction right away. She lives in one of the suburbs of Sydney and has three grown children. Her husband has retired, and they are in the process of opening a Bed and Breakfast establishment for tourists. My sister Cathryn has had a rough life. She developed leukemia when she was still a teenager, and in order to get it under control, they had to amputate part of her left leg. She acclimated herself to the situation pretty well. She went through college as an art history major and then did graduate work in physical therapy. I guess she figured that she could be a role model for others who had physical injuries or limitations. She married a guy with a criminal record when she was forty-four years old. At the time she lived in Minneapolis where she worked at a hospital doing physical therapy. She left her husband because he was beating her. That happened two years ago, and I have to admit that I've lost track of her since. She wanted to disappear for a while in case her ex-husband wanted to force her to come back to him. I know that my comments on my family show that we have all gone our own ways, and perhaps that is regrettable, but we are all individualists and very independent."

The other three exchanged glances, and after an extended pause Bobby turned to Edward. "I'm afraid that going in separate directions may not have been advantageous for your family. We have told you about the death of your half-brother William. We have had another mysterious death here, and there is at least a possibility that the victim was your sister Cathryn. We will need your assistance to find out for sure."

Edward paled. "You mean that you want me to identify the body of an unknown person? I'm more than willing to view the remains, but what makes you think that it might be she?"

Bobby glanced at Irma and Arthur, indicating that he wanted to control the discussion. "Edward, we found the remains of a woman in the attic of the church where William had been pastor until his death. She had a portion of her left leg missing. We also found a matching prosthesis for a woman's left leg among William's belongings.

The woman has been dead for so long that she would not be identifiable by anyone who simply viewed the remains. I studied the online listings of missing persons and found an entry for Cathryn

Middlemiss Slocum. That entry was posted by the Minneapolis police who were not sure whether she had left her husband voluntarily. The description indicated a missing portion of her left leg which appeared to match our victim. The Middlemiss name jumped out at me because of the recent death of William. I followed up by searching for other members of the family and found your name and relatively close location. From your description of the family relationships, you would be an even better source of DNA to compare with that of the victim than would be a sample Irma retained from the autopsy of William's body. You had both parents in common with Cathryn, and William had only one. At this point, DNA analysis is the only way to definitely establish the identity of this woman. Irma is an expert at performing that test."

"Chief, you're telling me that I have probably lost both William and Cathryn. I gather that William died under mysterious circumstances, and if your recently discovered body is that of Cathryn, she must have been murdered. This is a small and supposedly peaceful town. How could two such events happen here?"

"Edward, our investigating team doesn't think it was a coincidence, assuming the DNA tests show that our deceased woman was Cathryn. We think that Cathryn knew that William was here, either because they had kept in contact or because she searched him out through church records. As you said, she wanted someplace to go where her husband would not be expected to find her. She thought she had such a place here. Cathryn may have had a fight with William, and he killed her, accidentally or on purpose. Another possibility is that she was pursued and found by her husband, Carl Slocum, and he murdered her. It's also possible that she died in the process of a struggle between Carl on one side and William and Cathryn on the other.

"Irma, I'm going to ask you to get a DNA sample from Edward and compare it to the DNA sample you obtained from the remains. Please perform the test right away. In the meantime, I am going to prepare a bulletin to all agencies including the FBI, seeking the apprehension of Carl Slocum on suspicion of murder. I won't issue it until you confirm that our victim was Cathryn, but if you do, we can call upon the resources of the FBI because he would have crossed state lines to get to her. As I said, there are several possible scenarios as to how she died, but if it turns out that he did come here, he is the only living witness to what happened, and I want to hear what he has to say."

Arthur added, "Bobby, I think your analysis is reasonable. However, I think that only two of the possibilities you mentioned would explain William's keeping the prosthesis as a remembrance of his sister. Either she died accidentally in a fight with him, or she died as the result of a fight that the two of them had with Carl. He wouldn't have kept such damaging evidence if he had deliberately murdered her, and if Carl was involved there would have to be some reason such as William's partial responsibility for him not to have called the police afterward. The fact that he hid the body in the attic rather than arranging for a proper burial suggests that the more likely alternative is that she died accidentally and William was afraid to reveal what had happened."

"You may be right, Arthur, but I still want to find out what part, if any, Carl played in this. If we can establish that he followed her here, I'll consider him my prime suspect."

Irma and Edward rose to go into the office containing Irma's equipment. Edward was shaking his head in disbelief as he followed her.

After they left Bobby turned to Arthur. "I wanted you here in case Edward needed counseling and prayer after learning that he may have lost half of the remaining members of his family. He seems to be taking it well for now, but he may need your assistance if it becomes definite that the second body was Cathryn's. I also have another theory of what may have happened to her that I didn't mention. While she was staying here, Cathryn may have discovered something about William that he didn't want known, and he may have killed her because of it. If this were the case, the discovery must have been very important and at least damaging to his career if not to something he valued even more. The fact that he kept the prosthesis may have been his way of doing penance for his evil deed."

"I hate to be uncharitable to William, Bobby, but your theory may have some merit. Shortly after I first arrived, I started to go through William's possessions in his office including those which had been brought over to the church from his apartment. I made a cursory examination of only about one third of his accumulations, but there were enough unusual things there to give me the feeling that William was hiding something from people around him. I don't know that investigation of his past would lead to something sinister, but I do feel that William Middlemiss was unlike any other pastor that I've met. We pastors have varied backgrounds and ambitions, but William appears to have been unusually concerned with building a wall of secrecy around himself. He separated himself from his congregation rather than reaching out to them in service. If you wish, I'll get back to my examination of his belongings on a higher priority basis, and I'll share information on anything unusual that I find."

"I'd appreciate that, Arthur. I don't think your congregation needs to be bothered by excessive police activity at the church. Just make your continued sorting process appear to be a normal part of your taking control of church matters."

Irma and Edward reentered the conference room. "We're all set for now. I took a buccal swab of the inside of Edward's cheek, and I'll send it to the lab for evaluation alongside a sample that I've already prepared from the remains of the female victim. We should receive results within a few days. In the meantime, Edward, remember that everything that we discussed today is based on suppositions and probabilities. We won't know anything for sure until these DNA tests have been completed. Will you be staying in Parkville until the results are received, or will you be going back to the University in Platteville?"

"If you don't mind, I'll head back to UW Platteville. As I indicated, I never got along with William when I was young, and I feel his lurking presence here. I can come back on short notice. My schedule isn't tight, and putting family matters to rest, so to speak, is important. I only hope that my failure to keep in touch with my family wasn't partially responsible for this situation. You never know when your opportunities for contact with siblings will expire."

# CHAPTER 32
## COUNSELING

P rofessor Edward Middlemiss pondered the standing wave ripples on the surface of his coffee as he debated with himself about the sanctity or irrelevance of family relationships. He knew that he had been a bit hypocritical in ignoring family connections while he had been teaching his political science students the extreme value of connections in business and government. He concluded that the difference was that he didn't want anything from his family while he might want a lot from government and university connections. He heard a rather tentative knock on his door.

"Come on in. It hasn't been a very good day anyway."

The door eased open after this greeting, and Michelle Caspar entered, followed by her younger brother Kevin. "Is this a bad time to talk with you, Professor?"

"No, Michelle, I'm just feeling a little sorry for myself. Can I help you with something?"

"Kevin and I were just wondering if you might have some advice or resources to help with a family matter."

Edward laughed somewhat mysteriously. "I think God timed your inquiry to get even with me. What kind of family matter?"

"Our parents and their friends from Washington are trying to trace a war widow from England who came to the U.S. after World War II with her son and probably remarried here. There were so many war brides and widows that came over that it appears to us to be an impossible task. We were wondering whether your studies or connections might lead to information about associations or mutual help groups that these women might have formed after arriving here."

"The answer is yes and no. There is a War Brides Association, but it wasn't founded until about fifty years after the end of World War II, and it is relatively small. I doubt that they could be expected to locate one particular person. What information do you have up to this point?"

"Joe and Penny, friends of our dad, have determined that this woman came with her young son in 1947. Her first name was Carolyn and she may have been using the last name of Perkins, or she may have been using her maiden name which isn't known. Our parents are trying to trace her because her son may be the half-brother of our Aunt Bertha."

For the second time Michelle and Kevin were bewildered by a strange look that Professor Middlemiss had on his face. "What's the matter, Professor? Aren't you feeling well?"

"Your story hit just a little too close to home for me. I'm sure that the names are just coincidental, but my mother was a war bride from England whose name was Carolyn. I don't know her last name before she married my father because I wasn't born until five years later, but she was at least in a similar situation. If by some strange quirk of fate she is the one you are seeking, I have bad news for you. Both my mother and her son William are deceased. Mother died many years ago, and I have only recently learned of William's death. In any case, I strongly doubt that my mother Carolyn and the Carolyn that you seek are the same person. I do have a suggestion for you, Michelle, should you want to pursue this coincidence further."

"What's that, Professor?"

"In connection with the death of William, I have recently submitted to DNA testing. If your Aunt Bertha wanted to prove whether or not she is related to William, she could also be tested, and her DNA could be compared to William's DNA. She would have to go to Parkville, Illinois to be tested by the person who tested me and William."

Kevin perked up at this suggestion. Here was action they could take to contribute to the family effort. "Yes! Let's call home and arrange the trip. I'm sure that Aunt Bertha would be willing to go." The two students left Edward's office feeling very optimistic.

Edward picked up the phone and called the number on the card he had taken from his pocket. "Irma, this is Edward Middlemiss. I think I have another DNA test that I would like you to make. No, this one's alive."

# CHAPTER 33
## A NEW APPROACH

John sat on a park bench in the Boston Public Garden near the bridge that arches over the Swan Boat pond. He had begun to feel claustrophobic in his apartment, and the cobwebs in his creaky old mind cleared better when exposed to fresh air. He also felt younger when he was close to children who played and enjoyed the Swan Boats as he had when a child.

Hendrix had been working to concoct a plan for legitimately "discovering" art and jewelry treasures that had disappeared during World War II and then returning them to their rightful owners or to an appropriate institution. So far his plans consisted mostly of doodles, but he felt that he was on the verge of coming up with something. He owned a reputable import-export firm that he had created for hiding treasures, but it should work equally well for discovering them. All he had to do was to invent a bulk purchase of domestic estate goods and then find that among the many insignificant items there were a few unexpected treasures. These would catch his eye as possibly having been stolen during or after the war. He would have to be sure that the source of the shipment was cloudy, or if it had to be specific he would identify it as having come from the estate of someone with no relatives to react to the discovery. He felt that this scheme would work for finding a few items of value, but he had not yet figured out how he could repeat the process to find additional things without arousing suspicion from the authorities.

Perhaps a better approach would be to create a fictional estate owned by a shadowy individual and then innocently make a bulk purchase from the estate. After the few treasures in that purchase were revealed, he could notify the authorities, and they could raid the estate to find the rest of his collection, supposedly left behind by the fictional owner. He wouldn't mind if he lost the remainder of the collection, because he had already converted more items to liquid assets than he would ever need. By notifying the authorities he might also create a reputation as a civic-minded treasure hunter. Such a status might make it reasonable for him to be seeking the valuables that William Middlemiss had taken from him. The more he thought about this plan, the more he liked it.

If only Maria would not suddenly appear to announce that his whole operation was a charade. He would have to face this eventuality if it came. He hoped that she would see his actions as signs of contrition for his past deeds. This would be his last chance to get Maria to accept him again as part of her family. She would be sixty-one years old now, and he was about to turn eighty-five. Was he a grandfather or even a great-grandfather? John hadn't realized how much Maria's return and the answer to that question meant to him.

John started to develop his plans for Operation Payback. He would have the art and jewelry be found in an old farmhouse somewhere in the Midwest. This would make the transfer from their current hiding places relatively simple. He would select a farm that had a history of successful business practices and past ownership by people of German ancestry who had retired and moved elsewhere. The new owner would be a corporation with no traceable assets or personnel.

Because corporations are legal entities with indefinite lifetimes, it is always easy to find an existing corporation that survives in name only, all prior products, services, and activities having long been defunct. He might even be able to assume the identity of such a corporation without even purchasing it. The easiest way would be to have an intermediary pay the back taxes of a corporation that had failed to keep up with its obligations. State governments never question people who pay their taxes, only those who don't. After a quick online search for an available corporation and a suitable available farm, he would be ready to put his plan into operation. His man was still in Parkville awaiting instructions. Barry would enjoy this assignment much more than his nighttime encounter with Pastor Middlemiss.

# CHAPTER 34
## PETER BLAKE

Arthur had asked Bill Martin and the church trustees to refinish the top of the conference table, and they had done a very good job of it. The cigarette burns had disappeared, making it better aligned with Methodist views on smoking in the church. Even the initials from past infatuations had vanished. Conference attendees were now enticed to meaningful discussions by a broad expanse of highly polished two-inch thick oak of a quality that had long been absent from most lumber yards and furniture factories.

The Antiques Fair Committee was now gathered around the table, along with Arthur and a somewhat shorter and older individual who strongly resembled him. Arthur opened the meeting with a prayer for successful cooperation in organizing the Fair and for encouraging all people to appreciate the value of older items along with the memories and nostalgia they stimulate.

As leader of the group, Wally Sanborn followed the prayer with an invitation for Arthur to introduce their guest.

"Thanks, Wally. I'm pleased to have my father, Peter Blake, with us this evening. As I indicated earlier, Dad owns an antiques shop in Richmond, Illinois. Both he and my mother cherish anything that shows the caring craftsmanship, uniqueness, and beauty of the past. During my teen years I traveled with Dad on his searches for antiques. We acquired merchandise for him by visiting flea markets, garage sales, and estate sales. I learned to appreciate our ancestors in the process. Dad has agreed to be our appraiser for the Antiques Fair. He will also serve as one of the judges. Dad, do you have any preliminary comments for us?"

"Thanks, Arthur; I appreciate your admitting that you learned something on our trips to acquire antiques. I've already spoken with Wally by telephone, and I'm sure that I'll get to know each of you well as we organize and operate this Fair. Antiques and religion have a natural affinity for each other in that we turn to both of them for information about our forebears and guidance regarding what was important to them. The items that I study and sell give me detailed knowledge of aspects of our history during the last few centuries. The archeologists who are trying to find out more about life in biblical days get most of their knowledge of ancient people from the artifacts that they unearth. The process is the same; we study artifacts in order to learn more about their makers and users.

"As Arthur mentioned, I will be appraising items for participants in this Fair. Appraisals are a tricky part of the antiques business. Whenever you appraise an item, you are substituting a monetary ranking or exchange rate for its inherent value. Many antiques have beauty and craftsmanship that should bring delight to the owner or observer without reference to monetary value. Appraisals are required by the business side of exchanging antiques in order to obtain relative valuations of dissimilar items. Nevertheless, the true value of an antique is often found in subjective appeal to the individual. This cannot be quantified because any particular characteristic of an item may have a different appeal to you than it has to me. The other danger in appraisals is that as a dealer, I have a conflict of interest in telling you what I think an antique is worth. Collectively, antiques dealers have the power to raise prices in the market by their appraisals. In other words, we can be tempted to say things are worth more because we will then receive more money for similar items when we sell them. This temptation is enhanced by the fact that the owner of the antique being appraised is hoping that you will maximize the value of his or her possession. I will do my best to be objective in all of my appraisals, but I have to caution every client that the monetary value of each item is not what I say it is, but rather what someone else is willing to pay for it.

"That's enough for the disclaimers. I'm sure that you will have a successful Antiques Fair, and I applaud the format that you have chosen in restricting the sale of all judged items to the auction at the end of the Fair. This will undoubtedly maintain interest and attendance throughout the event."

Anna Santini's face glowed with pride. "That idea was mine. I suggested it so that everyone would have the opportunity to see the best items for as long as possible."

Wally acknowledged the value of Anna's suggestion and added, "It's obvious to me that this event is giving everyone an opportunity to contribute in many ways to the wellbeing and growth of our church. We will be having a continuing series of these meetings as we get closer to the Antiques Fair, and I want you all to encourage everyone in the church to feel that they are part of the planning and operating process. This event should be planned out in detail so that it has the greatest possible chance for success, not just to raise money, but to become an ongoing tradition that we will feel is part of who we are as a church. Thanks to Arthur's suggestion of the Fair, I think that we are changing from a church that finds comfort only in established traditions, to a church that wants to make a difference in our village and beyond. Thank you all for coming and for being part of this effort."

# CHAPTER 35
## TESTING

B ertha Calahan was nervous as she climbed out of Bob's car in front of the Parkville Police Department. She had never been in a police building in her life, and this made her almost as nervous as the possibility that she would soon learn something about the existence of her half-brother. She had been incredulous when Michelle and Kevin called home to say that one of their professors had a war bride mother named Carolyn. She knew that there was little chance that she was the Carolyn who had mothered her half-brother, but she did know that she had been surprised by God's timely providence in the past. She was not about to bar the door before she investigated what was behind it.

Bob and Aunt Bertha entered the building and approached the front desk, currently occupied by Sergeant Al Gomez. Given the small sizes of Parkville and its budget, the Police Department could not hire a receptionist, so all personnel had to take turns at the front desk. Even Chief Bobby Andrews was known to fill in during lunch hour when he happened to be available.

Bob spoke first. "Bob Caspar and Bertha Calahan, to see Irma Custis." Sergeant Gomez showed them a bench to wait while he went to find Irma. He said that he knew the Medical Examiner was expecting them.

Irma entered the room within a few minutes and greeted them warmly.

"Hello, Mr. Caspar; thank you for coming." Turning to Bertha, she continued, "Welcome, Mrs. Calahan; I'm Irma Custis, and I know that this must be as unusual a situation for you as it is for me. I frequently test to identify someone who has died by comparing the body's DNA with that of living relatives, but in this case we know the identity of the deceased, and we will be testing your DNA to see whether he was related to you. As I understand the situation from Professor Edward Middlemiss, there is at least a chance that his deceased brother, Pastor William Middlemiss, was your half-brother. I have the Pastor's DNA on file from his autopsy, and I will sample yours to compare with it. Similar patterns will emerge if there is even a distant relative in common, and we should see close matches of pattern segments in a case where two people share a parent."

"I didn't know what to expect, Dr. Custis, but I am relieved that you are so pleasant and approachable. I know that I shouldn't think in terms of stereotypes, but I admit that I was expecting the Medical Examiner to be a mad scientist with a sinister outlook on life. May I call you Irma?"

"Certainly, and with your permission, I'll call you Bertha, so that we'll just be two friends discussing relationships with just a little bit of science thrown in.

Edward Middlemiss has given me a brief history of your search for the woman with whom your father may have had a son during World War II. He said that you had found that her first name was Carolyn and that you had determined how and when she come to this country. Your story intrigues me, and I must admit that I was impressed by the detective work that you and your friends performed to get that far into the search. As I understand it,

Edward's mother has the correct background, arrival timing, and name to be a candidate for the person you are seeking. It wouldn't be the first time that objective analysis techniques were assisted by some good old-fashioned luck, if she turns out to be the correct person."

"Thanks, Irma, for that affirmation and support. Bob is too practical to accept the possibility of luck entering the picture, and I have to admit that I tend toward the old adage that anything that sounds too good to be true usually isn't true. It is intriguing that Edward's brother was named William, because that was my father's name, and I could see him wanting to have a son who was William, Jr. Anyway, I'm ready to be tested. What do I have to do?"

"It's a very simple procedure, Bertha. I'm going to swab the inside of your cheek to collect some epithelial cells. This won't hurt at all. I will then seal up the sample and send it to the laboratory we use. They will perform the test and will send back DNA information which we will be able to compare with the report that we have already received on Pastor William Middlemiss. If they match closely enough, we will know that you two are related with a great degree of accuracy. We have a similar report now being prepared for Professor Edward Middlemiss, but from his family history, he would have no parent in common with yours."

"It sounds simple enough, Irma, but I'm not at all sure what results to wish for. If we get a match, I have found my half-brother, but he is already dead. If we don't get a match, then I have more searching to do, but there is still a possibility that I will find him alive."

"That's a very good statement of the alternatives. Now let's take the sample so that we can find out which situation we have."

137

# CHAPTER 36
## FIRST TEST RESULTS

E dward had come to Parkville to receive the DNA test results in person. He didn't want to accept a brief summary over the telephone or by e-mail. He wanted to see both the data and the expressions on people's faces as the results were announced. He also felt partial responsibility for whatever had happened because he had been such a loner for most of his life. It was time to finally take part in investigating these family issues.

The first person he met as he entered the Parkville Police Department was Pastor Arthur Blake, and somehow he felt comforted by his presence. "Hello, Arthur, is your being here a coincidence, or have you been waiting for me?"

"Some of both, I guess. I've been in to give Bobby Andrews some additional results of my examination of William's belongings. While I was here, I learned that you were on your way here to receive the DNA test results on William's body and the unknown person in the attic. I felt that I should remain during the presentation because it will undoubtedly be a time of stress and tension for you. Being around at such times is part of my job description, you know."

"I appreciate that, Arthur. You realize that I'm not a member of your church, and the fact is that I haven't been part of any church for a long time. When I was young in West Virginia, church was a big part of my life, but I guess that I became a bit self-reliant and egocentric when I entered the academic world. The funny thing is that I was strongly feeling the need for support from others and interpersonal connections while I was driving down here. Your timing is impeccable, Pastor."

"Well, come on in. They're setting up the conference room now. After they finish their presentation, we can go over to my study and talk more over coffee if you wish."

Arthur and Edward joined Irma, Bobby, and a technician from the testing laboratory around the conference table. Irma and the technician were completing their review of data on a computer screen and some printouts when the newcomers sat down. Irma appeared to be reviewing and checking the data in a rather animated fashion. After a few minutes the paper-shuffling and mumbling between the two stopped, and Irma addressed the non-technical members of the group.

"I wanted to verify the results in several ways before sharing them with you because they are likely to have long-lasting implications both for police investigations and for family relationships. At this point I can state that the information that I am about to give you is reliable to a very high probability level. First, with regard to the remains of the individual who was found in the attic of the old section of Parkville United Methodist Church, we certify that the remains were those of Cathryn Middlemiss Slocum. I'm sorry, Edward; I wish I had better news for you. I also conclude that the cause of her death was blunt force trauma to the head and that she died somewhere else, and her body was then moved to the attic. We do not yet have enough information to determine whether Cathryn's death was accidental or a homicide, but it is obvious that a crime was committed in concealing both the body and the event of her death. The remaining circumstances of her demise will have to be determined through police investigation. The second set of results from our analysis and comparison of the DNA sample taken from Professor Edward Middlemiss was somewhat unexpected. In addition to comparing Edward's DNA to the unknown individual found in the attic, we compared it to the DNA of Pastor William Middlemiss through a sample which was taken prior to his burial. We pursued this procedure primarily for the purpose of thoroughness. As scientists we know better than to prejudge the results of any test, and we probably shouldn't have been as surprised by the results as we were. Edward, the fact is that William was not your half-brother at all. Our results show that he did not share either parent with you. Cathryn and you have very similar DNA, but William's is quite different. I have to conclude that if William was your mother's son, then he had to be her adopted rather than biological son. You told us that your mother was a war bride and that she brought her son, with her from England when she was transported as the widow of an American soldier. Given the hazards of wartime, it is quite possible that William was the son of friends who had been killed during the bombing of England. There is no way to prove the details of his background, but I can definitely state that he was not related to your mother, or his DNA would resemble yours. William may not even have known that he was adopted because he came over here at a young age. I doubt that this fact will affect any police matters, but in conjunction with the death of Cathryn, it will undoubtedly affect how you view your family relationships.

"Does anyone have any questions regarding the test results?"

Arthur turned to Bobby Andrews, "Chief, Irma assumes that William was adopted, but we don't know for sure. Would this have any effect on his career as a pastor? There wouldn't be any question about the legality of weddings, funerals, and other matters he conducted, would there?"

Bobby smiled, "That's an easy one, Arthur. The identity of William prior to coming to this country might be in question, but he was legally adopted by Edward's father, and both William and his mother became U.S. citizens through the naturalization process, so he was legally who he said he was. I'm sure that many people entered the country after the war with little or no authoritative identification. What counts is how well they blended into the system after they arrived here."

Edward spoke up as though he was airing his inner thoughts. "Until you called me a week ago, I thought that both William and Cathryn were fine, but I didn't know where they were. I had pretty much drifted away from the family into my own solitary life. Now I find that my only  remaining living relative is my sister Susan in Australia, which isn't exactly around the corner. William and Cathryn are both gone, and it turns out that William wasn't even my half-brother after all. I selfishly decided to be solitary, and now I have no choice in the matter. I have to adjust my outlook from wanting to be alone to having to be alone, and there is a subtle difference there which I will have to face. At least it is easier to understand why William and I never agreed on anything. Arthur, I think I'll take you up on that offer of coffee and counseling after this meeting. I hope you have a very large coffee pot."

Bobby Andrews stood up. "Irma, thanks for your analysis. I think we can adjourn the meeting now. I have to issue a multi-agency bulletin for Carl Slocum. He may be the only one who knows the details of what happened to Cathryn."

# CHAPTER 37
## DISCOVERY

T he small Ohio farm still seemed to echo the vibrations of machinery that had paraded up and down its fields relentlessly over many years. This year's exception was obvious from the bedlam of weeds and native plants that irresistibly infringed on plowed rows that had cradled corn. A two-story red brick house flanked by elderly apple trees greeted visitors at the end of a serpentine driveway. Four identical black off-road vehicles were stealthily approaching the house. When they came to a stop at a distance of ten yards from the building, black-clad individuals approached both the front and back doors while others held alert positions behind the vehicles. The peace was shattered by loud knocking on the front door.

"Federal agents—We have a search warrant. Please open the door." The speaker listened intently, but heard nothing. "We're federal agents with a search warrant. You have thirty seconds to open the door, or we'll break it in." Once again there was no response. This was a plausible result given the lack of a car outside or in the open barn. "Break it in." The speaker stepped back, and two men approached, one with a steel cylinder with handles along its length and the other with his gun drawn. There was a loud splintering sound as the battering ram hit the door adjacent to the lock. The man with the gun passed through the door quickly and crouched to one side to let three others enter while he watched for any possible resistance. They fanned out with weapons drawn to search the house, and periodic shouts of "Clear!" were heard as they moved from room to room.

After about five minutes the man who had entered first came out and spoke to the person who had knocked on the door. "It appears to be empty, Joe. We'll start our detailed search, but we'll keep our weapons handy in case someone pops out of a hiding place."

Joe nodded. "Thanks, Steve." He followed the armed man inside and started to examine his surroundings. Others entered carrying equipment cases, but two guards remained outside at the front and rear doors. An individual carrying a laptop computer approached Joe. "What do you think? Is this an ordinary farmhouse, or was our tip reliable?"

"Well, Penny, it looks like a farmhouse, but the interior is much more modern than the exterior. It has the appearance of having been empty for a while, but I think I hear an air conditioner in the background." He turned to the first man who had entered.

"Steve, let's check the basement."

Steve led Joe and Penny to a small door off of the kitchen, opened it, switched on the light, and led the way down the stairs with his gun drawn. When they reached the bottom of the stairs, the three spread out to search more thoroughly. After a few minutes, Joe stood still facing the back wall of the basement behind the furnace.

"I think I may have found what we're looking for. This house is old enough to have had a coal bin for its original furnace. The existing furnace is gas powered and is turned off for the summer. The coal bin was probably in the space behind that wall, and I think I hear the hum of an air conditioner coming from that direction. Call the others down here, and let's see how we can get to the other side of the wall without causing too much damage."

Portable high intensity lights were set up, and six sets of eyes scrutinized the wall behind the furnace for access clues. Tapping the wall had confirmed that there was hollow space behind it. The group was just about to conclude that they would have to demolish the wall, when Joe retreated and operated the furnace power switch. A motor started to operate, and the two-foot section at the right end of the wall swung inward, allowing walk-in access. Fluorescent lights blinked on in the hidden room.

Steve gave a thumbs-up sign to Joe. "That's a lot better than using sledge hammers to open it, and we don't have to worry about damaging the contents."

Penny was the first one to reach the open access panel, and she stood stark still as she stared at the contents of the compartment. "There must be close to three dozen paintings in there, along with several crates that probably hold other valuables. The climate control is good, so hopefully everything is in decent shape. If this really is stolen war booty, it has to be the largest collection we have found in decades. Look for clues regarding the identity of the person who stashed this hoard while I see if I can match any of the artists and paintings to entries in my computer listings."

Several people opened the equipment cases they were carrying and began to assess the basement as a whole and especially the hidden room as a crime scene, looking for any detail that would lead to the history of the valuable collection and the people who built the room and stored it there. Steve opened and examined the contents of the small wooden crates they had found. Others went to other parts of the house looking for clues. Penny entered information about the paintings into her computer. After completing a tour of the entire house, Joe returned to join Penny and Steve.

"Do any of the paintings or other items appear to match items in the lists we have from the Hungarian Gold Train or claims filed by Holocaust survivors and their families?"

Steve spoke first. "The crates contain mostly jewelry, and although I can't specifically identify any items, there are so many gold wedding bands, ornate bracelets, and assorted other old-fashioned jewelry pieces, that I would have to suspect a Holocaust connection. Each wedding band probably represents a life cut short and a story of suffering. They may very well be from the warehouse that held the treasures from the Hungarian Gold Train."

Penny looked up from her computer screen. "There appears to be one painting that matches one of the later individual claims, but none that were on the Property Control Warehouse inventory, although some of the artist signatures match. My guess is that they may have come from the Warehouse. The military authorities were so tardy in taking an official inventory that many paintings, possibly including these, disappeared before they were ever listed. When they did make the list, they estimated in advance that they had about two hundred paintings, but the actual count was slightly less than twelve hundred, so the officials had very little grasp of what was in there. Many things could have disappeared without a trace. I can tell you that these paintings are good quality but by relatively unknown artists. That would fit with their having been taken from middle class rather than aristocratic homes."

Joe smiled. "We did good work today. Pack everything, and ship it back to Washington with a security escort. Others will have to handle the laborious piece-by-piece repatriation. The people behind this stash have been hiding it for more than sixty years. They could have disposed of it without problems because there are no records, but they didn't know that. They surely could have melted down the rings and gold jewelry to make disposal easy. I think that they saw the wedding bands and felt that they would be treading on sacred ground by melting them. I'll get someone working on real estate records to try to learn who put this stuff here, but I have a feeling that they covered their tracks very well."

# CHAPTER 38
## FEEDBACK

T he ringing of the telephone jolted Bertha from her daydream. She had been watching the birds at the bird feeder, and had drifted off to thoughts of when she had been a child learning to climb a tree. She heard Paula call her name, and realized that the telephone call was for her.

"Hello. This is Bertha Calahan."

"Hi, Bertha. This is Irma Custis with information from the DNA test. I wanted to get back to you right away so that you wouldn't have unnecessary stress about the outcome. Summarizing the test, we were comparing your DNA sample with that of deceased Pastor William Middlemiss, the son of a war bride named Carolyn who came to the United States following World War II. Based on your private search efforts, you had suspected that Mr. Middlemiss might be your half-brother and the son of your father.

"Our results, somewhat surprisingly, showed that William was not Carolyn's biological son, but must have been adopted by her. We also found that your DNA does not match William's, so the natural conclusion is that Carolyn Middlemiss was not the person named Carolyn that you have been seeking. We all knew that it was a low probability that she would be the correct Carolyn."

"Well, Irma, thank you for contacting me so promptly. I really didn't know how long the process would take, but I expected to have to wait another week or so. In a way I am relieved by the results. I would love to find and contact my half-brother if he exists. However, I had mixed emotions about learning that a deceased person was my half-brother. This way, I can still hold out hope that I will someday find him and get to know him."

"What I can do, Bertha, is to keep your sample on file and submit your DNA test data for comparison with all of the available DNA databases. Such stores of information are very incomplete and in many cases are limited by law to only specific uses, but at least that process will cover some ground for you. I'll be sure to notify you if I do receive a positive match result. I really do hope that your search is successful and that you finally get to meet your brother."

"Thanks, Irma, for all of your efforts and good wishes. I hope we keep in contact regardless of the outcome."

Bertha put down the telephone and looked again at the feeding birds. She said a silent prayer that the bird she sought would fly into her life soon.

# CHAPTER 39
## NEWS REPORT

Maria Svenson scanned the news summary on her laptop as she sat on the front porch of her yellow-sided cottage outside Burlington, Vermont. Her grown children had left for challenging lives in major cities. She had stayed here because she preferred living where she was near a city of reasonable size, but where life still had a country scent. Besides, this area reminded her of her youth in Austria.

Maria had been a widow for eighteen months, but she still half-expected to find Erik at his workbench whenever she went down to the basement. He had spent many hours there over the years, fashioning wooden toys and mechanisms that he sold to small tourist trade shops. He had built a good business through shop and internet sales because of the uniqueness of his designs. Erik's toys were generally unpainted, but occasionally she had added some fine brush details for him. He had especially liked to make wooden construction equipment and intricate tops for spinning. His tops featured hidden pivoting arms that flew outward by centrifugal force while the tops were spinning.

Maria missed Erik's enthusiasm for life and his love of the outdoors. They had done an amazing amount of hiking and skiing, both as a couple and with their children. Maria had met Erik while they were both climbing Mount Washington in New Hampshire. At the youth hostel atop the mountain they had each been assigned to making sandwiches, and later Erik had joked that they had been making sandwiches together ever since. He had died from uncontrolled blood clots when surgery after a skiing accident had gone very wrong.

Katie and John had grown up with more time spent outdoors than indoors. Even during their school years, they took part in nature study courses, outdoor sports, and scouting whenever possible. Katie had majored in Environmental Studies, and now she had moved to Chicago to work at the Shedd Aquarium. John had studied medicine and was an intern at Georgetown University Hospital in Washington, DC. They were both unmarried, and that was fine with Maria. She was sixty-one years old, but she felt too young and independent to be turned into a doting grandmother. Maybe it would happen someday, but she wasn't going to rush it by turning into a matchmaker for her kids.

Maria returned her thoughts to the news she had been scanning on her computer screen. It had always been important to her to keep up with what was happening in the world. Whether it was news or sounds and smells in the woods, Maria wanted to be aware of everything around her. She felt that the absence of that constant awareness would make her existence less than a life fully lived.

Most of the news today was a continuation of what she had been reading all week, especially on the political scene. Whenever there was a presidential campaign in progress at any stage, the media gloried in trying to extract deep meaning and controversy from every nuance of change in the words each candidate used from one day to the next. Alarmists were worried about various international situations, and complaints about the state of the economy were rampant. Maria was about to complete her review of the news, when she saw an item headed *WWII Treasures Recovered.* The story described a large quantity of paintings and jewelry stolen by the Nazis that had been found hidden in the basement of a farmhouse in Ohio. Very few details about the discovery had been released by the federal agency that had recovered the items, but it was rumored that the raid resulted from information contributed by a Boston dealer in estate merchandise and art objects.

Maria stared at her computer screen. She knew that this story could only refer to her father, and that the recovered items must be part or all of his hidden cache. He had wanted that collection to benefit her and her children, but when she had turned her back on that possibility she had felt a great sense of release. She knew that she would never have met Erik and lived her simple and somewhat rustic life if she had followed the road her father had laid out for her. Now it appeared that he was turning away from that road also. She would have to carefully monitor future details about this story as they were released.

Maria considered what would happen if her father had really changed and if she decided to let him be part of her life once again. How would she involve the children? They had been raised for their entire lives thinking that their grandfather was dead.

# CHAPTER 40
## KNOW YOUR NEIGHBOR

A rthur was working on some papers in his study when he heard a knock on the open door. He looked up to see Irma Custis smiling at him, dressed in a colorful blouse and blue jeans. Her sandy brown hair had been shortened since their last meeting. Arthur rose, offered her a chair, and cleared the top of his desk in front of her.

"It's great to see you, Irma. You're always welcome here, especially when you're not wearing your CME coveralls indicating an official visit."

"Thanks, Arthur, I've wanted to find some time to talk, but things have been busy. I'd like for us to find out more about each other. The fact is that I've been feeling that today nobody bothers to learn about his or her neighbor or even about family members. My job is to determine how people died, and in the process I find out things about them that their loved ones never knew while they were alive. Edward Middlemiss didn't know the where-abouts of William and Cathryn, and if he had, might it have changed or delayed the fact of their deaths? Edward didn't even know that William was not his biological half-brother. Bertha Calahan has been searching to find out if she has a half-brother that her father concealed from her and the rest of the family. I have been working with Bobby Andrews and other police and medical personnel for years, and I know little or nothing about their non-professional lives. Does God want us to be isolated from each other? I thought that Christianity teaches the value of community both inside and outside of the church."

"Irma, I like the way you think, and I owe you a dinner at a good restaurant, because you just wrote my sermon for Sunday. I've been bothered by the fact that so many people at church worship together but know very little about each other. Thanks to the prodding of your comments, I'm going to speak to that topic this Sunday. I'm also going to try something new as a tool for increasing community. Each person will be asked to write down ten personal facts. The names and fact sheets will be posted on the bulletin board, and by browsing the sheets, people will be able to discover background facts or characteristics that they have in common with their neighbors. It should be a good conversation starter, and I'm hoping that increased knowledge of backgrounds will lead to more sharing and communication. Let's try it out now. We'll each take a piece of paper and write down ten personal details. Then we'll compare the sheets to see whether we can't discover some interesting things worth discussing. OK?"

"That's fine with me, Arthur, if we can't improve interpersonal knowledge right here, we don't have much of a chance of achieving wider acceptance of the concept."

Arthur and Irma each took a sheet of paper and a pen and concentrated on the assigned task. Periodically, a burst of pen-scratching could be heard, followed by an interval of complete silence as they each thought about what to write. Irma put down her pen first and studied Arthur while he continued to think and write. Two minutes later he set his pen aside.

"Well, Irma, I learned that it's hard to decide which facts to write down. I think the process would be much easier and less threatening    to people if we just asked them to fill in the blanks on categories such as birthplace and hobbies."

"You're probably right. It would also be more interesting to compare answers that each person gave to the same set of questions instead of comparing wildly different subject matter. For instance, I put down the kinds of toys I liked as a child, and I doubt if you did."

"I didn't, but I would guess you put down dolls and chemistry sets, just because of the field you chose for yourself."

"OK, smart guy, you're half right, but I won't tell you which half. I think you said that you liked anything to do with space flight and Chinese food. How did I do?"

"You're right on both counts, Irma. How did you do it?"

"I remembered that you worked for NASA before entering the ministry, and I saw your chopsticks on the shelf behind your desk. Don't forget that you're talking to a forensic scientist who has to extrapolate answers from small clues. Anyway, we're both pretty good at this game, and you said you owed me a dinner, so how about some of that Chinese food right now?"

"That sounds good to me. I'll get back to designing my personal information survey later."

# CHAPTER 41
## REPATRIATION

J oe was leaning back in his office chair with his feet comfortably perched on top of his desk. Through the v-shaped space between his feet, he was staring out the window, watching a hawk glide in spirals, searching for prey below. Penny walked through the open door and pondered his reverie.

"Are you being an intent bird watcher, or are you watching the bird but thinking about something else?"

"You know me too well. I'm watching that hawk go through all of his gyrations as he searches for food, and I'm thinking about all of the gyrations that the paintings and jewelry we recovered have taken in the past and will continue to take in the future. They started in individual homes, or perhaps in museums or universities. They were seized by the Germans or the Hungarians, and shipped off to avoid their capture by the advancing Russian Army. They were then discovered and captured instead by the American Army. After the war the paintings and other treasures were stored without adequate security, so they and many other items simply disappeared. Now that we have recovered them, they will go to several facilities where a bunch of so-called experts will try to determine how to repatriate them to their rightful owners. The descendants of multiple individual owners will present and dispute ownership claims as will museums. Governments will get involved due to the redrawing of several national borders in Europe following World War II. Issues of monetary compensation will be raised. The point that amuses me the most is that the creative artists and jewelers or their descendants will have no claim or hope for compensation from the huge increase in value of these paintings and baubles which have been hidden for so long. The notoriety of the paintings after this recovery will make them extremely valuable, and somebody will make a lot of money from them, now or in the future. That somebody will probably have little or no relationship to either the original owner or the artist."

"I agree, Joe, some opportunists or organizations with strong political ties will get a windfall out of the art and other treasures. If we do our job well, the public feels that points have been scored on the side of fairness, but very few people will follow the story all the way to the final disposition of this plunder.

"What do you think about John Hendrix, our source for the tip? He said that he found some suspicious ornate bracelets and rings among some mundane estate merchandise that came from an agent for this farm. Does that sound plausible to you?"

"You're very perceptive, Penny. It sounds plausible, but it's not realistic at all. My guess is that John Hendrix had something to do with the original disappearance of these items. I checked on him. He was based in Austria near the Property Control Warehouse after the end of the war. He is eighty-five years old now, and he may be revealing his treasures because he has found religion in his later years. There have been so many strange stories about supposedly honest people coming into contact with postwar valuables and not being able to resist them. Most of those folks would never even consider trying to take something from its rightful owner, but once the Nazis and their agents    looted treasures and amassed them in a way that made proof of ownership difficult, many people felt that such items were free for the taking. It's like the looting that occurs following a natural disaster or a riot. People yield to instincts that they keep subdued during times when there's a framework of authority and social justice. What do you think we should do about John and his tip?"

"Even if your feelings are correct, they would be difficult to prove, and the government is not going to make any friends among veterans and senior citizens groups by prosecuting an eighty-five year old man. I think that we should show gratitude for the information. We should treat John as being a public-spirited citizen, but keep an eye on his future activities in case he leads us to more treasure or additional people who accumulated postwar valuables."

"That sounds like a balanced approach to me, Penny. I'm going to issue a news release naming John Hendrix as the source of our tip and giving him a good measure of gratitude. I'll also indicate that an international team of museum curators and other experts will be studying the recovered items in the hope of determining their rightful owners. Beyond that, we'll just keep monitoring the situation as one of the many leads we always pursue."

# CHAPTER 42
# EDWARD

E dward Middlemiss unlocked his bicycle outside Pioneer Student Center at UW Platteville feeling less like a distinguished Political Science professor and more like a lost little boy. As he started to ride back toward his apartment, he thought about how he had deliberately distanced himself from his family. Now his only remaining sibling was his much older sister Susan far away in Australia. She had a family, but he would probably never even meet them because of the distance. He felt very lonely. He had never gotten along with William, and he had felt very close to Cathryn because they both had the same father and mother. Yet, upon learning that they both were dead, he knew that he was more upset about William's death than Cathryn's. Perhaps this was because his subconscious goal in life had been to show William that he, Edward, could achieve more and contribute more to society. Now he couldn't show William anything. In fact, the competition had been made meaningless when he had learned that William had not been a blood relative at all, but only an enigma with whom he had grown up. He had felt like a younger and rival sibling to William even if there had been very few of William's traits that he had wanted to emulate.

When Michelle and Kevin Caspar had suggested that perhaps William had been their Aunt Bertha's half-brother, Edward had actually wanted it to be true. He yearned for a family with which he could be close, and the Caspar kids seemed to be so family-oriented. The idea that they had wanted to help track down Aunt Bertha's missing relative showed family love that Edward had never experienced, even as a child. It bothered him that he had been so disappointed when Irma Custis had told him that William's DNA matched neither his nor Bertha's. The mismatch to his own DNA had been a shock, but the mismatch to Bertha's DNA had been a disappointment.

In the past he had turned his back on available family while he pursued his career. Now he would have to learn how to get value out of his career without the ability to share it with a family. He could foster closer relations with his students in lieu of family, but he knew that they would continuously move in and out of his life without the permanence that he sought. At the age of fifty-three, he would probably never have children unless he married a much younger woman, so he would have to turn somewhere else for a substitute family.

In stereotypical professor fashion, Edward had been concentrating on his personal relationship failures while he semi-consciously wove his bicycle between groups of pedestrians and past other bicyclists. He had become adept at thinking while charting this random two-dimensional course. Unfortunately, it was a cloudy, dreary day, with just enough reduction in visibility for him to miss the three-dimensional hazard of a backpack abandoned on the sidewalk of Hickory Street. His front wheel hit the backpack on an angle, causing the bicycle to slide downward toward the left, while Edward's momentum carried him off the bike to the right. His right knee scraped the sidewalk as he tumbled until his left wrist collided with a parked car. He felt a searing pain in his left wrist as he lay in the gutter. A crowd gathered. Several of his students in the crowd stayed with him until the ambulance arrived, and the paramedics eased him onto a stretcher, carefully supporting his left wrist and immobilizing it. On the way to Southwest Health Center they put a preliminary dressing on Edward's right knee, accessible through his torn jeans.

Suddenly, the trace of a smile appeared on Edward's lips despite the pain. It was a bit crazy, but he just might approach Bertha Calahan to see whether, in the absence of having found her half-brother, she might accept him as a substitute. It was a weird concept, but the more Edward thought about it, the more he liked it. After all, he was the son of a woman named Carolyn from England.

# CHAPTER 43
## INVITATION

J ohn Hendrix answered the telephone, and heard Peter Blake's voice. He listened intently as Peter introduced himself and then congratulated John on figuring out that his farm estate merchandise had contained loot from World War II Nazi victims. Peter explained that he was an antiques dealer and somewhat of an expert on American and Asian items, but was a little weak on those originating in Europe. He said that he would be providing expertise to an Antiques Fair in Illinois, and wondered whether John might be interested in being a judge and appraiser with emphasis on European items. Peter indicated that the people running the fair felt that it would be an honor to have John there because of his recent citation for helping to recover treasures confiscated during the Holocaust.

This wasn't the first call that John had received since he had become a minor celebrity, and in routine fashion he responded, "You probably aren't aware of the fact that I'm no longer a young man. I'm eighty-five years old now, and I can't accept very many requests that involve a lot of traveling. Where exactly did you say this Antiques Fair was located?" Peter had expected this line of conversation. "The Fair is in Parkville, Illinois, quite a bit west northwest of Chicago. It's on the grounds of the United Methodist Church there. You wouldn't have to worry about transportation from Chicago at all, because I will be traveling from my home in Richmond, Illinois, and I would pick you up at the airport and drive you to Parkville myself. My son is the church pastor, and he has made arrangements for us to stay at the parsonage during the Fair."

There was a lengthy silence that Peter took to be an indication that John was looking for the best words for declining the invitation. He was surprised to hear, "Peter, you said that this Fair is scheduled for October, didn't you? I might be able to make it, because I enjoy the opportunity to take in fall foliage in different parts of the country. Send me all of the details, and I will look them over and give you my comments."

"Thank you, John; I will send you a packet of information today. One other point I would like to raise is that we will be receiving publicity generated by the Illinois Bureau of Tourism. Do you mind if they use your name in the news releases and advertising?"

"That would be acceptable, Peter, if you think my name would have any value to you."

"I'm sure it would. You may not realize it, but you have become a bit of a celebrity. Thank you again for agreeing to come."

After hanging up the telephone John scratched his head and reached for a congratulatory drink. He had been trying to think of a reason to show up in Parkville so that he could search for William's portion of the collection, and the ideal reason had just fallen into his lap. He would have free run of the church and its grounds and would be expected to be inquisitive about all of the antiques at the Fair. If William had a partner who would be showing any of his items, he would spot them.

# CHAPTER 44
## CHINESE FOOD

P arkville didn't exactly have a Chinatown section, but the one Chinese restaurant, House of Ming, produced quite good food. House of Ming had a dark and serene atmosphere to offer customers who dined there. Those who dined at Ming's often felt that they were somewhere in the orient, even though the proprietor, Tony Fleming, had learned to cook Chinese food while growing up in Chicago and had shortened his last name for the oriental effect.

Arthur and Irma sat at a picnic table alongside Mallard Lake. On the way to Ming's they had decided to order their food for take-out so that they could enjoy the weather and sit on rocks at the water's edge across the road from the old portion of the church. Mallard Lake was usually quiet, because it was too small to attract people with high speed power boats. This fact was welcomed by Arthur and his congregation, who didn't want the roar of outboard motors and inboard engines to distract worshippers on Sunday mornings. As a precaution, the Church Council had arranged to have signs posted by the lake declaring quiet hours on Sunday mornings, but they really didn't have to worry. Virtually all of the power boaters went to Loon Lake on the other side of Swanson Hill because it was much larger and just as convenient to reach. There seemed to be an unwritten truce between the boaters and the fishermen, allocating Loon Lake to the former group and Mallard Lake to the latter group.

Arthur was pleased that Irma manipulated her chopsticks as well as he did, indicating that she was no stranger to Chinese food. He enjoyed having someone to join him in appreciating his favorite cuisine. In his earlier churches he had found himself going to Chinese restaurants alone or doing his own oriental cooking in the absence of a local restaurant. He let his mind wander while he ate, and a random thought percolated up.

"Irma, I've been wondering. Are you a descendant of Martha Washington? You share her maiden name."

"Correction, Spaceman, I share her married name from her first marriage. She was originally a Dandridge, but she married Daniel Parke Custis. He was much older than she was, and he died while she was still quite young. When she later married George Washington, she was only twenty-eight. You aren't the first one to ask me about my heritage. I've done some fact-checking in order to  be prepared for that question. It turns out that there were four Custis children, but two of them died in early childhood. Of the remaining two children, only one was male and able to keep the Custis name continuing. John Parke Custis had seven children, but only four survived longer than a couple of years, and three of those four were female. That left only George Washington Parke Custis who had one daughter, Mary, and she married Robert E. Lee. Therefore, there are no direct descendants of Martha with the Custis name. I may be descended from a Daniel Parke Custis cousin or brother, but I've never checked that because the question is always centered on Martha. I'll bet that's more information than you expected or wanted."

"I'll have to augment my history studies before I play trivia with you. That was awesome.

"I know that you've been in Parkville a lot lately, Irma, due to some nasty professional assignments. When things are quiet, how frequently are you here?" Arthur was skipping flat stones across the lake surface as he tried to keep this question casual.

"Things are quiet more frequently than not, and when that's the situation, I can usually set my own schedule to match my interests. The county isn't that big, and I just have to make myself available as required for crime scene and death investigations. I can pretty much get to any part of the county from any other in less than an hour. Parkville is close to the middle of the county, so it's a convenient location for departure to any rush assignment." Irma had a twinkle in her eye as she added, "Is there a reason why you asked about my schedule for being here?"

Arthur was a bit sheepish in responding. "I guess I enjoy talking with you, because we can cover a wide range of topics, both social and technical. Our conversations give me more of a feeling of confidence. When I converse with most of the people in my church they see me with my pastor's hat on and expect me to wax religious or provide counseling. That's all fine and goes with the job description, but there are times when I have to help them through tough times and sound sure in my advice, but I'm not sure at all."

"I know the feeling. When your profession includes autopsies, people look at you as a cross between a technical expert and a ghoul, at least on a subconscious level. It's hard to be seen as just a person who happens to have a particular job. I promise that if I do choose to attend your church, I'll see the man behind the words, and I won't have any awe of you because of your holiness."

"Thanks, Irma. I needed that. And because I know that the eternal soul outlives the worldly body in which it dwells, I promise to think of your autopsy work in the same way I think about the mechanic working on my car. By the way, how are you at diagnosing engine problems?"

"Probably about as good as you are at delivering a baby. Let's change the subject. Do you think William Middlemiss deliberately killed his sister? He had her prosthesis, so there's a high probability that he knew her body was in the church attic."

"I think we need a lot more information before we can reach a conclusion on that one, Irma. I do know that emotions and circumstances frequently lead people to take actions that they would never ordinarily consider. Look at the case of a parent accidentally shooting his or her own child coming home late at night and sounding like a prowler breaking into the house. Then there are people who get involved in illegal activities and feel they have to kill someone who is about to report them to the police. When people feel vulnerable, they sometimes strike out at someone who threatens them without even thinking about it. I'm sure that you've worked on the aftermath of such cases."

"I have, more often than I'd like to admit. You'd like to think that because we live in a highly-developed society, there are definite limits to how far people will go to hurt each other. I've learned that when a motive is intense enough, a person's sophistication is a very thin veneer that can be easily stripped off, revealing the savage beneath it. The value of any society can be measured by the degree to which it manages to keep its people from reverting to savage behavior."

"I agree. Somebody's savage core was definitely revealed in our church."

# CHAPTER 45
## CARL SLOCUM

B obby Andrews read the e-mail message from the Minneapolis Police with a funny feeling in his stomach. Following receipt of his bulletin, Minneapolis detectives had been sent to bring Carl Slocum in for questioning. They had found his apartment very recently vacated, with soup still warm on the stove and most of Carl's belongings strewn around the apartment in a haphazard way. His car was missing, so they had asked the Minnesota State Patrol to pull it over if they spotted it. Two days later, the car had been found abandoned on a side road near La Crosse, Wisconsin. Police there theorized that Slocum had taken a bus to disappear rather than continuing to drive a targeted vehicle with out-of-state plates. He had not been spotted on a bus, and nobody knew which direction he had taken from La Crosse, but Bobby had extended the general bearing from Minneapolis to La Crosse and come up with the theory that he was heading toward Parkville. It was just as possible that Slocum was heading for Chicago and the anonymity of a big city, but Bobby didn't think so. He would have each of his people carry a photograph of Carl Slocum for personal reference and for use in querying others as to whether they had seen him.

Bobby's gut feeling that Slocum was headed for Parkville stemmed from two sources. First, he was convinced that William Middlemiss had been in possession of something valuable and that Cathryn Middlemiss Slocum had been murdered either because she was about to reveal information about William's riches or because she wanted her share of them. His second reason for expecting Slocum was that Arthur Blake had more results from his study of William's personal belongings. Among them he had found a wedding ring engraved with Carl Slocum's name and Carl's Social Security card. Bobby had a hunch that Slocum would want to retrieve this proof that he had been at the site of Cathryn's murder, and Carl might also be looking for William's valuables if he had learned about them while he was in Parkville.

Bobby knew from his first interview with Edward that Slocum was an ex-convict. However, the background search had surprised him. Bobby had found that Slocum had never been arrested because of anything violent. He had served time for swindling two old ladies out of most of their retirement savings by posing as an investment expert. This nonviolent background was especially surprising in the light of the story that Cathryn Slocum had left home because of physical abuse from her husband. Was Slocum physically dangerous, or was he just a con man who had been in Parkville because he smelled the scent of easy money?

If, indeed, Slocum was normally nonviolent, was Cathryn's murder a crime of passion perpetrated by either her step-brother or her husband? She had died from blunt force trauma, but that might easily have been the result of a spontaneous triggering event and didn't require any special skill such as expertise with weapons or martial arts.

Bobby also wished he knew more about Cathryn. Had she been the innocent victim running to her brother for protection against her husband's abuse, or had she played a more sinister part in the saga that led to her demise? Could her actions have been the catalyst for her own doom? Edward had said that Cathryn had led a hard life. Perhaps her lifestyle had hardened her outlook, and she had become someone who was far from innocent. She had, after all, married an ex-convict, presumably with full knowledge of that fact. Cathryn may very well have been an unsuccessful perpetrator of a crime and not just a victim. Bobby would discover more about her as soon as Carl Slocum turned up. They would be on full alert for him throughout the Parkville area. He would request additional assistance from the Illinois State Police in case Slocum stayed at a hotel or motel outside of his jurisdiction.

Bobby's thoughts were interrupted by Sergeant Gomez entering the office to say that he had a visitor. Bobby took a last sip of cold coffee and went to the front office to learn what new direction his day would be taking.

The man standing by the front desk was Carl Slocum.

# CHAPTER 46
## CELEBRITY

M aria read the brief article in the travel section of the newspaper and almost spilled her coffee.

> **Antiques Fair**, *Parkville, Illinois*
> Opportunity to purchase family heirlooms and to have yours appraised and/or sold. Enter your special artifact or work of art into competition for awards and cash prizes. Judges are antiques dealer and expert, Peter Blake of Richmond, Illinois and John Hendrix of Boston. The knowledge of Mr. Hendrix concerning European art and jewelry recently led authorities to a cache of World War II stolen treasures. See displays of ecumenical religious art objects and antique toys. This will be fun for the whole family. *First weekend in October*

It was obvious that her father had decided for whatever reasons to give up his hidden collection, but she was amazed that he had managed to do it in a way that had made him a hero and a celebrity of sorts. Maybe he had changed. She knew that such mellowing did tend to occur as people grew older. Perhaps it was true that material things tend to lose their value as you approach the end of your life. In any case, she was sure that her father had kept his word and had never tried to find her or to monitor her activities. Her anger toward his misshapen values had waned with age anyway. She would definitely have to attend that event to see how things were developing. She wouldn't go so far as to involve the children, but maybe she would be willing to have them meet their grandfather later if he had genuinely changed.

# CHAPTER 47
## BROTHERHOOD

Edward Middlemiss had arranged to pay an informal visit to Bertha Calahan and the Caspars by means of a telephone conversation with Paula. While on the telephone, he hadn't gone out of his way to correct her impression that he was visiting because Michelle and Kevin were his students. His thoughts about blending himself into their family were unconventional to say the least, and he had known enough not to approach the subject during a telephone conversation. Edward was, after all, a professor of political science, and he would have to apply some political expertise to make this work. As he drove past the sign that welcomed him to Monticello, Iowa, he surprisingly did feel welcomed and thought that he was ready for this unique meeting.

He steered his 10-year-old green Jeep through the opening in the white horse-style fence and into the graveled courtyard in front of the barn-colored house. Edward saw Bob Caspar coming out to meet him from the open garage. He parked next to the front porch and stepped out.

"Hi, Professor, It's good to see you again. We met last year when Michelle took me along to hand in her paper. What did you do to your left wrist?"

"I remember you very well, Bob, and the name is Edward, not Professor. The cast on the wrist is from a bicycle accident when I was careless. I'm afraid it will be my companion for quite a while. I've been looking forward to visiting with the whole family. I'm not here on academic business."

"That's fair enough, Edward, but you'll have to take us blemishes and all. We haven't planned anything special. I've been out in the garage working on a carving project, and Paula has been sending out query letters for an article she wants to write. I don't know where the kids or Aunt Bertha are. Let's go into the house and check. I'm sure I can find you a cool drink."

They found Bertha, Michelle, and Kevin watching an old movie in the den. Bertha had been trying to convince the younger generation that Laurel and Hardy were the funniest comedians or comic actors ever. Kevin's favorite was Jim Carrey, and Michelle argued on behalf of George Carlin. As the newcomers entered the room, all three of the debaters were talking at the same time.

Bob tried to get their attention, "Order in the court please, we have a distinguished visitor."

The sound level tapered down, and they all stood up. Bertha turned off the television. Michelle was the first to speak.

"Hi, Professor; welcome to our great political science debate over comedians. Who is your all-time favorite?"

"Well, I know it dates me, but I always liked Groucho Marx. No matter what anyone said, he always had a funny comeback instantly available. As a comic actor, though, I would pick Jerry Seinfeld."

Bob patted Edward on the back and chuckled, "Bravo, Edward; you are good at politics and diplomacy. Without any hesitation you managed to pick one favorite each from the older and younger generation." They were all laughing as Paula walked in.

"With all of this uproar, I felt left out, so I thought I had better join you. You must be Professor Middlemiss. We talked on the telephone."

"Glad to finally meet you, Paula. I was telling Bob that this is a social visit, so let's make it Edward. I have also been looking forward to meeting Aunt Bertha. How are you, Bertha?"

"I'm pleased to meet you too, Edward. I've heard about you from the kids' college stories. I had some hope that your brother William might turn out to be my half-brother."

"Michelle and Kevin filled me in on your search effort. I was waiting with great curiosity to see whether the DNA tests would show that William was related to you. The results were more of a surprise to me than to you. You knew that a positive match would have been a long shot. I would have been mildly surprised if he had been your brother, but I was completely floored when I learned that he was not my brother except by adoption. This whole matter of relationships is actually the subject of my visit today.

"As you may have learned from Irma Custis, I have only recently discovered that both William and my sister Cathryn are dead. My remaining half-sister, Susan, is much older than I am. She lives in Australia. At this point I am effectively without a family. If William had turned out to be your half-brother, that would have made me part of your extended family, a thought which appealed to me more than I expected. Your search will continue, with only a small likelihood that you will find your father's son. I would like to propose something unusual. Would you consider accepting me as a surrogate brother to give you someone with similar background to your half-brother and to give me a substitute family? You are about the same age as my sister Susan, and I am the son of a war bride named Carolyn who came over here at the same time as your father's Carolyn. I know that this idea might sound a bit ridiculous and wacky, but it has advantages for both of us, and I have some background with Kevin and Michelle. What do you think?"

A stunned expression bounced back and forth across the faces of all the Caspars and Bertha. After about ten seconds Bertha's lips curled into a smile. "Do you promise not to refer to me as your *much older* sister? If we can get by that one, we might make it work."

Kevin brightened. "Do we call you Uncle Professor Edward?"

Michelle laughed. "I guess we could shorten that title to *Upward*."

That broke whatever ice remained, and everyone was soon debating the merits of making custom-designed extended families a new national movement.

# CHAPTER 48
## CATHRYN

B obby Andrews invited Carl Slocum into his office and poured iced tea for the two of them. Slocum reminded Bobby of his high school English teacher. Carl looked older than the fifty-five years indicated by his prison record. He had wavy gray hair, a scar over his left eye, erect posture, and a slight limp. His thick glasses made him look owlish. Bobby began the informal interrogation, "The feedback I received from the Minneapolis Police sure made it look as though you were running away."

"I can see how you would have come to that conclusion, Chief, especially with my background, but I just wanted to straighten things out. Along the way I've come to know several Minneapolis officers very well, and one of them called me about your bulletin. It said that you wanted me for questioning regarding the death of my wife Cathryn, so I came right away. You see, I didn't even know that she was dead. She left me almost two years ago, and I thought she had settled somewhere else. I started to drive here, but my car died in La Crosse. After that, I took buses and hitchhiked the rest of the way."

"Are you saying that this is the first time you've been in Parkville, Mr. Slocum? We have evidence that suggests that you were here when Cathryn was still alive."

"You probably aren't going to tell me the nature of your evidence which is good police procedure, but I can tell you that when Cathryn walked out on me, she took some of my things. She took my wedding ring so that people would know that we weren't married any more, she took my wallet, and she took my Harley-Davidson leather jacket. Right after she left I worked through the banks and the credit-rating agencies to cancel my credit cards and change accounts so that she couldn't bleed me dry. You can check with those agencies to confirm what I'm telling you. There is a paper trail. She even took the newer car, leaving me with the junker that died in La Crosse. I doubt if it's even worth repairing."

"What are you doing for a living, Mr. Slocum, and how long have you been doing it?"

"Call me Carl, Chief. You know how hard it is for someone who's been in prison to find a job in private industry. Instead of fighting my background, I decided to use it to help people. I have been working for three years for the Skyway Senior Center in Minneapolis. I teach classes and advise senior citizens on Medicare matters and community resources. I got into trouble because I related well to older people, so now I use that skill to help them. It doesn't pay a lot which was one of the reasons that Cathryn left, but now that I'm on my own it's enough."

"Carl, Cathryn told her brother that she left you because of your physical abuse to her. What's your response to that issue?"

"I think that if she made that statement, she was stretching the truth a bit. Cathryn has had problems with feeling sorry for herself, ever since her partial leg amputation. When I couldn't get a high-paying position, and she lost her job doing physical therapy, she started to drink more than she had before. The only physical abuse I ever gave her was to restrain her on several occasions when she was drunk and wanted to go out driving late at night. The combination of her inebriated  condition, her attitude toward the world, her bad leg, and the time of night, told me that she might not be safe, so I restrained her and made sure she stayed home. Each time she would be sober by the next morning. I thought that her anger at my restraining her disappeared when she sobered up. I guess her resentment against me built up each time it happened, and she finally left me for good. She even trashed our apartment as a final act of vengeance before she left."

"Why did Cathryn lose her physical therapy job? That's a scarce skill. Couldn't she get another job doing it?"

"She couldn't get another job in the Minneapolis area because she was fired for hurting people during her therapy sessions. Her arms were very strong, and even during the early days of her drinking, her patience had become limited. On several occasions Cathryn became frustrated over frequent sessions of repetitious small movement therapy for people recovering from joint replacements. She overstressed their artificial joints, damaging them, putting her clients into agonizing pain, and making them face the prospect of new operations and expenses. When Cathryn was fired, her name was placed on a blacklist for agencies hiring physical therapists."

"What do you know about Cathryn's brother, Pastor William Middlemiss? Did you ever meet him?"

"I knew of him, but I never met him. I learned that her brother was a minister while we were still dating. I suggested to her that we ask William to perform our wedding ceremony, but she refused. She said she had never gotten along with William and that he didn't want anything to do with the family. She said that she would prefer a    civil ceremony. I let her have her way, and we were married by a judge."

"Did you know that William was pastor of a church in Parkville?"

"Chief, please don't take this as a putdown, but until I learned about the bulletin saying you were looking for me, I never heard of Parkville. Cathryn may have known he was here, but she never shared that information with me. She didn't like to talk about her background and family matters. I don't even know whether her folks are still alive. I think she may have once mentioned another brother in addition to William, but she never told me his name."

"OK, Carl, you are making the case that you are a reformed person who has a steady job helping older people. You say that you never abused your wife except in a therapeutic manner. You also say that you have never been here before and that you knew little or nothing about Cathryn's family. Now the big question: Why haven't you asked me how and when she died? You were her husband. Don't you care?"

Carl shifted in his seat and stared out the window. "Ours was a marriage of convenience. She wanted to have someone who would help her present herself as fully capable so that she wouldn't be regarded as handicapped. I needed someone to help me restore my reputation so that I could have a fresh start. It worked for a while, but then things went sour for her, and she no longer wanted me. I lived with that and moved on. I look at life with the viewpoint that it could end today or tomorrow, and all I'll have to show for it is what I've done in the past. I'll keep trying to improve so that when my time comes I'll have a better balance sheet to present to God. Cathryn and I helped each other for a while, but when she left, we became history for each other. I had nothing to do with her death, but I accept the fact of it, however it occurred. I haven't filed for a divorce because I have no desire to remarry. Beyond that statement, I have no interest at all. Cathryn is past tense in every sense of that expression."

"Thank you, Carl. I have no further questions for you. Please make sure that Sergeant Gomez has all of your contact information, and thank you for taking the initiative in coming to us. I'll cancel my bulletin with all of the authorities. For your information, there is a rental car agency sharing space with the Ford dealer on Main Street."

# CHAPTER 49
## EXTENDED FAMILY

Joe Gonzalez finished his telephone conversation with an amused expression on his face. He walked to the door of Penny's office and waited until she looked up from her computer.

"Bob Caspar just called me. There have been some unusual developments regarding our spare-time job of searching for Bertha Calahan's half-brother. Michelle and Kevin happened to be talking with their political science professor, and he turned out to have a recently-deceased brother who matched our profile. The DNA check was negative, but this professor liked the idea so much that he has applied to be a surrogate brother for Bertha, and everyone in the family thinks that it's a great idea.

The professor's name is Edward Middlemiss. His brother William, a minister, died under suspicious circumstances. His sister Cathryn was murdered, and her body was hidden in the attic of William's church. The police, the CME, and the current pastor of that church are putting their heads together to try to figure out the details behind the two deaths. Professor Edward feels he has lost his family, so he volunteered to be the family that Bertha is seeking. I guess it's good for both of them. It probably wouldn't make much difference if we found the missing half-brother, and he joined the party also.

"One very interesting detail about all of this family merging is that the church where the deaths occurred is the same church at which John

Hendrix is scheduled to be a judge for their Antiques Fair. This, of course, means that we will soon be visiting there to see whether anything of professional interest to us happens during that Fair. Mark your calendar to keep the first weekend in October open."

Penny did not share Joe's cheerful expression. "You just gave me a large dose of very interesting information, but while some of it is amusing, I don't like the sound of the rest of it. Sure, it's good that Bertha is getting at least some satisfaction from her search, but you just mentioned valuable antiques and murder in the same conversation. When we go to that Fair, we should have plenty of backup by people who are used to dealing with violent crime. This project has just become potentially dangerous.

# CHAPTER 50
## NEEDLE IN A HAYSTACK

A rthur entered the Parkville police station and found Bobby and Irma talking by the front desk.

"Is this a private conference, or are you open to including an amateur sleuth?"

Bobby chuckled, "Are you one of the Baker Street Irregulars overhearing key bits of information as you go about your clerical duties?"

"I'll accept that designation with a few ethical constraints. I'll be very tight-lipped about information that has been given to me in confidence in the course of my official duties. However, you've already seen that I have been able to find and identify interesting items among my predecessor's belongings. By the way, were you able to contact Carl Slocum to ask him about his property that I found?"

"He actually came to see me, Arthur. His visit is what I was discussing with Irma. He had reasonable answers to all of my questions, and I believed him. I don't think he was involved in the murder of Cathryn Middlemiss. Here, read my report, and reach your own conclusion."

Arthur took the stapled pages and scanned through the interrogation notes item by item. "It doesn't read as though he was being evasive. I see him as feeling that he had a well-documented case to present to you, Bobby. It doesn't appear that he was worried about you finding flaws in his story."

"The straightforward nature of his answers plus my knowledge that he had never been known to use violence, led me to thank him for his information and send him home. I'm sure we will be able to find him again if we need him."

Irma nudged Bobby. "I perceive that your Baker Street Irregular came here because he has significant information for you. If you don't stop talking and let him present it, he may explode."

They all laughed at this, and Arthur took an envelope out of his inner pocket. "Irma perceives very well as usual. I've spent some more time going over the belongings of William Middlemiss. I've been reading a large number of his voluminous and completely unsorted papers. Anyway, I got lucky. This envelope contains his ordination, marriage and divorce documents. He married one Maria Schmidt, an Austrian citizen. The marriage took place in London in 1968. Apparently, it didn't work out very well, because they were divorced in the United States in 1969. William was a U.S. citizen, and they were married just a few months after his ordination.

"The point of my bringing you these papers is to show you that there is someone else who knew William well, albeit a long time ago. If we could trace William's ex-wife Maria, we might gain insights into his personality that would help us to learn what happened in connection with both deaths. At the end of the investigation, we should return these papers to Edward as William's closest surviving relative."

Irma was impressed by this new information. "This gives us a new direction to take in going for background information and for learning about the personality of William Middlemiss. Before we start a laborious search for his ex-wife, I think we should explore this further with Edward. He was young at the time of his brother's marriage, but this new information might trigger some forgotten memories."

Bobby scratched his head as he thought through the situation. "I agree that we should continue to try to learn more about the old pastor's background and personality, but the policeman in me says that we should spend more time determining what happened on the night that William died and on trying to figure out how, when, and why Cathryn died. We don't know for sure whether William's death was a murder, but we're sure that Cathryn's death was. If I accept my own conclusion that Carl Slocum was not here and was not responsible for Cathryn's death, then William becomes the prime suspect. We don't know for sure that he did it, and we don't know the motive or exactly what happened, but all of this happened long after William and Maria parted. I agree with Irma that we should take the simpler course. Add this information to the file and use it in questioning Edward more deeply about relationships within his family. Let's start with the family member we already have nearby."

# CHAPTER 51
## MALLARD LAKE

A l Gomez entered the office as Bobby was starting to make a telephone call. "You'd better forget about the phone call, Chief. I just took a call from a very upset fisherman. He said that he was fishing on Mallard Lake and snagged what he thought was a piece of junk. He pulled like mad and finally pulled up a jacket sleeve with a man's hand sticking out. He's still sitting in his boat staring at it. He says we'd better get down there in a hurry to help him pull up the rest of the body. I already called Jerry Johnson at the Fire Department. They'll bring the boat they use for drowning cases. We're supposed to meet them at the Mallard parking lot."

Bobby put down the phone and grabbed his camera. "We'd better be sure we get pictures of the victim as he's pulled up. We'll need evidence to decide whether this was an accident, suicide or murder. Judging by the proximity of Mallard Lake to Blake's church, my guess is that it won't turn out to be an accident. Have someone call Irma and tell her she has more work to do here."

Al turned off the siren as they turned into the Mallard Lake parking lot, and parked next to the Fire Department ambulance. Jerry Johnson was standing next to the fire truck from which they had launched the rescue boat. Three firemen were in that boat about one hundred yards out into the lake, alongside the fisherman's boat. They watched as one of the firemen transferred over to be with the fisherman so that there were two people in each boat. One fireman from each boat reached over the side with a grappling hook on a pole. When they both had their hooks secured to the body, they nodded to each other and slowly pulled the sunken object upward. As the body broke through the surface of the water, the fisherman leaned forward and retrieved his hook from the jacket sleeve. The firemen wrestled the body into the fireboat and prepared to head for shore. Jerry Johnson gave a command into his radio, and then turned to Bobby. "The fisherman's name is Charlie Turner. He's retired, and fishes this lake several times each week. He was arguing with Sam that he should be left alone to continue fishing, but I told Sam to make sure Charlie comes ashore to give us a statement about what happened. Charlie doesn't want to get involved. He says he did his duty by calling the police, and now we should leave him alone to fish. I see that you brought your camera, but missed the boat. Don't worry; Andy took a few pictures out there while the others were raising the body. According to Sam, you won't have to do a lot of forensic work to determine whether it was an accident. He said that there was a concrete block tied to the victim's feet in a way that would have been almost impossible for him to do himself. I think we have a murder and disposal of the body in a way that was supposed to keep us from finding it for a long time. Charlie's tenacity in trying to avoid cutting his line when it snagged gives you the opportunity to examine a fairly fresh corpse."

Bobby wrote down a few notes and returned his notebook to his pocket. "Thanks, Jerry; your men handled the retrieval well. Irma will do her thing and try to learn enough from the body to tell us what happened." As he finished this comment Bobby looked up to see two more vehicles entering the parking lot. One was Irma's white CME van, and the other was a green Pontiac Grand Am with a large *PRESS* card showing through the windshield.

# CHAPTER 52
## NEWS

A rthur Blake's telephone rang twice before he picked up the handset. This was only his third call since the new telephone system had been installed. Now Shirley didn't have to answer all of the calls and buzz the proper person. Callers just keyed in his extension number.

"Hello, Pastor Blake speaking."

"Arthur, it's Bobby. I wanted to let you know that we fished a body out of Mallard Lake. Someone named Barry Silvers, according to the name printed in his undershirt. Looks like a murder—the killer removed all identification from his pockets, but he had his name written in his underwear. He must have been associated with some large organization where there was a chance of underwear getting mixed up. We don't know much more about him, but I wanted to warn you that this may cause you some trouble. A reporter showed up, and one of the firemen that he interviewed mentioned the two deaths at your church. My police know that we want to keep things quiet because it helps our investigation. Sometimes suspects talk about things that have never been released to the public. Anyway, the fireman said too much, and the reporter put out a story that this body is connected to those found at the church. It's pure speculation. We don't know anything about this victim. I thought that I should warn you so that you could head off any panic in your congregation. Tell your people that the police have no information that links this body to events at the church. When I learn more, I'll pass the information along to you."

"Thanks, Bobby. It's too bad that the church situation is getting publicity through pure speculation. I thought we had a pretty good lid on news of the developments that actually happened here. I'll let you know if I hear from anyone who has information about this Silvers person. May God have mercy on his soul. Goodbye."

Arthur returned the handset to its cradle. He had just taken his hand off of the telephone when it rang again. "Hello, Pastor Blake speaking."

"Blake, this is Angela King. I've just shown the Bishop a clipping that someone gave me from the *Rockford Register Star* about a body that was retrieved from the lake near your church. The article says that the person was murdered and that he was possibly involved in two earlier murders that occurred at the Parkville United Methodist Church. The reporter also says that officials at the church and at the Parkville Police Department are refusing to speak with him. I told you that I didn't want any more bad publicity from your church. Why didn't you deny the things he said in this article? Who gave him this information? Last time I talked with you about bad publicity, you said that you couldn't be held responsible for things that happened before you got there. Well, you can't use that excuse this time. This killing happened on your watch. What are you going to do about it?"

"News reaches you very rapidly, District Superintendent. I learned about this killing just before your call. There is no evidence that this person had anything to do with our church or with anything that happened here. The reporter was trying to put a sensational spin on his story. It's too bad that he talked with a fireman who wasn't clear on the facts and mingled several deaths together as though they were connected. I will inform the press that the church has no knowledge of the person whose body was found in the lake. With regard to any past deaths involving the church, I will say that they are the subject of an ongoing police investigation, and I am not permitted to talk about them.

I hope that a calm response to questions will convince everyone that we are being cooperative and that we do not feel that this new development involves our church. If I learn anything more about this new death, I will inform you."

"You had better smooth things over, Blake. We are about to launch a new fundraising drive covering the entire Northern Illinois Conference, and it won't be successful if we have bad publicity and rumors about troubled churches circulating. The next time I have to call you about this sort of thing, you will be out of there."

Arthur put down the telephone. He stared at it for about thirty seconds, wondering if it was going to complicate his day once again.

# CHAPTER 53
## RECOLLECTIONS

F our people were sitting around the conference
table at the Parkville Police Department.
Edward Middlemiss was being interviewed by Chief
Bobby Andrews while Pastor Arthur Blake and CME
Irma Custis played supporting roles. The
atmosphere was cordial and somewhat familiar.

Bobby initiated the session. "Edward, I want to
thank you for coming to talk with us again. You
may turn out to be extremely helpful to our efforts.
We are going to talk about personal relationships,
so I have asked Arthur to be with us because of his
pastoral and counseling background. I have also
asked Irma to join us because I believe that it will
be useful to call on a woman's point of view as we
continue our informal discussions.

"I asked you to visit us again because we've
found some new information about William that
might remind you about additional aspects of his
personality. We are trying to get to know him so
that we may more reasonably speculate on how he
would react to different situations. We also have
some new information about Cathryn's life in
Minneapolis."

"Go ahead, Chief. I'm just as anxious as you are
to find out what happened to William and Cathryn."

"Do you remember anything about William's
outlook and behavior when he was married to
Maria Schmidt?"

"I had almost forgotten that William was
married. They were only married for a year or so,
and I think I was about thirteen at the time. I    was

the cute little kid brother. I wasn't really involved in the adult conversations, nor was I interested in them. I do remember Maria, but only from a few visits. She was enthusiastic, and she treated me a lot more respectfully than William did. Their first visit as a couple was a celebration, but the subsequent visits were tense. Maria wanted to get close to the rest of us, but William just treated us as background material. He would have been happy to leave us all behind as he carved out his new life. In fact, once Maria had left him, he did just that. He only contacted us when it was absolutely necessary. He was a minister, but he refused to conduct the funeral services for our parents. It wasn't that he was too broken up to do the services; he simply wanted to keep his distance from everything and everyone."

"Was William closer to Cathryn than to the rest of the family?"

"William didn't want to be close to any of us. On the other hand, Cathryn always went out of her way for William. In the light of recent events, I'm beginning to wonder whether Cathryn knew that William wasn't a blood relative. She may have had a crush on him. Cathryn spent a lot of time talking with Mother about anything and everything. Maybe it comes with the territory in a mother-daughter relationship, but I didn't have talks like that with Mother. Cathryn may very well have learned more about William's origins than I did.

Bobby and Arthur exchanged glances. It might be significant if Cathryn had come to Parkville because she had always had romantic feelings for William.

Arthur voiced his thoughts first, "From what Bobby has told me about his conversation with Carl Slocum, Cathryn's husband, I could see Cathryn as wanting to find a relationship with someone    other than Carl. He was literally holding her back when she got drunk, and she wanted to go away to release her frustrations. I'm willing to assume that because of her feelings for William when they were younger, she might have wanted to turn to him. She might easily have managed to keep track of his location. After all, the United Methodist Church publishes the appointment list for all pastors, and it wouldn't take much searching on the Internet to find William's posting. I wonder how William would have reacted when she suddenly appeared."

Irma continued this line of thinking. "When Cathryn arrived in Parkville to contact William, she would have been pretty much out of control. Slocum has indicated that she was drinking heavily; she had very little patience; and she was frustrated because she had lost her longtime job and couldn't find a new one. William, on the other hand, had built walls around himself so that hardly anyone dared to disturb him. He had made being left alone the foundation of his comfort zone. Suddenly, he found himself confronted by this hysterical woman who wanted him to rescue her from her problems. If he had tried to simply reject her, her emotions would have changed to anger. Legally, he was her brother, and her affection for him may have gone beyond brotherly love. It is quite possible that under these circumstances Cathryn would have attacked William. Carl Slocum indicated that she had sufficient arm strength to seriously hurt her therapy clients."

Bobby looked thoughtful. "We're starting to develop a theory that is radically different from those I've already considered. Suppose that Cathryn was the initial aggressor, and William grabbed something and hit her in self defense. Would this make sense, and if so, would there be any way to prove it?"

Everyone looked at Irma. She paused and then began, "We would have to get very lucky to prove this scenario, if it actually happened. Any blood evidence would be old, and if William had cleaned the scene and the weapon, it might be difficult to detect. On the other hand, if the weapon could be found and identified, it's possible that we might find some damage to it that might be linked to Cathryn's death. If William killed her in self defense after she attacked him, he would have used some easily available object as a weapon. It wouldn't have been what you would normally consider a weapon at all. Cathryn's assault would have taken him by surprise. He would have considered his negative response to her to have been quite reasonable and unlikely to cause a problem.

There is one potentially worthwhile result of this discussion. If we're talking about a death which resulted from an emotional confrontation, then we have pretty much found the timing of her death. It would have happened shortly after she left Carl, which is a definite date that can be identified."

Arthur continued, "If Cathryn's death had been caused by William in self-defense, the keeping of her leg prosthesis would have appeared reasonable for him. He would have kept it as a reminder of his sinful action and also as a reminder of his rejection of his family. He may have thought afterward that if he hadn't rejected his family, Cathryn might still be alive. I really have no explanation for his putting the body in the attic. You knew him, Edward. Why might he have done that?"

"One possibility might lie in the way he always seemed to have made up his mind before he even heard the arguments in a debate. This is why I got extremely frustrated with him as a child. William wanted to take a strong position and to show no vacillation from that position because he considered openness to a different conclusion to be a sign of weakness. As a minister, he had built up a reputation as being a strong but reclusive person. Perhaps he felt that his emotional counter-attack, if revealed to the police and his congregation, would negate his stature in their eyes and ruin his career."

Bobby interjected, "We may be getting completely carried away by hypothetical possibilities. If William killed Cathryn, we have no way of knowing who the initial aggressor was. I do think that we can rule out an accidental death. If it had been an accident, William would have had no reason to fail to report it. He must have felt that he would be accused of her murder if he called the police. He felt threatened by the circumstances, and he felt that he had to conceal the body so that no one would know that a crime had occurred. The thing I don't understand is how he thought that the body would never be discovered. He had to realize that someday, someone would look in the attic."

The meeting ended, and Arthur drove back to the church, bothered by the hypothetical nature of their discussions. They had been earnest in their speculations, but he doubted that theories were going to solve this mystery. He entered the church from the upper parking lot, checked that Shirley had no messages for him, and headed down the long hallway alongside the sanctuary toward the old church building. Arthur entered his office, threw his notepad on his desk, and stared at his *blue monster* covered pile of stuff. The tarp had definitely been removed and replaced haphazardly. The shape of the pile had also changed. He leaned over the pile to remove the tarp and determine the changes, but as he reached for the blue fabric he felt a terrible pain on the back of his head. The last things he remembered were wondering if the pile would    be comfortable when he fell on it and realizing that the investigation was no longer a matter of speculation.

He woke up to find Sue Willoughby bending over him. "Arthur, are you all right? I called 911. What happened?"

He pushed off from the pile and stood up. "I'll be all right, Sue. Someone hit me when I wasn't looking. Thanks for your help. You can go now. While I wait for the paramedics, I want to check to see if anything has been stolen."

Sue wanted to stay in the hope that Arthur would turn to her for comfort. She thought that this might be her big chance to let him know how she felt about him. She had the competing desire to leave and spread the word about what had happened so that others would see how close to Arthur she was. When Arthur gave his full attention to determining whether items were missing, she followed his instructions and left. As he continued to search he glanced at the mirror behind the door. He had a small rivulet of blood meandering from the back of his head to the right side of his neck. He also had a red lipstick kiss mark on his left cheek.

# CHAPTER 54
## CHURCH FAMILY

"Wally Sanborn reporting for duty, Sir. Wow, what happened to you?"

Arthur had a gauze bandage wrapped around the top of his head, and his eyes had a slightly vacant look. "Come on in, Wally, it's not as bad as it looks. No, it's not due to someone taking exception to one of my sermons. I must have surprised a burglar when I returned here yesterday. As I came into my office, I was greeted with a blow to the back of my head. I don't think I was unconscious more than a few minutes, but it was enough for the intruder to get away undetected. At least nothing appears to be missing. This bandage will only be on for a day or so. I notified Chief Andrews, and he sounded almost happy to hear about it, because it gives him something current to investigate. "Have a seat, and we'll move on to more pleasant topics. Thanks for stopping in. There's fresh coffee in the pot. Help yourself."

"If it's any consolation, I had several similar hits on my head while I was in the Army, and I managed to bounce back in pretty good shape." Wally revealed a coffee mug he had been holding behind his back. "We've been getting along well, Arthur, and I've enjoyed these discussions so much that I think it's time to make them an official function of friendship. I hereby install my personal U.S. Army coffee mug on the tray by your pot. Just call on me whenever you need a soldier to stand guard over your office or a fellow coffee drinker."

"That's an impressive gesture, Wally. Thank you, and please accept one of my NASA mugs to use at home.

"Now that we are officially co-conspirators, I'd like to test your memory a bit, and I'd also like you to help me with a potential church project."

"OK, Chaplain, test away."

"This conversation has to be kept confidential. It's about that body that was found in the old church attic. Whatever happened took place about two years ago, maybe a little less. I don't know exactly what occurred, but it was something that might have significantly upset Pastor Middlemiss. Do you remember anything unusual about his behavior during that time period?"

"He was always a bit unusual, but there was a period of about a month or more back then when he preached every week about Hell and damnation. I had thought that sermons of that type had gone out with the nineteenth century, but at the time I attributed it to his old fashioned straight-laced outlook on life. We all questioned his choice of sermon topics when we mingled after church, but we all forgot about it after he stopped that series. I hadn't thought about it again until you just now raised the question. Thinking back, I remember that sometime around that period Middlemiss started to show up for church in older clothes that were more disheveled than the tailored black suits he usually wore. It wasn't that he was being informal; it was more like being sloppy. In reality, it didn't make much difference, because he wore a robe over his clothes during the services, but I noticed the change right away. I'm sure that most people never even realized that anything was different. I'm more observant because I spent years inspecting the gear of my troops for neatness and completeness. In the army, a sudden change in appearance and preparedness would be looked upon as an indication of possible psychological problems."

Arthur made a few notes on a small pad while Wally was speaking. After Wally finished, Arthur asked, "Did this sloppiness continue forever, or did it stop after a while?"

"I think that it must have been around the same time as the Hell and damnation sermon series, but I think it lasted a month or two longer. Then, it suddenly stopped, and he was back to his neat black suits. Once he got back to dressing neatly, he never lapsed again."

"Were his sermon topics more cheerful after he became neat again?"

"Your predecessor never preached a cheerful sermon, Arthur. He mostly tried to do theological interpretation, with only limited success. I did detect a change in his direction at that time from attempts at biblical scholarship to frequent preaching about Jesus as a healer. I think the congregation was relieved when he made that change. All of us can use healing, but very few of us could follow his more academic sermons."

Arthur made a few more notes, and then put his pad away. "Thanks, Wally; you have a good memory for detail. I'm beginning to get the feeling that I know William, but it will take more work before I'll be able to say that I understand his thought processes.

"Now, on to a new topic. I'm thinking about a project to help people in the church get to know each other better so that they will feel more like family members and less like a group of random strangers. I'm planning to have each person fill out a form listing ten specific personal traits or background experiences. The completed forms will be posted on a bulletin board, and by looking at the forms you should be able to quickly find other people in church with whom you have something in common. I'm hoping that this project will lead to more in-depth conversations and friendships. What do you think of the concept?"

"It should work, but you might run into problems with the women if one of your form items is age or date of birth. If the information you request is not too personal, most people will cooperate."

"I'm glad you feel that way, Wally, because I'm asking you to be my test guinea pig. Here is my first try at the form. Complete it, and we'll see how much time it takes and whether the answers are useful conversation starters."

Name_____

1. Place of Birth_____
2. Years in Parkville Area_____
3. Occupation/Career_____
4. School last attended_____
5. Favorite Subject/Major_____
6. Hobbies_____
7. Marital Status_____
8. Childhood Church_____
9. Favorite Bible story_____
10. Most memorable childhood event_____

Wally looked at the form briefly, and then he started to work on it. Arthur made a note of the starting time to see how long Wally took to complete his assignment. The room became quiet, and

Arthur devoted his full attention to his coffee. Five minutes later, Wally broke the silence.

"I'm done, but I have some comments. First, I think you need longer lines to give people space to write. Second, I think some people will have problems with the education section. Those who never went beyond high school or had less education may not want to publicize that status. Those with several college degrees may want to mention more than one college and major. I also think you should include something about cities lived in before Parkville. I'll bet that we'll have quite a few people who lived in the same places, maybe even at the same times. I do think the approach will work, but you may want to test it in a small group before giving it to everyone. I suggest that you try it during the next Church Council meeting. That should be a big enough group of people, and they're the kind of people who would have strong opinions one way or the other."

"Thanks, Wally, I think I'll do just that, and I'll make a few revisions to the form by that time."

They stood up. Wally placed his empty mug by the coffee pot and left. Arthur looked intently at the answers Wally had written, and then he filed the form in his desk drawer.

# CHAPTER 55
## STAKEOUT

I n the Parkville Police conference room, Chief
Bobby Andrews was briefing Sergeant Gomez
and two detectives on the status of each of the
three death investigations. Al Gomez looked fairly
alert, but Gene Murphy and Hank Robbins were
having trouble staying focused because they were
night shift people, and it was now ten o'clock in the
morning. Gene and Hank heard Bobby's words as
though they were echoing down a long tunnel.

"The second death, that of the woman whose
remains we found in the attic, was most likely a
crime of passion, although we are not at all sure
who was the aggressor. The woman, Cathryn
Middlemiss, died earlier, but her remains were not
found until after the death of Pastor William
Middlemiss, her step-brother. It's likely that Pastor
Middlemiss was the perpetrator of Cathryn's death,
but he may have killed her in self-defense. At this
time we don't know the circumstances of the
pastor's death except that he was found with a
wound on his head at the foot of a ladder leading to
the locked attic hatch. The hatch was still covered
with cobwebs and did not appear to have been
opened at the time of his death. The death of Barry
Silvers, whose body was fished out of Mallard Lake,
is probably not connected to the church deaths, but
we can't be absolutely sure. If it was a completely
independent crime, we have no leads on it at all so
far. Hopefully, we'll get lucky and learn something
about him while we're going through our other
inquiries.

"During the course of the church investigations, we have heard several references to Pastor Middlemiss having alluded to valuable property that he possessed. He never gave any specific information about that property, and nothing of significant value has been discovered. As I said before, my advisors and I think that the death of Cathryn was the result of some kind of emotional confrontation. It may or may not have had something to do with the valuable possessions of Pastor Middlemiss. On the other hand, it is quite likely that the pastor's death was the direct or indirect result of a conflict with someone looking for that property.

"Assuming that Middlemiss' death had something to do with his property, It is likely that he died before his assailant could find it, and the pastor probably never revealed its location. I believe that someone is still looking for it because Pastor Arthur Blake was hit from behind and knocked out when he surprised an intruder in his office. I also believe that either the property or the key to its location is located somewhere in or near the church. Because of this, I want to have a stakeout of the church every evening for the next few weeks, up until the time that they are actively involved in their Antiques Fair. I think that whoever is looking for the pastor's property will try again to find it, but I don't think they will take another chance during daylight hours when people are around, and I don't think they will try in the midst of all of the activity preparing for the Fair. If these assumptions are correct, we have a limited time window to cover, and a reasonable probability of success. We know that an outsider was there at the time of the pastor's death because somebody had to bring the ladder to the church. Arthur's injury proves someone is still trying to find something. Hopefully, this stakeout will lead us to the identity of that unknown person or persons when they come back to search again.

# CHAPTER 56
## PREPARATIONS

Wally Sanborn entered the church office as Shirley Hadley was working on Sunday's service bulletin in her computer. She held up her right index finger in a request for him to wait, and she continued her typing. When she reached the end of a paragraph, she swiveled her chair to face Wally.

"What's up, Wally? Would you like an almost fresh piece of pastry?"

"I'll have to waive the pastry, Shirley. I have to keep in shape for taking the youth group camping. They think I'm way over the hill, and I'm out to prove to them that when it comes to wilderness survival techniques, a fit old man can beat a young person whose life is video games and snacks."

"Well, don't be too down on snacks; I am the baker's wife, and we're saving for Jeremy's college education. Let's just say everything in moderation."

"Fair enough, Shirley. I've been running down my checklists of everything we have to do before the Antiques Fair, and I came across a couple of things that are naturals for you to handle."

"I want to be part of the team. Whenever you have something for me, just let me know. What do you have for me now?"

Wally unrolled a large sheet of paper he had been carrying. "Here's a layout of the booths, tents and presentation areas for the church grounds outside the building. I'd like you to contact the Fire Department and ask them to mark on the layout where they think we will need fire extinguishers and any other required safety equipment. When you talk with them, offer them the use of a spot by the outer ring of booths if they want to have someone there to promote the use of smoke and carbon monoxide detectors. In addition, I'd like you to make a copy of this layout for Bill Martin so that he can look into lighting the area well enough for us to continue the Fair into the early evening hours. I'm sure that I'll have more for you later, and I appreciate your enthusiasm, but that's all for now."

"Consider it done, Wally. I'll start on it as soon as I finish working on the bulletin for Sunday's service."

"Thanks, and Shirley, do you know where I can find Arthur?"

"You can't find him. He took the day off to go meet his father somewhere."

# CHAPTER 57
## SHOW AND TELL

A rthur walked into the restaurant and waved to his father who was already seated in a corner booth. As he slid into the booth Arthur said, "Sorry I'm a little late. There was a minor fender bender accident that slowed everyone. Have you been here long?"

"Just long enough to have a cup of coffee and to get very curious about what you wanted to show me, Arthur."

"Well, Dad, do you remember how you used to like to come home with an unusual antique or artifact, and after dinner you would ask me to tell you what I thought it was?"

"That was part of your education process. After you gave me your opinion, I would always tell you the true history of the item in detail. By the time you were in high school you were coming very close to identifying the items I brought home every time."

"Today you're going to get to play that game, Dad; but you know the rules, no discussions until after we finish our meal."

They each ordered soup plus a sandwich. Arthur had vegetable soup with a roast beef sandwich, and Peter had tomato soup with a tuna salad sandwich. They enjoyed reminiscing while waiting for their food and while they ate. Peter was getting very curious about what Arthur had for him to see, but Arthur insisted that they have dessert just to build up the suspense. Finally, he took something out of his pocket and handed it to his father.

"I found this in a metal box in the attic of our old church building, and I'm pretty sure that I know what it is. I wanted to see whether you would agree with me. I also think it signifies something else that is interesting."

Peter looked at the item carefully, and then he checked it a second time using a powerful magnifier that he retrieved from his pocket.

"I see what you mean. It definitely looks genuine. Was this the only one?"

"No, there were eight of them, but one is sufficient for this discussion. Do you agree about the implications?"

"Absolutely. I think we should discuss it further while I'm at your church for the Antiques Fair. I want to get the feel of the place, so I'll arrive a bit early. In the meantime, I think that we should both treat this as confidential and not talk about it with anyone else."

"I agree. You may discuss it with Mother if you wish. She may have something to contribute. Will she be coming to the Fair?"

"She'll be there acting as a third judge specializing in paintings. She'll also judge antiques from parts of the world not covered by Hendrix or me. Do you think she would forego any opportunity to show her pride in her son?"

"Please ask her to subdue that part. I have to live among the people she'll be meeting, and I don't want to give them any unnecessary ammunition for embarrassing me."

# CHAPTER 58
## WOOLWORTH'S

W ally sat at a small table in a dark corner of Marbury's Parkville Pub and nursed his Bass ale as he thought back to what his mother had told him during her final illness. He had been eighteen years old when she died, facing adulthood by himself because his father had died three years earlier. Mum had said that she hoped he wouldn't hate her after she told him something she had kept secret for many years.

"Wally, something terrible happened when you were just a baby. It was November of 1944, and I had taken you shopping with me at Woolworth's in the New Cross section of London. The store was crowded that day. People had the feeling that the war would be over soon, so they had started to enjoy going shopping again. You were in your pram, and the store was pretty full. I was wheeling you past the clothes for infants when the whole world exploded. I found out later that we had been hit by a German V-2 rocket. People were buried under debris everywhere. Some were screaming; some were moaning; and a lot of them weren't making any sounds at all. The whole neighborhood was a shambles. They said afterward that it was the worst V-2 strike of the war. One hundred and sixty-eight people died, and one hundred and twenty-one more were badly injured. Many more were separated from their loved ones and didn't know whether they were alive or not for many days. I looked everywhere when I regained consciousness, but I couldn't find you. I was hysterical at the site, and I couldn't sleep for the next several nights. After a week and a half, I was directed to a hospital where they were said to have infants rescued from the blast who had been treated for wounds. I was so happy to find you. I snatched you up and hugged you ever so carefully as soon as I saw and recognized you. I had thought that I would never see you again.

I took you home to Dad, and with the war ending a few months later, things got much better. We were all happy as you grew up and started school. One day at school you fell onto some pieces of sharp metal and hurt your leg. They called the ambulance and took you to hospital. Then they called me to meet you there. When I arrived, they said that you had lost a lot of blood, and they asked me to donate some to replace it. Dad came along shortly, and he donated some blood too. In a little while, the doctor came out and said that he wanted to have a private talk with us in his office. Dad and I were both petrified that he would tell us that you were dying, but in some ways what he told us was even worse. The doctor told us that you would recover fully, but that neither of us had the same blood type as you. He said that it was clear that you were not our son. I broke down at that point and just cried and screamed for quite a while. When they finally managed to calm me down, I told them that it must be my fault. I must have identified the wrong baby as mine after the V-2 bombing. In the midst of the post-bombing trauma and their overflow patient load, they hadn't confirmed the parental identifications by doing blood typing.

"Years had passed, and there were insufficient records to locate and re-examine all of the parents and infants who had been involved in the reclaiming process, so the doctor said that we should continue to raise you but that we should go through the legal process of adoption if we    wanted to be absolutely sure that there would be no later difficulties for you. I was afraid of legal people and government agencies, and although we told the doctor we would take that path, we never did. To this day, I believe that I selected my own child in good faith, but I know that I walked into that nursery being very afraid that my son had been one of the ones who had died. Perhaps I subconsciously wanted to be emphatic in my identification so that there would be no doubts, and I would have a son again.

"Wally, I'm so sorry to have to tell you this. I've always loved you, enough so that I can't allow myself to go to my grave without telling you. Please forgive me."

Wally remembered how tightly he had held his frail mother as she lay there. Of course he had forgiven her. She was the only mother he had known, and they had loved each other very much and been very close, especially after his father had died.

Following his mother's death, he had read everything he could about the V-2 rocket that had hit Woolworth's and the traumatic aftermath. He had collected related obituary notices and newspaper clippings about family members being reunited afterward. He remembered being amazed at the amount of newspaper space that had been given to the event for so long, and he began to realize how much the bombing had affected the feelings of the nation as a whole. As he continued to gather clippings and place them into scrapbooks, he had reached two surprising conclusions. The first was that for a very long time afterward people would be partially identified in newspaper articles by the fact that they had been at Woolworth's that day. The second conclusion was that a much larger number of people had claimed to have been there than could have fit into the entire neighborhood.

Wally remembered the day that he had found the article mentioning that Woolworth's had been a popular shopping spot for American soldiers and their families. This was due to nostalgia for the many Woolworth stores in the United States. That article had also stated that many of the dead and injured had been Americans along with their British wives and children. It had been this article that had made Wally in his newly-orphaned situation think about the possibility that he was actually the son of an American soldier. He had latched onto that thought in order to keep from just drifting through life. Wally had decided to emigrate from Britain to the United States. He would start his adult life there. Once he had settled in America, his youthful desire to join in and help others had led him first to the Peace Corps and later to a career in the Army. These organizations had rapidly made him feel part of the fabric of American life and had given him desires for creativity and leadership. Now that he was retired, he was compensating for his uncertain parentage by doing his best to be a father figure for youth at the church.

# CHAPTER 59
## HUSBANDS

M aria reminisced as she walked through the woods. Her choices of husbands had certainly been eclectic. William had been up-tight, controlling, frail, introverted, and introspective. Erik had been almost the exact opposite: relaxed, open to change, robust, extroverted, creative, and interested in everything that was going on around him and in the world. Erik had also been a much better lover, expressing his zest for life in every aspect of love. She smiled as she thought about what her life would have been like at this point if she had stayed married to William. Maria had left William because of his overwhelming desire for wealth and the material treasures that her father possessed. She knew now that if she hadn't left him for this reason, she would have had to invent another. She hadn't been in love with William. She had been in love with the idea of being a minister's wife and with becoming the catalyst that made an ordinary church congregation become something special. William would want to control every aspect of his flock's activities, or at least to control their expectations for his involvement in those activities. Maria wondered where he was now and whether he had changed at all.

Erik had been one of those rare people who are good at everything they attempt. She knew from close observation that he had always done his homework and had planned and researched before tackling any new challenge. Outsiders who didn't know about his penchant for preparation had always thought that everything was just easy for him. He had been fun to be around because he had been humble and free of ego. She honestly felt that she had grown to be a better person because of the time she had shared with him.

As she trudged along the winding path up a steep hill, Maria wondered whether her father still hated William as much as he did at the time of their divorce. She also wondered how her life would have developed if she hadn't married William before coming to America and contacting her father.

# CHAPTER 60
## FINAL PREPARATIONS

Arthur entered the church office as Shirley was hanging up the telephone. She wrote a name into a blank space on the chart on her desk and then turned to him. "That does it. I now have volunteers for all of the work assignments for the Antiques Fair. That was Bob Murray, and he took the last booth-sitting assignment for giving exhibitors a rest break. His wife Martha also volunteered for the packaging booth. That was a last-minute thought that may turn out to be a good fund-raiser. If people are buying valuable antiques, they will want to buy packaging materials and services to protect them on the way home.

"What can I do for you, Arthur?"

"I'm just going around dotting I's and crossing T's to be sure that everything will be ready on time. I know that the committee has everything under control, but because I suggested this event, I feel that it is in a sense still my baby, and I want to be useful."

"Well, you brought the baby to the church, but we have all adopted it, and we're nursing it quite well, thank you. If you really want to help, you can call the garbage company to arrange for their largest dumpster for cleanup afterwards, and at least twelve sets of garbage cans and recycle bins to be distributed around the grounds and adjacent to the inside displays. To protect the appearance of the church, we are going to restrict food and drink sales and consumption to outside areas, but we'll need a few bins inside for the benefit of those who don't obey the rules."

"You have the right guy for this job, Shirley. My mom always had me in charge of garbage cans when I was a kid. Do you know if the Illinois Bureau of Tourism has mailed out brochures yet?"

"We're part of their *Illustrious Illinois* promotion with TV commercials, a featured page on the state website, and newspaper ads in other cities. They've cut back on bulk mailings because they're not cost effective, but they have a mailing piece and a downloadable brochure that they are supplying to anyone who requests it on the website. Sue Willoughby and her boss at Tourism, Sarah Sanders, have done very well by us."

"Will we have T-shirts for sale?"

"They've been designed, printed, and they're now sitting in a huge carton in the next room. They come in various colors, and they say *Parkville UMC* on the back and *Collect me, I'm a Fair Antique* on the front. We didn't put a date on them so that we can use any leftovers next year after this event becomes a successful tradition."

"You've convinced me. Everything's going per the plan, and you're all enthusiastic. What more could I want?

"I'll be in my study working on my sermon. I expect my mother and father to arrive sometime today. If they come during the next hour, please call me. I want to do my genial host imitation."

# CHAPTER 61
## THE BLAKES

I rma was talking with Arthur in the lower parking lot of the church when Arthur's parents arrived in a plain white van with the small inscription *Blake Antiques, Richmond, Illinois* on the doors. As Arthur started toward the van, Irma began to walk away, but Arthur stopped her.

"You might as well meet these folks. It may turn out to be an experience that will make your day."

"I don't want to barge in on family matters, Arthur."

"Too late, family matters are about to barge in on you."

Irma saw two people practically running from the van toward them. The man was quite lean and shorter than Arthur at about five feet ten inches tall. The woman was about five feet six inches tall and well-proportioned. They both had graying hair that seemed a mismatch for relatively youthful faces featuring broad matching smiles. Irma thought that they were probably in their sixties, but they looked as though they were in their early fifties.

The woman spoke first, "Hello, Arthur, I finally made it out here. I should have come when you were first assigned to this church. That just shows that I must be an unconcerned mother. And who is this sweet young thing, the choir director?"

"Mother, you've been extremely patient and considerate to let me get established here before making your grand entrance. You kicked me out of the nest to fly by myself, but I always know that I can fly back and be welcomed, so don't worry about making impressions. You're the best.

"In response to your question, I'd like you to meet Irma Custis, our County Medical Examiner and a good friend. Irma, meet my mother and father, Janice and Peter Blake."

Everyone shook hands, hugged, and exchanged greetings as appropriate. Then Arthur's mother turned to Irma. "Are you descended from Martha's first husband, Colonel Daniel Parke Custis?"

Irma laughed. "I can see that this family specializes in history, but you'll have to give Arthur two demerits. He thought that Custis was Martha's maiden name. As far as the genealogy, I might be related to a cousin, but not directly to Daniel."

Peter finally had a chance to join in the conversation, "Don't mind us, Irma, we come on pretty strong when we're together with new people. We talk about historical aspects of things all the time when we're alone, and it just spills over when we encounter people who are new to us, especially those with interesting names. The funny thing is that we're old New Englanders, and everyone who knows that expects us to be very reserved and terse in our conversation. We can be when the circumstances require, but our natural inclination is to erupt with loquaciousness and curiosity."

Irma smiled. "Did you come from the same part of New England?"

Janice was quicker to respond. "We grew up one block away from each other in Berlin, New Hampshire; and be absolutely sure that you avoid pronouncing our town like the German city. You have to put the accent on the first syllable or everyone in Berlin will yell at you. We went to the same schools all the way through the University of New Hampshire in Durham. I majored in Art History, and Peter majored in Archeology. The most interesting part was that we didn't date until our senior year, and then we got married the week after graduation. All those years we traveled in the same crowd but were only friends. It was only when we both had breakups at the end of serious relationships that we turned to each other for consolation. The rest is history. We've been married for forty-three years now. My folks were none too happy when I changed from being a Catholic to being a Methodist."

Arthur turned to Irma, "I told you this would be a different experience. You have now known my parents for five minutes, and you have heard most of their life stories."

Peter joined in, "Don't worry that we'll run out of things to talk about, Arthur, we have many more stories to tell Irma, and we'd like to learn from her what it's like to be a County Medical Examiner."

"Well, Dad, let's save that for another day when we have plenty of time to relax and talk. Just be sure that we do it during the daytime, because Irma has stories that can give you nightmares that you wouldn't believe. Whenever she tells me about her work I hold up a cross to protect myself. Now, why don't we all adjourn to the parsonage and get you unpacked. Then I'll treat for supper. Irma, please come and join us."

"Not tonight, Arthur. You folks have a lot of catching up to do, and I have to write an autopsy report. Give me a rain check, and I'll join you the next time you schedule a feast."

Irma waved and walked toward her black Ford Mustang which was her off-duty car. She enjoyed it much more than the white GMC Yukon she drove when on duty, but she knew the Mustang could never handle all of her crime scene gear nor reach some of the remote off-road accident investigation sites. When she reached her car Irma opened the trunk to store something that Arthur had given her for DNA analysis. He hadn't given her much explanation. She assumed that it had something to do with the deaths of William Middlemiss and his sister Cathryn.

# CHAPTER 62
## EDWARD AND BERTHA

T he Caspars had thrown their annual *End of Summer Barbecue* halfway through September and had invited all of the nearby neighbors. Edward had been able to get away from UW Platteville, and he brought Kevin and Michelle with him. When they arrived, they walked down the path to the rear of the house, rounded the corner to reach the barbecue patio and shouted, "Here we are!"

Bob responded, "This new expanded family arrangement is certainly good for taxi service."

Everyone laughed, and the newcomers filled plates with food and dispersed to join in various conversations. Edward sought out Bertha, and found her sitting on a chair under a tree.

"I really do appreciate your letting me be part of the family. I actually feel younger for having people I can relax with and engage in non-academic conversations."

"It's funny that you said that, Edward, because I had the same feeling after Bob and Paula moved me down here from that old house in Iowa City. I guess independence only goes so far as a positive virtue. At some time you have to start sharing yourself with others if you want to feel that your life has been worthwhile."

"Speaking of sharing how would you like to have a pseudo sister-brother outing? During all of that follow-up to the deaths of William and Cathryn, I became friendly with Pastor Arthur Blake and Irma Custis in Parkville. I know that you have been there and conversed with them too. They are about to have an Antiques Fair at Arthur's church, and I thought that it might be fun for us to drive over there for a day to enjoy the Fair and to get to know each other better. Would you be interested?"

"That sounds like a great idea, Edward, as long as you don't refer to me as being one of the antiques. I'm getting a bit sensitive about age."

"Bertha, you're young in my eyes, and you've been a breath of fresh air coming into my life. I'm sure that we'll both enjoy it, and we'll feel quite young next to some of those old artifacts, meaning the displayed pieces and not the people."

# CHAPTER 63
## JUDGES

As promised, Wednesday morning Peter Blake met John Hendrix at O'Hare International Airport in Chicago. The Blakes had driven to Parkville early, so Peter had driven back to O'Hare alone. He recognized John from a picture in a newspaper article, and he was surprised to see how physically fit Hendrix looked. He appeared to be about six feet tall, and he had very good posture for a man his age. John effortlessly carried a small suitcase by a strap over his shoulder while he carried an attaché case in his hand. Peter introduced himself as soon as John had cleared the security area, and then they proceeded to the baggage claim area and Peter's car.

During the long drive to Parkville, they exchanged anecdotes about unusual antiques and art pieces that they had encountered and about the many misconceptions that people had about why something old is or is not valuable. They soon felt relaxed with each other and found that they had similar senses of humor. John told a joke about an old man who kept repeating himself, and then with an impish look in his eye he told it again. Peter countered with a story about a lady who had come to him for an appraisal of a beautiful old flowered soup tureen. He said that she was very enthused about it because it matched her China dishes, but that he had to very diplomatically suggest that perhaps she shouldn't use it for serving because it was actually a chamber pot. In between stories Peter explained the way the Antiques Fair was laid out and what their duties as judges would be. By the time they reached Parkville and pulled up at the parsonage, Peter and John were interacting like old friends and professional colleagues.

While the two men were unloading John's luggage, Arthur and his mother came out of the parsonage to greet them and to tell them that everyone was supposed to go over to the church for a final briefing by Wally Sanborn. Within ten minutes they had John's belongings stowed in his assigned room. When they drove up to the church grounds, they found that a long table full of sandwich ingredients, potluck salads, and casseroles awaited them. Wally and the other committee members greeted them, and then Wally began his briefing.

"I want to start by thanking everyone for the work that has been done to date to get us ready for this special event. When Pastor Blake first suggested this idea, it sounded perfect for us because we would make good use of those portions of the new building which are not normally occupied. At this time I have to announce that the reaction to our Antiques Fair has been so good, thanks to the publicity campaign of the Illinois Bureau of Tourism, that we have overflowed the building. Fortunately, the weather is expected to be good enough for outdoor exhibits. We have arranged for a large number of booths to be set up in the lower parking lot for both antiques displays and food sales. We had expected almost all of the exhibitors to be local, but we have had display space requests from as far away as Michigan. The good news is that the Fair will be bringing in considerably more money than we expected. The bad news is that we will have to work very conscientiously to keep all of the exhibitors and the visitors happy. We have plenty of volunteers, so there shouldn't be a problem. If we can't cope with it, Father McGraw from the Catholic Church has offered the services of his youth group. We will let him know by Friday afternoon if we need assistance. I also have added something to give the Fair a good start. As you know, all booths are supposed to be set up and ready for customers by ten o'clock Friday morning. In order to attract early attention for the exhibitors, I will ask Pastor Blake to give the Fair a blessing at precisely ten o'clock. Following this benediction, we will have a unit from the Illinois National Guard present the colors with the playing of a recording of the National Anthem. After the Anthem has concluded, a friend of mine from the Army will parachute into our midst. All of this is being described in advance on several radio stations, so we should see a good-sized crowd at the opening on Friday. Do you have any questions?" Arthur spoke first, "Do we need any special permissions to have the man parachute over the church property?"

"The permissions have already been obtained, and for the record it will be a woman parachuting."

Bill Martin added, "This isn't a question but a clarification. Because the lower parking lot will be used for additional booths, parking will be in the upper parking lot plus the lot across Jeffers Street alongside Mallard Lake. I think these two lots will be adequate, but if not, we'll allow some parking on the grass behind the lower lot."

Wally wrapped up the meeting by inviting people with remaining questions to see him privately. He told the booth setup crew to start their work immediately. Then he reminded those who were registering the exhibitors to be there Thursday evening and early Friday morning. There was a loud cheer when Wally closed the meeting with a "Here we go!"

After eating, those who didn't have immediate tasks drifted away for a final afternoon of planning or relaxation. The final preparations and opening of the Antiques Fair would bring a complete change of pace to Parkville.

# CHAPTER 64
## NOCTURNAL VIGIL

D etectives Murphy and Robbins had the stakeout duty for Thursday, the final night before the Antiques Fair would open. Chief Andrews had said that this would be the last night that they would watch for unusual activity at the church because there would be nothing but unusual activity once the Fair opened. Besides, once the Fair started uniformed officers would be watching the church at night to be sure that valuable antiques didn't disappear.

It had been dark for about three hours when Hank Robbins in the lower parking lot behind the new building radioed to Gene Murphy near the entrance to the old church that he had seen someone approaching the old building very quietly while trying to stay in the darkest shadows. The two detectives moved toward each other with guns drawn, and after they exchanged a synchronizing signal they both turned on their flashlights and aimed them at the shadowy figure. That person cringed and cried out. The detectives ran forward, ready for anything. Gene was the first to speak.

"It's an old lady. Hold your fire."

That utterance so scared the woman that she screamed, "Don't shoot! Don't shoot!"

Hank followed up. "Who are you? What are you doing here at this time of night?"

"My name is Rose Nowicki. I live in the house next door, and I wanted to see what was happening with the preparations for the Antiques Fair. I've been worried that I'll be having people walking all over my property while this thing is going on."

The detectives lowered their guns, thanking God that they hadn't been so trigger- happy as to shoot an old lady. Her story sounded plausible, so Gene told her that she could go home, but that she had better not walk around in the dark because they were giving security to the Fair. He made this last comment to keep her from wondering why armed detectives were around the church.

After Mrs. Nowicki left, Hank and Gene decided that they had experienced enough excitement for the night and called off the stakeout in favor of going back to the police station to write their report about the incident. As they walked toward their car, Gene had the feeling that they weren't alone in the darkness, but he attributed that feeling to tension remaining after intercepting the old lady.

# CHAPTER 65
## INTERVIEW

F riday morning Gene and Hank looked for Bobby Andrews to give him their report. They found him in the conference room with two strangers and Rose Nowicki. When they saw her, they got the feeling that they were not going to enjoy this meeting.

Before Bobby could say anything, Gene spoke, "Chief, if these lawyers are claiming that we did anything bad to Mrs. Nowicki, they are absolutely wrong. She was just in the wrong place at the wrong time and got caught in our stakeout."

Bobby frowned. "These people aren't lawyers, and Mrs. Nowicki is here to be interviewed, not to file a complaint. It appears that you fellows accepted her story at face value when you shouldn't have. Meet Penny and Joe Gonzalez who work for the Federal Government."

They shook hands, and the detectives joined the others at the conference table. Joe was the first to speak.

"As I was telling you, Chief, there are aspects of this Antiques Fair that are of interest to our agency. Because of that we have our own security people in the area, just quietly watching things. We knew about your stakeout, and we were monitoring what went on there. Your detectives should be congratulated for intercepting Mrs. Nowicki because she was doing her best to stay hidden. Far from simply taking a walk to see what was going on, she was doing a very good job of slipping between shadows, and you may have noticed that she    was dressed entirely in black. What you didn't notice is that she was carrying a knife in a sheath and that she had two old keys, one of which is the missing key to the front door of the old church building and the other of which fits the lock on the pastor's office. After you told her to go home and left, we detained her. Our conversations have been very helpful. Rose, please tell these gentlemen why you were really out there last night."

"Pastor Middlemiss was my tenant in my basement apartment, and we had become friends. He told me that if anything ever happened to him I should use the keys that he had on a special hook in his apartment to enter the old church building and his office. I was to retrieve a camera he had there with some unexposed film in it. I was then supposed to process the film, and the pictures would give me instructions on how to proceed with retrieving and distributing his estate to his heirs. He wanted me to get in there without being seen so as not to create any controversy in the church. I have been waiting for an opportunity ever since he died, but between the activities of Pastor Blake and the visits of the police, I had not dared to try to enter until last night. I finally decided that the preparations for the Antiques Fair would give me adequate cover and an excuse for being there if I was caught trying to enter the church."

Bobby said, "I think you'd better revise your story a bit. You knocked Pastor Blake unconscious when he interrupted your earlier visit to his office."

Joe added, "You did a good job of slanting your story toward being an innocent bystander, Rose, but we have been going through your house, and we found evidence that you and William were a lot more than casual friends. We have documents indicating that William had items of great value and that he planned to share them with you after he retired. He was planning to continue to live in your house after retirement and to work with you to convert his possessions into cash. We did retrieve that camera, and we processed the film to find pictures of a collection of art and jewelry that we believe were stolen from their rightful owners during World War II. The pictures in the camera did not give any clues as to the location of those items, but I have to believe that they're not far from here. Pastor Middlemiss always wanted to be in control of things. We have also checked your background, and we have learned that you were once employed by the military intelligence agency in your home country, a fact which you failed to reveal when you applied for American citizenship. Consequently, you had better cooperate and give us all the information we need, or you will at the very least face the prospect of deportation."

At this point Sergeant Al Gomez entered with Arthur.

Bobby Andrews greeted Arthur and introduced him. "Joe, Penny, I'd like you to meet Pastor Arthur Blake. Joe and Penny work for a little-known agency of the Federal Government. Arthur has been quite helpful in assisting our investigations of the two deaths at his church. I suspect that he will have useful contributions to make in connection with this interview. It was his office that Mrs. Nowicki was trying to burglarize, and I'm sure that she was the person who knocked him unconscious during an earlier burglary attempt.

Joe and Penny greeted Arthur, and Joe summarized Rose's statement and the information that he had revealed about her background. He then told Arthur to feel free to make comments or ask questions.

"Well, Mrs. Nowicki, I've seen you from a distance, but I didn't realize that there were still possessions of Pastor Middlemiss at your house. I thought that the trustees had returned everything to the church. I guess the camera you were seeking must have been returned to the church by mistake, and you needed a cover story to look for it. In case you're wondering, my head still hurts when the weather is damp.

William lived with you for most of the four years he was here, so your relationship has been growing throughout that period. The police might even be interested in checking when you came to Parkville to see whether you and William might have had a relationship that predated his arrival. I want to applaud you for keeping yourself in such good physical shape with the passing of the years. Your ability to move stealthily through the darkness is what surprised the detectives when they en-countered a person of your age. They expected the prowler to be much younger. I just have one additional question. Was it difficult getting Cathryn's body up the scaffolding and into the attic?"

# CHAPTER 66
## ENCOUNTER

T hey all saw Rose flinch at Arthur's surprise question. It had come out of nowhere, and it had shocked her. Bobby was the first to speak.

"Arthur, how did you connect her to Cathryn's murder?"

"Well, for some time it has been obvious to me that William Middlemiss was not physically capable of lifting his sister's body into the attic by himself. He made it easier by asking the trustees to move the rented scaffolding into the multi-purpose room so that he could see what was in the attic. I was pretty sure that Cathryn died shortly before the scaffolding was moved, but I felt that he would have needed a second person to help move the body. I had been waiting to see if a close relationship between William and someone else would be discovered. Upon meeting Mrs. Nowicki and learning of her relationship with William plus her prior background, I realized that she needn't have been William's helper; she could have moved the body by herself. Now, Rose, would you like to tell us how Cathryn died? I suspect that you can tell us exactly how it happened."

Bobby added, "You might as well tell us the truth, because at your age, you'll spend the rest of your life in jail whether you were William's accomplice in the murder or whether you acted alone."

Rose hesitated for about thirty seconds, as though she was in the midst of an internal debate with herself. Then she began. "William and I met in Chicago while we were both visiting the Art

234

Institute. He was studying paintings in a display of twentieth century European artists, and I was looking to see whether that display had any paintings by my uncle who had been fairly well-known in Europe. We got into a conversation about the effects of World War II on European art and soon found that we had other common interests. William was pastor of a church in the Chicago suburb of Elgin at that time, and I was living within easy driving range of him, so we became good friends and eventually lovers. Two years later he was transferred to Parkville UMC, so we were separated for a while. A few months after he arrived in Parkville, he called me and said that the old house next to the church was for sale at a reasonable price. He suggested that I buy it with his help and then advertise for a tenant for a basement apartment. He would become the tenant, allowing the church to rent out the parsonage for extra income, and we would get to live together without attracting attention.

"William went out of his way to create the feeling among church members that he wanted to be alone whenever he was not actually conducting church business. This image discouraged people from trying to contact him when he was in his apartment and gave us privacy. From the beginning of our relationship William had implied that he had more wealth than I would normally expect from a clergyman. After we became very close, he revealed that he had a collection of valuables that had been stolen by the Nazis during World War II. He never told me how he had come to own this collection, and I didn't ask. He never revealed where it was hidden. He gave me expectations that we would get married after he retired from the ministry, although he didn't specifically propose. He wanted to call upon my background and contacts in European intelligence circles to help convert various pieces in the collection into cash. William alluded to plans he had for starting a new church denomination so that any cash he acquired could be treated as donations that would be exempt from taxes. Everything was going very well for us until his sister showed up about two years ago.

"Cathryn didn't know about me, and William intended to keep her from discovering our relationship. When she showed up at the church one day, William tried to be cordial but distant in keeping with the lack of attention he had given his family ever since he had become an adult. However, Cathryn surprised him by saying that she was in trouble and that she wanted to move in with him and have him support her for a while. William asked her how long a stay she needed, and Cathryn replied that it would be a year or two. William told her that she could stay for a week, but no longer. At this response, Cathryn got furious. She told him that he had better agree to anything she wanted, or she would tell the church authorities about the sex games he used to play with his half-sister when she was eight and he was twenty-two and working toward his ordination. William realized he had a big problem. He told her he would work on finding her a place to stay. He called me from his office and explained the situation while Cathryn waited outside in the hallway. I told him to tell her that the lady who ran the boarding house next door was coming over to meet her. When I got there I started asking her typical background questions, and when she had her back turned to me I hit her with a rock that I had brought with me in my purse. It took two or three blows to be sure she was dead. William hadn't been quite sure what I would do, but he looked very relieved after I did it. You were right, Pastor Blake, I took the body up the scaffolding    to the attic by myself two days later. We were a little worried that someone would find or smell the body while it was temporarily rolled in an old rug I brought over, but we had to take the chance. We knew it would take a day or more for William to have the workmen set up the scaffolding in the multi-purpose room. We were going to leave her body in the attic until there were only bones left. Then we would crush the bones for easy disposal. We never got to that point before William died. Except for that it all went smoothly."

Rose sat thoughtfully as though she was re-living the episode of killing Cathryn and climbing the scaffolding with the body. The silence was finally broken by Bobby Andrews.

"Thank you for the completeness of your statement, Rose. We have recorded it, and it will be transcribed for your signature. Now, can you tell us anything about what happened on the night when William died?"

"I can tell you some things, Chief, but not everything. William had been contacted by a man who wouldn't give his name but who told him that he had found out about William's hidden wealth and wanted a share of it. He threatened to ruin William's career and alert the press. It sounded like Cathryn's blackmailing all over again. William said that he would comply but that the stranger would have to bring a tall ladder for him to do so. The stranger arrived with the ladder, and they set it up for William to go to the attic where he had implied the treasure was hidden. William said that he would take care of this killing without my help. Just to be on the safe side, I watched the church to see whether William would signal for my help. He had a clever idea, actually, because the ladder would be all set up for us to move the body to the attic afterward. Then we would just dispose of    the ladder, and nobody would ever know that it had been used in the church.

"As I said, I was waiting for William to signal for my help with the body, but apparently something went very wrong. I saw the door to the old church building open, but instead of William it was the stranger who came out. He looked around searching for witnesses, and I ducked out of sight. When I felt it was OK to come out, the stranger was gone. I hurried into the church, being careful not to leave any signs of my presence, and I found William dead at the foot of the ladder. I couldn't tell whether he had fallen or whether the stranger had hit him with something, but William was just as dead either way. I slipped back out without disturbing anything and went home to avoid any involvement.

I thought that I would never have to concern myself with that stranger again, but after the police found and removed Cathryn's body, he reappeared and started asking questions all around the town. I was in the bar when he questioned the Medical Examiner's assistant, and I decided that if the stranger didn't quit snooping, he would cause me some serious problems. I told him that I had information about the body at the church but that I wouldn't talk about it in a public place. He agreed to meet me that night down by Mallard Lake. I had the rope and concrete block hidden in a fisherman's boat that was there. When the stranger arrived, I injected him with a sedative. Then I rowed the boat out into the middle of the lake and threw him over with the block tied to his legs. I thought that it was deep enough that no fisherman would snag him, but I guess I was wrong. The stuff I pulled out of his pockets said that he was a private detective from New York City. I don't know why he would have been working on a case in Illinois. Whoever hired him must have wanted someone who was completely unknown around here.

"The church became a much busier place with Pastor Blake here. He did interrupt me the first time that I dared to search the office for clues to the location of William's treasure, and I had to knock him out so that I could escape undetected. Pastor, please understand that I deliberately softened the blow so that I wouldn't kill you too. Last night was going to be my second attempt to find William's secret. That treasure may never be found."

Arthur smiled at the conclusion of Rose's statement. "It will be found the day after the Antiques Fair ends. I know where it is."

Everyone stared at Arthur as he turned and walked out of the room.

# CHAPTER 67
## FRIDAY AT THE FAIR

T he Antiques Fair opened on time Friday morning with the military precision and flare that Wally Sanborn considered essential. Loudspeakers outside and inside the church began issuing recorded music starting at 9:45 AM. The music was being played from a small podium that had been set up near the entrance to the church in the lower parking lot. Fifteen feet in front of the podium was a square space twenty feet on a side, that was outlined in wide red tape. This square space was in the center of an open area that was surrounded by the many outdoor booths. A large red tape "X" connected its corners. As the music started to play, many people started to approach the podium, but members of the church youth group prevented them from going in or near the red-outlined square. At 9:55 AM Wally Sanborn and Pastor Arthur Blake came out of the church and stood behind the podium, accompanied by the three judges and the rest of the committee members. At 9:59 AM Wally stepped to the microphone and announced, "I now declare the Parkville Antiques Fair open. The Fair Committee extends to each and every one of you a hearty welcome. As our first order of business, Pastor Arthur Blake of the Parkville United Methodist Church will give us his benediction."

Arthur stepped forward and raised his right hand toward the crowd. "Bless all who gather here this weekend for our First Annual Antiques Fair. May they find insight into things that were part of life in the past. May they find antique items that will provide them with a sense of continuity with the past as they carry them forward into the future. Most of all, may they find fellowship with others attending this event, that we may all come to appreciate each other and build lasting friendships. This we pray in Christ's name. Amen."

A chorus of answering *Amen's* was followed by Wally taking the microphone once again. "Please rise for the presentation of the colors by members of the Illinois National Guard, and remain standing for our National Anthem."

The color guard entered from the speaker's left and marched into position in front of the podium. Precisely as they turned to face the crowd, the strains of *The Star-Spangled Banner* began to issue from the speakers. As people stood in respectful silence, they heard the engine of a small plane in the distance. When the music had come to its end, Wally again approached the microphone.

"I now direct your attention to the sky above you, where Captain Claudia Reid of the U.S. Army will jump from an aircraft and parachute to land on the red-outlined area in front of us. I ask you to be sure to stand back to give her plenty of landing space. Captain Reid will be jumping from thirteen thousand five hundred feet altitude. She will free-fall to a lower altitude before opening her parachute."

All eyes were turned toward the sky and the small airplane that was barely visible as it entered their field of view from the east. The crowd concentrated in silence as a small dot appeared below the aircraft and increasingly separated from it. Soon the dot became a person, and after a painfully long interval the crowd saw the jumper's parachute open. There were cheers at the sight of the parachute, followed by murmurs that she was off course and that she would miss her mark. The crowd watched in fascination as the jumper   pulled on the lines of her specialized chute to steer herself gradually and steadily toward her target landing zone. As she drifted lower, the people saw that a small American Flag was attached to one of the parachute lines. The jumper steered her parachute so that she moved sideways until she was over her target landing zone. Then she floated straight down and landed in the exact center of the red-outlined square. The crowd cheered as Captain Reid detached herself from her parachute and approached the podium while two army assistants who had been protecting the landing zone gathered and stowed her chute. She took the microphone.

"On behalf of the U.S. Army and the Antiques Fair Committee, I welcome you to this event for your enjoyment and education. My assistants and I will remain in the area for about an hour in case you have questions about the U.S. Army or about military parachuting operations. Thank you for giving me your hearty welcome."

The crowd drifted away toward the various exhibits, and Arthur turned to Wally with a very impressed look. "Now that's what I call a grand opening. Well done."

During the first few hours of the Fair, people circulated at random through all of the display and sales areas, getting an overall feel for what there was to see and buy before they focused their attention on anything specific. Peter Blake and John Hendrix were presiding over two Sunday school classrooms on the lower level of the new church building. The sign over the door to Peter's room read *Appraisals—American and Asian Antiques* while John's room's sign read *Appraisals— European Antiques*. Janice Blake occupied a third school room bearing the sign *Appraisals—Art and Miscellaneous Antiques*. Despite the fact that they were charging fees for analysis and appraisal services, all three had waiting lines, indicating that the church would derive a good portion of the Fair's revenue from their services.

Arthur was touring the outside displays, greeting people he knew and welcoming strangers to the Fair and the church. He checked in at the official Parkville UMC Welcome Booth to be sure that it had enough brochures and to encourage the church members who were running it to be cheerful and friendly to all the visitors. He was walking around the back end of the new building on his way to the upper parking lot when he heard someone call his name. He turned to find Joe and Penny Gonzalez approaching him.

Penny spoke first. "Hi, Pastor, we wanted to let you know how impressed we were with your insights while we questioned Rose Nowicki. We had some knowledge of the deaths of William and Cathryn Middlemiss, but neither we nor the Parkville Police saw how Rose fit into the puzzle the way you did. Then you completely floored us by saying that you know where William's valuables are located. Are you sure that you won't give us a hint before Monday?"

Arthur smiled but then went serious, "My responsibility right now is to make sure that this Antiques Fair is a successful event for the church. If the cache was revealed during the weekend, we would disrupt the Fair and gain additional unwanted notoriety in the press. We'll do our treasure hunting on Monday after the people attending and exhibiting at the Fair have gone home. In the meantime, enjoy yourselves. We do appreciate the extra layer of security that your presence gives us. Some of the antiques being exhibited and sold are pretty valuable."

Joe patted Arthur on his back. "We would like to spend some time with you after this is all over so that we get to know each other better. I have the feeling that some of our other projects could benefit from your particular blend of science and religion."

Arthur pulled out a notebook and made an entry in it. "I'm recording that offer to make sure I follow up with you. I'd like to know more about your agency and some of the other government groups that hide in the bureaucratic background."

They all shook hands on the prospect of further discussions. Arthur continued his tour of the Fair, while Penny and Joe headed for the Appraisal area. When they arrived there, they invited John Hendrix to shut his room temporarily and take a break with them. They went outside to the youth group refreshment booth, where Joe bought cold drinks for the three of them. Then they found a picnic table in a quiet area under a tree.

Penny spoke first. "John, we want to thank you for the tip that led to the recovery of that large collection of plundered items from World War II. There are still massive quantities of similar items out there. We and others are continuing to search them out in order to repatriate them and to find the original owners or their heirs. As you know, time is running out for the original owners and also for those who *liberated* valuable property after the war."

Joe continued, "We know that you were stationed near the Salzburg Property Control Warehouse during the critical time period when many things went missing. We strongly suspect that the stash you located was actually planted there by you or your associates for us to find. Everything was in good condition. Experts are now trying to determine rightful ownership for those items. Given your age and your apparent willingness to voluntarily return misappropriated items, we have no desire to prosecute you, but we would like your help in finding additional stashes if you know of any. We don't want to do anything that would damage your reputation, but we hope that you will want to share any additional information you have with us."

John looked thoughtfully over their heads at the people moving from one display of antiques to another. He thought about what an antique he had become while he had devoted his life to his material treasure. He looked at family groups strolling across the grounds and wondered how things might have been different if Maria and even Helga had been at the center of his life. Then he responded to Joe and Penny.

"There was a time when I thought that I was truly blessed because of the head start on civilian life that I stumbled across while serving in Austria. We had all been through so much during the war. Then they made me stay in Europe to help displaced people put their lives back together. A lot of our people felt that winning the war meant that we deserved some kind of prize. When all of the warehouse riches were so easily available, it was just natural for soldiers stationed there to take a small bit of them. There were even generals who requisitioned fancy furnishings and accessories from the warehouse for themselves and for the offices of all of their staff.

"I spent a lot of years learning how to live off of my collection of trophies without appearing to be doing anything illegal. In the process, I turned my back on a woman who loved me, and our daughter later rejected me. I'm not sure that I ever really accomplished anything worthwhile with my life after the war. Now that I'm in my final years, I want to try to make up for that.

"You were absolutely right. I arranged for that farmhouse to be set up so that you could find what was left of my collection. I wanted to be rid of it, but I couldn't just give it away without causing trouble for a charity or for myself. You probably don't know that my daughter was married to William Middlemiss when he first became a minister. It only lasted for one year, but during that time, Middlemiss blackmailed me into giving him some of my collection. When my daughter found out about the blackmail and the collection, she divorced him and turned her back on me. I haven't seen her since, because she made me promise not to try to find her. When Peter Blake invited me to be a judge at this Antiques Fair, I agreed because I knew that William was dead and that he had been Pastor of this church. I wanted to see if I could locate William's part of the collection, return it, and expose him as having been anything but saintly.

"That's the whole story, and I still hope to detect whether someone is trying to sell any of William's items."

Penny had been secretly recording John's statement, and she nodded to Joe that she had a good recording as she turned off her hidden device. Then she turned to John. "Thank you for opening up to us. We believe you because your comments confirm some information that we had obtained from other sources. Keep watching for anything that looks as though it might have been plundered during World War II, and notify us if you see anything. We'll take care of confronting anybody who looks suspicious to you."

As they walked away, Joe noted that neither he nor Penny had seen any reason to tell Hendrix that they expected to find William's treasure on Monday.

Arthur had completed his tour of the grounds and his mingling with the visitors and church members. He was about to go in to talk with his mother and father when Jeremy Hadley ran up to him.

"Pastor, I was working at the refreshments booth when I saw a man walking toward the appraisal area carrying an old statue of an Italian baker. That statue was stolen from the window of my father's bakery last year. Someone broke the window during the night and took two statues. This is definitely one of them. I think the guy I saw sometimes hangs around outside our school, and I've heard that he sells drugs, but I don't know for sure. What should I do?"

"Head back to your booth. I'll get the police to take care of this. He won't be hard to identify with that statue he's carrying."

Arthur called Bobby Andrews on his cell phone and told him Jeremy's story. He requested that Bobby send a plainclothes detective if possible to minimize the disruption and possible danger to visitors. Bobby said that he didn't have a detective immediately available but that he wouldn't object if the federal security folks on the grounds handled it. Arthur agreed and beckoned to one of Joe's men who had been watching the scene from beneath a tree. After receiving a brief summary from Arthur, he talked into the small microphone he was wearing.

"Joe, this is Steve. We have a situation developing in the appraisal area that needs a soft touch. We may have a drug dealer trying to sell a stolen statue. The local police say we are in a better position to handle it quickly and quietly."

"No problem, Steve, let's just give him the first class greeting."

"That sounds good to me. We'll be in position in three minutes."

Five minutes later a somewhat rotund man wearing a Cubs baseball cap and carrying a colorful statue walked out of the appraisal area on the lower level of the church. He headed toward a pickup truck that was parked on the grass beyond the sales booths. By the time he was about a third of the way to the truck he realized that he was not alone. Three men in dark clothing were walking quietly on each side of him. As he started to react to their presence he felt the statue leave his arms to be simultaneously replaced by handcuffs on his wrists. The men guided him to continue walking straight ahead toward a black Jeep that had moved into position alongside the pickup truck. Three minutes later he was on his way to the Police Department, and none of the visitors at the Fair realized that anything had happened.

Friday evening at House of Ming, Arthur and his parents celebrated the successful conclusion of the first day of the Antiques Fair with a special bottle of wine that Peter had brought from home. He had purchased it at a convention for antiques dealers, where the motto at the wine vendor's booth had been *Antiques and Wine—Two Things That Improve with Age!* The wine was excellent, and they thoroughly enjoyed their first evening together in quite a while. As they prepared to head back to the parsonage, Peter told Arthur, "I'd like to come along when you reveal the location of the World War II plunder on Monday."

Arthur thought about it briefly and replied, "You can come along if you stay in the background. There are too many people involved already. You'll have to promise that you won't tell anyone else about my plan to reveal the cache location. This has to be a low key event free of outsiders and media coverage."

# CHAPTER 68
## SATURDAY AT THE FAIR

S aturday morning's Fair opening was a smooth continuation from Friday afternoon. Exhibitors returned prized antiques to their displays from overnight security storage locations; refreshment stands were resupplied with food and drinks; and church volunteers reported for duty wearing their colorful *Collect me, I'm a Fair Antique* T-shirts.

The weather was perfect, sunny and mild, and the advance publicity appeared to be paying off. By the ten o'clock opening four chartered buses had unloaded their passengers and were parked in the extra lot by the lake. Passenger cars were rapidly filling the regular parking lot, and gaily clad people were strolling among the many outside booths or waiting for the doors of the church to open for the inside displays and sales booths.

Among the visitors to the Fair were Bertha Calahan and Edward Middlemiss walking arm-in-arm beneath the old trees on their first pretend brother and sister outing. They were enjoying each other's company, and they both felt privileged to be alone together on an outing. As they passed by many of the outside booths one or the other of them would say, "Look at that gadget. I used to have one of those. It's hard to believe that it's considered an antique now." They were discovering the strong similarity of their experiences, and they were recognizing that fact in virtually identical statements. This became humorous with repetition, and they were soon laughing out loud as they found more and more items they had owned or used in the past. Bertha was surprised to find that Edward even remembered having items that she thought would have been obsolete by his time. He attributed this to both of his parents having had a fondness for history and for whatever they had considered rustic or quaint. They were continuing to exchange old memories when Bertha suddenly stopped and stared at some people under a tree.

"Look, there are Penny and Joe Gonzalez. They're Bob's friends from Washington who were helping me to search for my biological half-brother. I hope that term doesn't bother you, Edward. I just used it for contrast with you as my adopted half-brother."

"No problem, Bertha—I'm an academic, and I'm used to people trying to be precise in their speech. Were you expecting Penny and Joe to be here?"

"I didn't even expect them to be in this part of the country. Let's go over and greet them."

They walked slowly toward the group under the tree, and were surprised to see everyone except Penny and Joe drift away as they approached. Penny called out to them, "Hi, Bertha, it's good to see you again. Who's the handsome young man you have in tow?"

"Hello, Penny; I certainly didn't expect to find you and Joe here. I'd like you to meet Edward Middlemiss. He's my new adopted half-brother. We didn't quite track down my biological half-brother, although you two got us very close. Edward volunteered to fill the position, since he's pretty much on his own now."

Joe and Penny shook hands with Edward and hugged Bertha. Then Joe turned to Edward. "We're actually pretty familiar with what has been happening here. We work for a part of the government, and we're here on assignment, but the Parkville Police have told us what happened to your brother and sister, Edward. Please accept our sympathies."

"Thanks. It has been rough getting my mind adjusted to being pretty much on my own, but Bertha's willingness to be my adopted sister has been a big help. Is your agency under the Treasury Department?"

Penny and Joe exchanged surprised looks, and Joe responded, "I didn't think we had it written on our backs."

Edward laughed. "I teach Political Science, and I have a pretty good feeling for the organization charts of the Federal Government. I just took a stab at what might be of interest to the government at an Antiques Fair."

"Well, we're just being flies on the wallpaper here, observing but probably not taking any action, so please don't draw attention to us in your conversations with others. We're glad that you two are getting along so well together."

Bertha gave Penny and Joe a big smile. "Our lips are sealed, and we never saw you, but please look us up later when you're off duty." Bertha once again took Edward's arm, and they walked off toward the lower level entrance to the church. When they entered the church, Bertha and Edward passed by the appraisal area and headed for the display of antique toys, hoping to once more reminisce about old possessions.

Inside the appraisal area for European items, John Hendrix was examining a Swedish hanging sconce. It was a ceiling-mounted light fixture for five candles. It was salmon-colored, and the candle receptacles were set into metal flower blossoms which sat upon curved metal leaves. This object had been brought to him by a lady who appeared to be about sixty years old and walked with a cane. She was wearing a kerchief and sunglasses.

John completed his examination and turned to her. "Swedish pieces like this are quite simple in concept and line, and because of that they have a wide range of prices. I would say that this sconce is late nineteenth century because it hasn't been electrified. This can command a relatively high price among purists who are looking for an authentic piece of Swedish history, but it has much less value for others who may not appreciate the style or the lack of electrification. I have seen pieces like this priced at about twenty-five hundred dollars, but I have also seen some sold for just a few hundred dollars by people who were happy to dispose of them. You would have to decide whether you are willing to set the price high and search for the ideal customer, or set a much lower price in order to sell it sooner. Of course, if you intend to keep it and are just looking for valuation you won't have to make a decision at all. Where did you get this piece?"

"It came from my late husband's family." Mrs. Svenson straightened up as she said this and put down her cane. Then she removed her kerchief and sunglasses and continued in a younger and stronger voice, "You would have liked Erik, Dad. He was the most creative man I ever met."

John had been only half paying attention to his client while he was appraising the sconce, but he stiffened and stared in disbelief as the older Mrs. Svenson morphed into his very recognizable daughter.

"Maria, I thought that I would never see you again." He couldn't believe how damp the corners of his eyes were. "How have you been? We've missed so much of each other's lives, and it has been my fault. Forgive me if you can. I have spent far too much time cherishing things when I should have been cherishing people, especially you. Where have you been living? Tell me more about your Erik. Are their children? Are you well?"

Maria laughed and cried at the same time. "There's a lot of telling required on both sides. I wasn't sure when I came, but I think you've really changed. Even if you're still the same problem you were for me, it's time for us to work things out. We've spent too many years apart, and we have too few left to share."

John went to Maria and rather tentatively hugged her, but Maria responded with a hug that was both warm and enthusiastic. When they separated after the lengthy hug, John felt that they were both much younger than they had been a short while before. He was cradling his little girl once again, and she had found the fantasy that had been hers while she grew up in Austria.

After what seemed like a very long time of just looking at each other, they decided to take a walk so that they could be alone together. John put the CLOSED sign on the door to his room and went next door to where Janice Blake was talking with a young man about a painting.

"Janice, I'll be gone for an hour or so. This is my daughter, Maria. We've been lost to each other for many years, and now we need a little time by ourselves."

"Congratulations to both of you. Take your time, John. I can cover European antiques as well as my own stuff for a while. Just remember that we have to do our judging rounds this afternoon."

John and Maria went outside to the lower parking lot, and he suggested that they go across the street and sit by Mallard Lake. As they started to walk in that direction, he stopped and told Maria to wait for him. John disappeared among the many outside booths and returned carrying two chocolate ice cream cones.

"If I'm going to have a talk with my little girl, I'm going to make sure we enjoy it."

They went beyond the parking area and found a large rock between the water and the edge of the woods. Ice cream cones in hand, they climbed up onto it, and sat facing the lake. Maria started the conversation by saying how happy she had been with Erik and his manufacturing of wooden toys in Vermont. She told John all about their love of outdoor living and about the children. Maria noted the reappearance of moisture in his eyes when she described the children. She especially enjoyed seeing the smile burst onto his face when she told him that he had a grandson named John Hendrix Svenson. Maria knew that this one bit of news was sufficient to tell her father that he had been banished but not forgotten by her during the past forty years or so. The smile broadened further when she told him that Katie's full name was Katherine Helga Svenson. He knew that in some convoluted way the family had been reunited through Maria's children. She was continuing to tell him about the children's interests and occupations when John interrupted her.

"Maria, before we get completely absorbed in the happy aspects of your life, I have to give you some information which may disturb you. William Middlemiss was the pastor of this church until he died here under strange circumstances several months ago. One of the reasons why I agreed to be a judge at this Antiques Fair is that I wanted to see whether anyone would be selling his portion of the collection at the Fair. If I spot anything familiar, I will alert the authorities. They know about his treasure, but they don't know where it is. I feel that by helping them if I can, I will complete what I can do toward my redemption."

"Dad, I'm sorry to hear that William is dead, and I appreciate your working to return his tainted treasures, but I hope that you are not doing this as one final act of vengeance against William. Even at this stage of things, he's not worth it. You should know by now that acts of hatred hurt you as much as the person you hate. William is past the point of vulnerability. He's gone. Don't let hatred for him tie you up in knots. I found Erik, and when he entered my life, all thoughts of William disappeared. I've learned that the worst thing you can do to people is to ignore and forget them. Hatred isn't even required. I've been apart from William for as long as I've been apart from you, but I ignored and forgot William, while I daydreamed about you and forgave you. There's a big difference between those two ways of treating people from whom you are separated. He doesn't matter, but you matter very much to me."

John just said, "Wow," and held Maria's hand.

At the other end of the Fair, Arthur was also sitting on a rock. He was at the back end of the lower level parking lot, and he was finishing up his latest cup of black coffee. He shaded his eyes from the bright overhead sun and scanned the individuals and groups that were visiting outside booths and entering the church building. He felt that all of the people charged with running the Fair were doing their jobs well, and that he actually had the easiest part of it. Arthur stood up, stretched, and scored a basket throwing his coffee cup into the nearest trash can. He was still admiring the accuracy of his throw when he heard, "You are the most psychic man I've ever met!" Seconds later someone hugged him and planted a big kiss on his right cheek. The next thing he knew was that Irma was laughing at him for looking so shocked and having his mouth wide open.

"What's the matter? Haven't you ever had a sneak attack kiss before? I should have kissed you on the lips, but I didn't want to embarrass your holiness in front of this crowd."

Arthur finally found his tongue. "What did I do to deserve that? Whatever it was, I should do it more often."

"I think that you should organize a meeting in your office so that we can discuss the analysis I did on the sample you gave me—and do it this afternoon. Here's the list of those who should attend."

"OK, but give me a half hour to get substitute workers for those with Fair responsibilities. You round up those who aren't working on the Fair, and I'll get the others. If you see Bill Martin, ask him to get extra chairs for my office. It's going to be a bit cramped, but the church conference room is being used for the display of antique toys."

Irma and Arthur went off in different directions to find the necessary participants for the meeting and to rearrange the duty schedules as needed to cover Fair operations. Thirty minutes later everyone had assembled in Arthur's office without any advance explanations for why they were there.

Arthur motioned everyone to seats and opened the meeting."I want to thank you all for coming on such short notice. I think you all know each other, and if not you soon will. Irma Custis suggested that we get together immediately because everyone was already here for the Fair. As many of you know, I have been very examining the possessions of Pastor William Middlemiss that were stored in this room. I have cleared enough of them away so that you can all fit in here, but I apologize for the cramped quarters. Chief Bobby Andrews of the Parkville Police Department is here on an unofficial basis to keep him informed about matters that may have some impact on his cases. None of you are in any trouble with the police unless you are illegally parked.

"Wally Sanborn is the head of the Antiques Fair committee and is a very busy man right now. I had to convince him that it was more important for him to be here. His efforts are resulting in an excellent event. In my mind there is no doubt that we will make this an annual project for the church. A discussion that I had with Wally a few weeks ago led to this meeting. The two of us were evaluating a sample of a brief questionnaire that we could use to get members of the church to know more about each other. One of the questions I asked on the form dealt with your most memorable childhood event. Wally's answer to that question reminded me of some newspaper clippings that I had found among the belongings of William Middlemiss. Although it is an amazing coincidence, it appears that William and Wally as babies were both caught in a tragic German V-2 rocket bombing of a Woolworth store in London in 1944."

Arthur's revelation produced low murmuring among most of the people who were present. Then Wally spoke up.

"It wasn't that much of a coincidence. As I grew up, I collected clippings about that event. I filled several scrapbooks. Most of those clippings were of a general nature or about the monstrosity of warfare against civilian targets. I continued to search out information about the Woolworth's bombing after I moved to this country and became a U.S. citizen. While I was in the Army, I used their archive resources as well. Then, four years ago I discovered an article saying that William Middlemiss had been appointed Pastor of this church and that as a baby he and his mother had been caught in the Woolworth's bombing. That article was probably among the clippings that you found, Arthur. Anyway, I was single and retired from the Army, so I decided to move here, join the church, and find out more about the pastor.

"My reason for doing all this was that my mother told me on her deathbed that she had made a terrible mistake and claimed the wrong child after the bombing had separated parents and children. I came here to see whether William's parents were my true birth parents. I gave up on the effort when I learned that both of William's parents were dead. It didn't seem right to completely disrupt a family when I wouldn't be able to gain from it anyway."

Arthur took up the story, "Wally and I have become friends, and we frequently gather in this office to talk and drink coffee. As an indication of the permanence of this arrangement, Wally installed his favorite U.S. Army mug on my coffee tray.

"Some of you may not know Bertha Calahan of Monticello, Iowa. She has been trying to search for a possible half-brother, a son that her father may have had with an English woman he met during World War II. Penny and Joe Gonzalez, who are over here, have been helping her with computer searches. The search has not been successful, although it led to the time and place of the arrival of the mother and son in this country. Edward Middlemiss, who has lost all his family members who lived in this country, has established himself as Bertha's *adopted* half-brother. Bertha and Edward are here visiting the Fair on their first outing together.

"At this point allow me to turn over the meeting to Irma Custis, our County Medical Examiner."

"A few days ago, before the Fair opened, Arthur asked me to do some DNA testing on this." She pulled an object from her attaché case and removed its tissue paper wrap to reveal Wally's coffee mug.

259

Then she removed several documents from her case and held up two of them. "These are DNA profiles. The profile on the left results from Wally's DNA sample, and the profile on the right results from Bertha's DNA sample. Please note the similarities." Irma pointed at corresponding sections of the two charts. "Bertha, allow me to introduce you to your half-brother, Wally."

There was loud applause and cheering in the room as Wally and Bertha rose and went over to hug each other.

Edward got up from his seat near Bertha. "Wally, you sit here. I'll switch with you."

Irma called out, "Stay where you are, Edward." She held up two documents once again. "The left profile is Wally, and the right profile is Edward. Please note the similarities again. Wally, allow me to introduce you to your half-brother, Edward." There were a few moments of stunned silence. Then Irma continued. "It's quite simple. Bertha and Wally are half-siblings through their father, while Edward and Wally are half-siblings through their mother. The common father was William Perkins, and the common mother was Carolyn who came to this country as the supposed widow of Ralph Perkins. We don't know her real maiden name."

Once again, everyone cheered. Bertha, Wally, and Edward joined in a three-way hug. When the cheering ended, Penny mused, "If the babies hadn't been switched after the Woolworth's explosion, we never would have united Bertha with her half-brother. It was only because Wally was also looking for answers that this worked out."

Arthur called for silence. "Would the three of you please come over here?" Bertha, Wally, and Edward approached him. "Modern science has given us an answer that we believe to be true. Now we are going to test it. I have in my hand a photograph from the belongings of William Middlemiss. It shows a young man with his pregnant wife. Please look at it carefully, and tell me what you see."

Bertha put on her reading glasses and peered at the photograph. "That's definitely my father."

Edward took his turn. "That's a younger version of Mother."

Wally smiled. "Those are my parents, and that's my first picture."

# CHAPTER 69
## SUNDAY AT THE FAIR

B ecause the Antiques Fair was a function of the Parkville United Methodist Church, the opening on Sunday was delayed until eleven o'clock so as not to interfere with the church service. Arthur was pleased to see that many of the Fair visitors came to church so that he had a full sanctuary. The title of his sermon was *Age Can Be a Good Thing: There Are No New Antiques*. The events of the last few days and the obvious success of the Fair had relaxed him, and he showed it by making his sermon very humorous.

Although the church was full for the service, there were some who deliberately played hooky. Bob and Paula Caspar were hosting a major party brunch at their home in Monticello, Iowa in honor of the *half-triplets*: Bertha, Wally, and Edward.

Edward proposed the first orange juice toast. "Please join me in toasting my new half-brother and his half-sister. I toast especially the fact that I no longer have to say *pretend* in saying that I think of Bertha as my sister also." Everyone laughed and cheered.

Bertha added, "I raise my glass to all of those who helped in the search for my half-brother, and I applaud the fact that somehow we succeeded in finding him and his half-brother too. May we all live *halfily* ever after."

Wally made the next toast. "Let's drink to the fact that I finally know who my natural parents were and the blessing that I have two new siblings who can tell me about them. At the same time, I drink to the love and care I received from the parents who raised me both during the period when they thought I was theirs and even after they learned about the mistaken baby exchange."

Not to be outdone, Edward completed the quartet of toasts. "I drink to the fact that I now understand why William always seemed so different from me. I would have had much more fun growing up with Wally as my big brother."

After the laughter simmered down, Bob approached Bertha. "I hope you realize that you're going to have to go through the photographs that we found among your father's things and label which ones show Wally and which ones show William. It will be interesting to see whether the change in appearance is obvious when you are looking for it. The two babies must have closely resembled each other because both sets of parents were fooled."

"Bob, both sets of parents were so relieved at being reunited with a child they thought had died, that they were bound to overlook any minor nuance and attribute it to the trauma that both they and the child had been through. Finding their child once again saved them from going through the rest of their lives feeling guilty and thinking that they had been terrible parents."

Penny added, "Even if we had been able to complete our computer search all the way, we would have told you that William was your half-brother. The computer would have only tracked the movements of Carolyn and her son and would not have been sufficient to give you a true result. It was only due to the circumstances of William's death that we turned to DNA comparisons. We didn't have enough information to even consider that the child Carolyn brought might not have been biologically hers."

Bertha thought about this for a time. "You know, I keep going back to feeling that there is a reason for everything that happens. If events had occurred even a little bit differently, I doubt very much that the three of us *half-siblings* would have ever found each other. I don't know whether I should call it a miracle, but it at least says that we defied all of the logical probabilities."

Back at the church Peter, Janice, and John were compiling the results of their judging in order to post their results and hand out ribbons and checks to the exhibitors. The judges agreed that most of the items that had been entered into the competition were interesting and amusing but not particularly valuable. Nevertheless, they decided that some of the prize ribbons should go to lower value items if they were unusual enough and in outstanding condition. Prizes would not directly correlate with value, and some of the more valuable items would not be eligible because of they lacked sufficiently pleasing aesthetics. Based on these principles, they would tour all of the exhibit booths together and award the prizes. Peter would announce the awards for American and Asian items; John would present the awards for European items, and Janice would recognize paintings plus antiques from other parts of the world.

The three judges started their awards tour with the outside booths. They tried to be very systematic in going up and down all the aisles so that each winning exhibitor would be surprised when the group stopped to present a ribbon and a check. As they circulated around the grounds, they gathered a fairly large group of followers who wanted to identify the winners and applaud when each award was given. This entourage continued to follow    the judges as they moved to tour the exhibits inside the church.

As more ribbons were awarded, the procession of judges and their followers increased in gaiety and noise level until it became a continuous stream of celebrants. Everything appeared to be going very smoothly to the casual observer. However, Joe Gonzalez, who had joined the following crowd, was watching with a trained eye, and he quickly noted the brief expression of concern which crossed the face of John Hendrix when Janice awarded a blue ribbon at one particular booth displaying old paintings. Joe signaled Steve to remain behind to keep an eye on that booth while he continued to follow the judges as they completed their rounds.

When all the prizes had been awarded, the three judges separated, and the crowd dispersed. John Hendrix, who had been studying the following crowd, approached Joe and motioned him toward a quiet area.

Joe nodded expectantly. "I saw your reaction when the ribbon was awarded at that painting booth, and I left Steve there to watch it."

John smiled. "That was a smart move. I had a feeling of *déjà vu* when I visited their exhibit. This was the first time I had been there because Janice was handling the exhibitors of paintings. The problem is that several of their paintings were from the batch that I led you to recover. You said that experts were now in the process of studying the recovered items in order to return them to their rightful owners. It appears that your system has some leaks. Some of your experts or their friends are trying to discretely sell pieces of the art rather than to repatriate it. I guess they figured that this Fair's location was remote enough that they wouldn't attract any attention."

Joe's usually placid expression briefly turned to one of anger. "Thanks for being so alert. It seems that greed and avarice are not just wartime problems. This case is worse because it is evident that someone is betraying a position of trust. We'll have to correct the situation and do so without attracting any attention that might disrupt the Fair or endanger people. We'll also have to move in quickly before those paintings can be sold in the auction to unsuspecting bidders." They shook hands, and Joe hurried away. As he walked he called Penny, briefed her, and suggested she head back from Bob's house in Iowa. Then he radioed for everyone in his on-site group except Steve to meet him under a large oak tree. He also informed Chief Bobby Andrews so that the local police would know that they were handling a situation. Finally, Joe called headquarters in Washington to request that they check out all of the people working on art repatriation in order to learn whether this was an isolated circumstance or part of a larger problem.

During the meeting under the oak tree, the group decided that the best way to handle the arrest without attracting attention would be for them to convince the exhibitors to come to them voluntarily. They would do this by setting up a tent next to the parking area where their unmarked vehicles were parked. Then they would request that the exhibitors who were going to auction off items come there for a pre-auction interview and recording of item specifications while official security was provided for their exhibit. The exhibitors should be expected to cooperate because the auctioneer would likely receive a higher selling price if he had detailed information about the item.

To make the pre-auction interview ruse believable, Joe had his people explain the procedure to every exhibitor in the room where the suspected party, Astral Art and Antiques, was located. Then they proceeded to conduct actual interviews for each exhibitor in that room who had items to sell at auction. Eight such interviews were conducted in routine fashion prior to reaching the turn of Astral Art and Antiques.

At the booth, Joe introduced himself as the auctioneer's assistant, and learned that the exhibitor's name was Warren McCarthy. Warren said that he was a graduate student at the University of Wisconsin in Madison and that he had participated in three similar shows over the past two months on behalf of one of his professors. Steve stayed behind to provide security for the booth while Warren and Joe carried three paintings that were to be auctioned to the interview tent. Once they arrived there, Joe asked Warren what he knew about the paintings.

"I don't actually know a lot about art; I'm an English Literature major. I've been told that the history of these paintings is unknown beyond the fact that they were included in the estate of an old lady in Pennsylvania. She was of German descent and may have brought them to the U.S. after World War II. I understand that the artists are fairly well known in Europe, but that few people have heard of them over here. Professor Stringholtz indicated that I should tell the auctioneer to set a minimum bid of five thousand dollars on each of them. He said that the other paintings could be sold at the fixed prices he had set, but that these would have to be sold at auction."

"Have you sold any paintings at the Fair so far?"
"I sold two that were priced at four hundred dollars each. They looked old but amateurish to me, although I'm no expert."

"Just out of curiosity, Warren, do you have records of the people who bought those paintings?"

"Well, they paid by credit card. Why do you want to know?"

"Warren, I'm actually associated with an agency of the Federal Government that is charged with determining the proper ownership of art treasures, and I have reason to believe that some or all of the paintings you have been exhibiting for sale are not yours to sell. We are going to have to ask you to come with us so that we can ask you some more questions. Some of our people will also be visiting Professor Stringholtz to determine his connection to these paintings as well as the history of Astral Art and Antiques. You don't have to worry about the safety of the remaining paintings in your booth. They are being packed up right now, and they will be coming with you to the office where we will be having our additional discussions."

"Am I being arrested? If so, I want an attorney present while you question me."

"You aren't being arrested. We are just going to check out the truth of the information that you have already given us, and we will give you the opportunity to add to that information or make clarifications. You may be totally innocent and may have been unwittingly used by the Professor and his associates, or you may be more deeply involved in a crime than you have told us. Until we determine the complete facts of the situation, no one is being arrested. Are you willing to come with us voluntarily?"

"I have no reason to object so long as you guarantee that the paintings and I will both be safe from any harm. How do I know that you are who you say you are?"

"That's a fair question. Here is my identification. As a further confirmation of the truth of my statements, I have arranged that we will continue our discussions in the conference room of the local police department. Chief Bobby Andrews will be there to vouch for my identity, although he will be present as an observer because we will be discussing the possible violation of federal rather than local laws."

Joe led Warren out to the parking lot where they were joined by several others from Joe's agency. The remainder of Warren's exhibit was being loaded into one vehicle while they got into a second one. The Astral Art and Antiques display area had been very quickly and efficiently converted from an exhibit booth to a rest area for Antiques Fair visitors so that no one would be surprised by the bare area in the midst of the other exhibits. As the two vehicles drove away, other members of the team took down the pre-auction interview tent.

At three o'clock the auction began in the lower parking lot in the same space where the Fair had been declared open and where the parachutist had landed. Chairs for bidders were arranged in neat rows within the jumper's target zone. Wally Sanborn served as the auctioneer. As tourists and declared bidders watched intently, Wally presented and described each antique or art object and with a staccato sales pitch encouraged bids from all interested parties. He sold each auction item with military efficiency. At the end of the process, he announced that the Antiques Fair had reached its successful conclusion.

Wally encouraged all of the visitors to register for the mailing list so that they would be contacted with early information about the second annual Antiques Fair next year. Pastor Arthur Blake delivered a closing benediction.

The exhibitors were released to close up their booths with grateful thanks for their participation and application forms for participating again next year. Arthur told Wally he had been very impressed by his meticulous handling of everything and asked him to commit to chairing the committee again next year. Wally responded that he had planned on doing so and had already been thinking about improvements and innovations.

# CHAPTER 70
## EXPOSITION

O n Monday morning Arthur was drinking his coffee while he inspected the church grounds for trash remaining from the Fair. He was pleasantly surprised to see how well Wally's youth mission group had cleaned the grounds immediately after the Fair had closed. His morning rounds revealed no sign of the weekend event except for a few tire tracks and some tent stake holes in the grass. He walked back toward the door to the old church building fingering the key that had been returned to him when they arrested Rose Nowicki. Now he no longer had to go in and out through the new building in order to reach his office in the old building.

As Arthur approached the steps of the old building, he found a cluster of people gathered there. Sitting on the stairs or standing talking to each other were: Penny and Joe Gonzalez, Bobby Andrews, Sergeant Al Gomez, Peter Blake, Irma Custis, John Hendrix, and a woman he didn't know.

Arthur announced his presence with, "Good morning, everyone. Are you here to join the church or just for a Morning Prayer service? I'm sure that a service of thanksgiving is in order following the success of the Antiques Fair."

Bobby Andrews stepped forward. "You know why we're here, Arthur. You mystically volunteered that on Monday you would reveal the location of this treasure that was the focus of Pastor Middlemiss' life."

"I was planning to finish my coffee and take care of a few of my pastoral duties before thinking about that, but if you folks are so impatient, I guess I can change my schedule. Bobby, do you suppose you can ask Bill Martin to join us to assist me, without giving him the impression that he is under arrest? Ask him to bring his toolbox."

"I'll be just as diplomatic as can be, but don't start your magic until I get back." Bobby headed for his unmarked car. "He won't mind coming back in this, but I think he'd walk rather than be seen in a black-and-white with sirens and lights."

Arthur turned toward the woman he didn't recognize. "I'm sorry, but I don't think we've met. You're not here from the press, are you?"

"No, Pastor, I'm Maria Svenson. John Hendrix is my father, and many years ago for a short period of time William Middlemiss was my husband. Dad and I were talking with your father, who suggested that I should be here as a matter of closure to my connection with William."

Arthur gave Peter a mildly annoyed look and said, "I'm pleased to meet you. I've been trying to learn enough about William to understand how he thought, but I've found it difficult. Perhaps you can assist me."

"Pastor, you're trying to do the impossible. I could never understand William. He was a very up-tight person, and he deliberately took steps to keep people from getting close enough to understand him."

"Well, thank you for that information, Maria. That confirms my thought that he was hiding behind a mask. He didn't want to lose control of those around him or to be vulnerable to emotional attachments."

Bobby's unmarked police car pulled up and parked on the street. He got out and helped Bill remove his tools from the back seat.

Arthur continued, "Here come the Chief and Bill Martin. We can proceed with the revelation of William's secrets if you agree to two rules. First, everyone must promise not to talk with the press about what happens today. This church has had enough negative and sensational publicity. Our Church Conference officials have been unhappy about it. Those of you representing legal agencies will have to treat anything you learn or recover as privileged information restricted to communication on a need-to-know basis. This should be reasonable for the agencies that are involved because sensationalism would hinder their future work. My second requirement is that those who are not officially assigned to pursuing this case stay behind and let the investigators do their work. After they have processed the evidence and given their permission, the rest of you will be allowed to inspect things. Do you all agree?"

Arthur heard a chorus of affirmations. "OK, let's go into the church and assemble in the multi-purpose room." He unlocked the church door, and everyone filed in, including three additional members of Joe and Penny's team. When they had gathered in the multi-purpose room, Arthur began his discussion. "Everything appears to center on this room and the attic above it. William wouldn't allow the youth to play basketball here. William died in a fall from a ladder leading to the attic. That fall may or may not have been accidental. William opposed Bill Martin's effort to create an easy access to the attic. I found Cathryn's remains in the attic while I was investigating the merits of Bill Martin's proposed entrance from the new building.

273

"On the day when I climbed up to the attic, shortly before I discovered Cathryn's remains, I brought down a metal box that turned out to be labeled *Items found in the old church foundation upon which this church was built*. For those of you who do not know the history of this church, the old church building in which we stand was constructed upon the foundation of a much older church that had been destroyed by a fire. A long time passed before I remembered the metal box and inspected its contents, but when I did, I began to understand things. I even met with my father, Peter Blake, to confirm my findings.

"Inside the box were a collection of miscellaneous items including old nails and other hardware plus eight oval-shaped discs that were very dirty. I cleaned them up and discovered that they were ceramic. I recognized the very special design on them. This design was the emblem of the Society for the Abolition of Slavery. It depicted a kneeling slave in chains surrounded by the motto, *AM I NOT A MAN AND A BROTHER?* This ceramic cameo was designed by Josiah Wedgwood in 1787. It became known as the Slave Medallion. Wedgwood sent a large number of these cameos to Benjamin Franklin in Philadelphia, and Franklin circulated them onward to his sympathetic friends.

"The significance of finding the eight Slave Medallions is that it is pretty convincing evidence that the original church on this site was a station on the Underground Railroad for escaped slaves trying to make their way to Canada and freedom. Many clergymen and committed Christians protected runaway slaves during the period leading up to the Civil War despite federal laws that made such activity illegal. There was a lot of conflict and many legal suits over the pro-freedom stance of these Christians. Many on the other side of the argument took the abolitionists' actions as participation in the theft of slaveholders' property. It is even quite likely that the old church was burned down because pro-slavery people found out that it was an Underground Railroad station.

"I asked Bill Martin to be with us today for two reasons. First, he gave me the initial clue to the hiding place of William's treasure when he told me that the only church renovation that Pastor Middlemiss requested was the installation of wall-to-wall carpeting in his study. William was not one to look for improved décor, so the only reason I could see for the carpeting was to conceal something, and the only something I could see him concealing was a trapdoor to the basement. The second reason for requesting Bill's presence is to help me pull up the carpeting in a way that makes it easy to replace it for future use.

"I'll ask the rest of you to remain here while Bill and I partially remove the carpet and find the trapdoor."

Arthur and Bill left to go to the study, and with an exchange of nods Joe and Steve followed them in case they needed additional assistance. Two other members of the federal team went to get lighting equipment from one of their trucks.

Once they were in the study, Arthur took command. "Let's start by removing the desk from the room. On several occasions I've felt something under the carpet with my toe, and William would have immediately thought of protecting the entrance with the heavy desk."

The old desk was indeed heavy, and it took four of them to pick it up. Arthur told them to put it down again.

"We have to remember that William would have set this up so that he could have access by himself. He couldn't have carried that desk away. When I went through all of his stuff in here, I found a long steel bar with a pair of wheels attached to it. Let me get that and see what it does for us."

Arthur found the bar device and put the wheeled portion under the side of the desk. Then he got down on his hands and knees, looked under the desk, and smiled. "We're on the right track. There are scratches on the bottom of the desk that line up with this thing." He stood up, pressed down on the end of the long bar, and the near side of the desk lifted easily. He rolled the raised side of the desk away from the room corner by a foot or so, and then he repeated the procedure with the far side of the desk. After he had wheeled aside both ends of the desk three times, the floor space that had been under the desk was completely exposed.

"Now, Bill, see how hard it is to remove the carpeting in that area."

Bill was kneeling down, examining the carpet and the way it was installed. "I think there's a trick to it, Arthur. This may not be bad at all. If you look closely, the trim molding above the carpet on both sides of this corner is screwed to the wall instead of nailed. I think that if I remove the screws the whole corner of the carpet will fold back as a triangular piece still attached to the moldings. Then when the moldings are screwed back onto the walls the carpet is stretched tightly again. It's a clever setup." They watched as Bill removed the screws and pulled the triangular corner of the carpet with moldings toward the center of the room. As expected, they found a trapdoor under the carpet where the desk had been. Bill inspected the trapdoor. Then he took two screwdrivers and used them to retract two spring-loaded pins that lay in grooves in the flush panel. Once the pins were retracted, he pivoted the screwdrivers slightly to enhance his grip and pulled the trapdoor open   on its concealed hinges. As soon the trapdoor started to swivel upward, Joe grabbed it with his fingers and opened it the rest of the way until it lay flat on the floor.

Joe took over. "Arthur, I think that my crew should be the first to enter the basement. We're trained to examine these sites and to avoid safety or booby-trap problems." Arthur nodded his affirmation. "Steve, go get Penny and the folks with the lighting equipment; then let's do a very careful descent. There are stairs, but they look flimsy."

The two people with the lights plus Penny and Steve came in, and the others stepped back out of the way. They found the most convenient electric outlet, tested the lights, and then Joe climbed down carefully followed by the others in his group. The opening to the basement was now a square source of bright light, illuminating Arthur's study from below.

After a few minutes, Arthur called down to Joe, "Have you found anything? What do you see?"

"I see absolutely *nada* except an empty, dirty basement. Your magic may not be working today."

"OK, Joe; that was only Act One of the magic show. Let me get my father to assist me, and then we'll have Act Two."

Arthur and Peter climbed down to join the others. "The whole point of the design of a station on the Underground Railroad was that you wanted to conceal runaway slaves so that no one could find them while they were hiding there. When the station was a church, some of the members might disagree with helping slaves to freedom and might reveal their presence if it was obvious. William might have had his cache in the main basement, but if he also realized how the old church was used, he would have looked for concealed compartments. My guess is that if such compartments are here, they are very well hidden, because the people who built our original church never found them during construction. Let's fan out and look very carefully; Dad, you've seen places like this before, so you lead the group on that side while I take this side."

Joe and Penny accompanied Arthur while Steve and the others went with Peter. Arthur pulled a candle from his pocket and lit it. Penny noticed that Peter was doing the same thing at the other end of the basement.

"I brought this candle because you have to remember that even hidden slaves have to breathe. They designed the hidden compartments to have air flowing through them. Let's walk along this wall and look for the candle flame to deflect."

The basement walls were constructed of brick with large vertical wooden posts between the brick wall segments. They walked along the walls placing the candle flame at different points on the brick walls and also near the wooden posts. There was no flame deflection along one wall and most of the next one until they reached a brick section next to double vertical wooden posts. At this point the flame went horizontal and pointed toward the wall.

Arthur smiled. "Apparently there is lower air pressure in the compartment than there is in the main room so that air flows from the big room into the compartment. If the air pressure in the compartment was higher, the flame would point away from the wall." He called over to Peter, "Dad, we have something over here."

Everyone gathered by Arthur and joined in examining the wall.

Arthur continued, "It always amuses me in treasure hunt movies when they find ancient secret rooms that open with the touch of a button or by moving a special brick. That would require a power source, and there's no way they could have that after many years of being abandoned. The best they could do would be to release a latch and then have the explorer supply the energy to open the room."

Arthur was examining the double post while he talked. "If I were designing a hidden room with an access latch, I would probably use a double vertical post, one to support the ceiling and the other to use as a release lever." He grabbed a bolt sticking out of the post on the left and pulled. The top of the post moved forward, pivoting about a point near the bottom of the post. Arthur continued pulling until the top of the post had moved outward about one foot from its original position and would not move out any more. Then he moved left to the brick wall section next to the post and pushed on the near end of it. Slowly it started to rotate inward. Others helped, and soon the wall section had pivoted about a vertical axis halfway across it to reveal a room behind the wall. Joe shined his light into the recess and saw a room eight feet deep filled with crates and stacked paintings. "We've found what we were looking for."

Penny took out her camera and started to document the paintings, jewelry, and other items that they had found. Arthur surveyed them briefly and then exchanged a few words with Joe. After Joe nodded, Arthur went back upstairs and invited John Hendrix and Maria Svenson to join them below.

When John and Maria reached the basement, they looked into the brightly-illuminated hidden room, and John gave a sigh of relief. "This is just about all that William had. In all those years he held on to virtually everything. I would have expected him to have sold most of it, but with his vocation and lifestyle he really didn't need any more cash."

Maria added, "That's what made life with him so difficult. He wanted things he didn't need and scorned things that were basic to a happy life like friendships."

John and Maria winked at each other, shook hands with Arthur, and then headed back upstairs. Before they left, Arthur told them that they could send down the others.

Bobby Andrews soon descended the ladder followed by Al Gomez and Irma. Bobby looked into the hidden room, whistled, and said, "I'm glad this aspect of the case isn't my responsibility. You're going to have to do a tremendous amount of documentation and follow-up paperwork on this collection. You'll have job security for years."

Penny laughed. "When you have an organization the size of the U.S. Government, all of the follow-up work goes to different agencies and departments. We're just supposed to find things like this   and pass the results to others. Pretty soon we'll be off looking for more."

Irma looked at the treasure in the hidden room with a feeling of amazement. She had never seen such a collection except in movies. She turned to speak with Arthur but didn't see him. She thought at first that he had left the basement. As she scanned the whole area, she spotted him studying a wall at the other side of the main room where there was another double post set. She approached him with a feeling that something else was about to be revealed. "Are you being anti-social, or are you about to do another magic trick?"

"More likely the latter." Arthur pulled on a bolt head on the right-hand post of the pair, and once again the top of the post swiveled out one foot. He called for Bobby to come over with a light and then began to push on the end of the brick wall segment as he had before. The wall pivoted inward, but instead of discovering another large hidden room, Arthur found the opening to a rather small passageway. He turned to Irma and Bobby.

"Do you know what that is?"

Bobby was the first to respond, "It looks like another way out of the basement."

"Right you are, Chief. The designers of Underground Railroad stations knew that they might have trouble with hoodlums trying to recapture escaped slaves on behalf of their owners or for reward money. To avoid confrontations they sometimes designed escape routes from the building. This tunnel appears to have been constructed for that purpose. From the direction it takes, it probably connected with the basement of the original house that was on the property where Rose Nowicki now lives. My guess is that William was planning to continue living in Rose's basement apartment after he retired in order to connect a tunnel from her house to this passageway. Once he had made that connection he could remove his valuables from the church basement at his convenience without anyone knowing what was happening."

Bobby shrugged. "I wouldn't have believed that he had that much planning and perseverance in him."

"Like I said, William hid behind a mask that made him appear humble, mean-spirited, and somewhat pitiable; but he was actually very shrewd and in control of everything that went on around him. When I was first assigned to this church after William died, the District Superintendent cautioned me that there was more to William than met the eye and that he had scared off members of the congregation by his antisocial behavior. The D.S. had been worried that the investigation of William's death might lead to something that would cause embarrassment for the United Methodist Church nationally. She was correct in seeing the potential for difficulties, but if we keep press reports to a minimum, we'll avoid major problems. William was an anomaly. Whatever he did was due to his twisted character and should not taint the reputation of the Church."

Sergeant Al Gomez approached with additional flashlights. "Shall we explore the tunnel? I've done some spelunking in the past, and it's great fun."

Gomez led the way, followed by Arthur, Irma, and Bobby. They were surprised to discover that the tunnel had two side branches, but they found that these ended less than ten feet from the main route, and both were blocked by cave-ins. The main passageway was high enough for them to walk without crouching, and it continued for about one hundred feet in the direction of Rose Nowicki's house. Then their flashlights revealed that it ended in another cave-in. Sergeant Gomez went on ahead to see if he could clear the obstruction while the rest discussed the amount of work that must have been required to create the tunnel. Suddenly, Al Gomez called out to them.

"I said before that exploring caves is fun, but I should have said it usually is. This exploration just lost its charm. I've discovered skeletons."

Irma and Bobby hurried to the end of the tunnel. After examining the bones for several minutes, Irma stood up. "These are definitely very old, probably the same vintage as the original church. There are three skeletons, although some parts of them are buried under the cave-in as though they were trying to dig further when the tunnel collapsed. I don't see any shovels, but there are two very old and rusty knives that may have been their only tools for digging. The skeletons appear to be those of a man, a woman, and a young girl. If I had to guess, I would say that they were fleeing the smoke from the fire that burned down the church when they became trapped in the blocked tunnel. I don't see any signs of trauma that hadn't already healed by the time of their death, so I would guess that they died from smoke inhalation. They appear to be a family of runaway slaves who were burned out of their hiding place by their pursuers. Their only chance of escaping was this tunnel, and they found it blocked."

Arthur said a silent prayer for these people who had died so cruelly and so long ago. "It appears that you do have jurisdiction over something that we're finding today, Bobby."

# CHAPTER 71
## FAREWELL

P astor Arthur Blake looked out at the sanctuary and surrounding balcony that were completely full of people. Seated with him in the raised altar area were the Bishop, all of the District Superintendents from across the Northern Illinois Conference of the United Methodist Church, and all of the other clergy from Parkville churches. The two front pews were filled with political dignitaries, including the Governors of Illinois, Iowa, and Wisconsin. The U-shaped surrounding balcony was filled with the massed choirs of twelve Chicago churches in their colorful robes.

The organist completed the playing of the musical prelude, and Arthur stepped up to the lectern.

"I want to welcome all of you to this memorial service for a very special family. We don't know the names of this Mother, Father, and Daughter who have been with us but not among us for more than a century and a half, but we owe them our deepest sympathies as well as a debt of gratitude. It is said that a journey of a thousand miles starts with a single step. This family, along with others, took that first step by running away from slavery. They did so with the assistance and kindness of Christian believers who operated a station of the Underground Railroad within a small church. That church stood on the same ground as the church in which we worship today. For a very long time, Mother, Father, and Daughter have laid at the site of their tragic death without benefit of either a memorial observance or proper internment. Today, we are going to rectify that situation with the help of all of you who are present. Today, we are going to honor them with a memorial service that will give them, in death, the dignity and recognition that they were never accorded in life. Following this service, the remains of this family will be escorted by members of all of the military services of the United States of America to a final resting place within sight of the tomb of Abraham Lincoln in Oak Ridge Cemetery in Springfield, Illinois. There they will be forever watched over by the Great Emancipator and all who visit his shrine.

"Thank you all for coming. The rest of this service will be led by our Bishop and the District Superintendents who have honored us with their presence on this special day. I also want to recognize the participation of many clergy members who have joined us within the congregation from other Christian denominations and from other religions as well. Today we all gather in unity as we at last honor this very special family."

Arthur sat down, and the Bishop approached the lectern to initiate a memorial service which was emotionally and spiritually beyond anything that those present could remember. All who were there knew that they were paying their last respects to real people who had suffered through the bleakest period in American history. This was not a rally for a concept; this service was an expression of love for three neighbors whose lives had been cut short a very long time ago, but who remained in the midst of those present for one final opportunity to ask their forgiveness and their fellowship.

When the service ended, everyone remained standing as a Military Honor Guard marched in from the two sides of the sanctuary. With precision that showed the utmost respect, they hoisted the single flag-draped coffin containing the remains of the unknown slave family and carried it with synchronized steps to the rear of the sanctuary and outside to a flag-decorated hearse that would bear it to Springfield as part of a special convoy of military vehicles. Once in Springfield, the coffin would be transferred to a horse-drawn wagon that had once carried the body of Abraham Lincoln, for its final journey to internment.

Two hours after the end of the Memorial Service, Arthur was sitting alone on the steps of the old church when Ed Jensen came around the corner of the building and sat down on the step next to him.

"Arthur, when you were first assigned to this church and took part in your first Church Council meeting, we complained to you that, years previously, when we built the new building, we made it too large for our needs and our economic situation. We also said that Pastor Middlemiss had driven away quite a few members of our congregation due to his attitudes and behavior. You expressed your belief that if we did our part in serving others, that building would someday be filled. Here we sit, just a few months after you joined us, and the new church building has been filled twice, once for the Antiques Fair and once for the Memorial Service today. We've even had some of our former members come back because they see positive things happening. I just wanted to stop by to tell you that everyone on the Church Council thinks that we are very fortunate to have you here and that we've petitioned the District Superintendent to give you a long-term assignment with us. The members of the Church Council managed to get Superintendent King aside for a private discussion following the Memorial Service. We presented her with our written petitions, and we each individually told her why we wanted you to stay. At first she seemed to be hostile to the idea, but after we completed our verbal statements, she softened her voice and relaxed her posture, almost as if she were giving in after a long argument. Then she said, 'It is the duty of the District Superintendent to listen to the needs and wishes of the laity. Without the lay members the church cannot carry out its mission to grow discipleship.' Then Superintendent King walked away to join Bishop Chandler who had been standing nearby. As she approached him, he smiled and shook her hand. They left with the other clergy notables and were discussing something as they entered the car."

"Ed, you've just served one of my biggest needs, the lack of stability in my ministerial career. Until now, my lack of seniority and my unconventional outlook have tended to shorten the length of time that I'm welcome in a particular assignment. I appreciate the fact that you've become comfortable with me and my ways. I've come to value and enjoy fellowship with the members of this congregation and the rest of the people of Parkville. We've had a lot of excitement around here since I arrived. Hopefully, the future will be more mundane and relaxed. This is a great congregation. We'll build our membership based on our shared church family experiences."

"Shirley wanted me to tell you one additional bit of news, Arthur. She said that Jeremy is going to get an Outstanding Citizen award from the Village Manager for helping to apprehend that drug dealer with the stolen antique statue. Shirley says that this development has redirected Jeremy's career outlook toward becoming a detective or an F.B.I. agent. He had been interested in law enforcement in the past, but thought that he had blown his chance because of his underage drinking run-in with the police. Shirley says that Jeremy must have been paying attention when you first came, because he now thinks that he really will be the hero of his life story."

# CHAPTER 72
## THANKSGIVING

K atie ran from her car onto the front porch of the wonderfully familiar yellow-sided house, and hugged her mother as though she had been away from her for a very long time.

"Mom, it's so good to be back at home. Chicago is great, but there's no place like Vermont."

Before she could say any more about how she felt, Katie was interrupted by the sound of another car entering the driveway. The car door slammed shut and young Dr. John Svenson ran up to join in a three-way hug with his sister and his mother.

"You guys won't believe what happened yesterday at the hospital. They let me operate rather than just assist, and I saved a guy's life. It was amazing. I think I really am meant to be a surgeon."

Maria laughed. "Well, hello to you too. You mean after all that investment of time and money, you're only now deciding you made a good choice? Congratulations on both the career choice and the life saved. I'm really impressed."

Katie's enthusiasm boiled over. "When this guy drove up and interrupted my news, I was about to tell you that I've been assigned at the Aquarium to be the primary caregiver for our one-year-old beluga whale, Miki. He's the cutest creature ever. They even gave him a big public birthday party in August. Now they're renovating the Oceanarium where the belugas live, so the whales have been moved to the Mystic Aquarium in Connecticut, and

I've been temporarily transferred with them. I'll be closer to you for visits."

"I see that my children are both very satisfied with their careers. That's the way it should be. You both have good news to share; that makes it even better. Now, is anyone interested in whether I have good news to share?"

Katie raised an eyebrow. "Do you have news that's better than spending time with a baby beluga whale?"

John stared at his mother. "I don't believe that you could have better news than saving a life."

Maria hugged them once again in appreciation of their zest for life. "I'm sure that you remember my telling you that my father, your grandfather, died before you were born."

Both Katie and John nodded assent, not knowing where their mother was going with this conversation.

"Well, we're going to have a special Thanksgiving this year, because he's waiting in the family room to meet you. Come inside with me so that we can have the best family reunion ever!"

# Epilogue

On September 26, 2005, the United States Justice Department issued a statement saying that the government "regrets the improper conduct of certain of its military personnel" with regard to the theft of valuable items from the "Hungarian Gold Train" after it was captured by U.S. forces in May of 1945. The statement further said, "The United States expresses its sympathy and solidarity with these victims and hopes that the settlement approved by the district court will provide meaningful assistance to those survivors." This apology by the U.S. government was required as part of the settlement approved by a federal judge in Miami on September 26, 2005. This action ended a suit filed by Hungarian Jewish survivors in 2001. Under the agreed terms, the United States will distribute 25.5 million dollars to needy Jews around the world through social agencies, principally those in Israel, Hungary, the United States and Canada.

New York Congressman Jose E. Serrano commented, "The resolution of this issue brings closure to a sad episode in our nation's history—both in the initial actions of the U.S. Army, and also in the 60-year delay in justice. Our nation is stronger for having admitted this mistake."

Suggested Further Reading

Kenneth D. Alford, *The Spoils of World War II*, Birch Lane Press, Carol Publishing Group, 1994

# WORKS BY THIS AUTHOR
NONFICTION:

*DECISION TIME! Better Decisions for a Better Life,*
VBW Publishing, Inc.
ISBN 978-1-60264-063-4 (paperback)
ISBN 978-1-60264-064-1 (hard cover)
RADMAR Publishing
ISBN 978-0-9829160-7-0 (2nd edition paperback)
ISBN 978-1-4581-8395-8 (Smashwords eBook)
ASIN B0052GOZEO (Kindle Edition eBook)

Where you are in life today is the result of all of the past decisions you have made or which have been made for you in response to the various situations and events that have impacted your life. The decisions that you will make from this point forward will determine the degree to which your future will be positive or negative. *DECISION TIME!* gives you insight into the subjective decision-making process as applied to both small and large choices you will face. It includes dynamic aspects, cultural effects, and morality as applied to decision-making for individuals, teams, corporations, and societies. *DECISION TIME!* prepares you to face the continuous impacts of decision situations confidently and without hesitation.

# FICTION:

*Lead Us Not into Temptation (The Lord's Prayer Mystery Series, Volume I),*
VBW Publishing, Inc.
ISBN 978-1-60264-407-6 (paperback)
RADMAR Publishing
ISBN 978-0-9976381-0-3 (2nd edition paperback)
ISBN 978-1-4581-7381-2 (Smashwords eBook)
ASIN B0052MGI6Q (Kindle Edition eBook)

Arthur Blake, former NASA engineer turned minister, receives an emergency appointment to be pastor of the United Methodist Church in Parkville, a distant suburb of Chicago, following the bizarre sudden death of the church's unusual former pastor. Pastor Blake's attempts to unravel the mystery that shrouds his predecessor become involved with tracking the child of a possibly bigamous soldier in World War II England, art and jewelry treasures plundered by the Nazis and their sympathizers, and the eventual results of childhood sibling conflicts in combined families. Arthur's allies in his investigation include Parkville Police Chief Bobby Andrews, County Medical Examiner Irma Custis, and the married team of Penny and Joe Gonzalez who work for a clandestine government agency. During the course of *Lead Us Not into Temptation*, the reader discovers how seemingly minor historical events lead to major present-day dislocations in church, village, and family relationships.

*Give Us this Day Our Daily Bread (The Lord's Prayer Mystery Series, Volume II)*
RADMAR Publishing
ISBN 978-0-9829160-0-1 (paperback)
ISBN 978-0-9829160-5-6 (2nd edition paperback)
ISBN 978-1-4580-6717-3 (Smashwords eBook)
ASIN B0052MQI66 (Kindle Edition eBook)

Arthur Blake, Pastor of Parkville United Methodist Church, has to deal with the aftereffects of a traumatic communion incident. He works to assist the authorities in investigating the cause while doing his best to convince members of his congregation that it is safe to return to church. Working with the police and federal agencies, he discovers that the terror of the initial event is minor compared with the potential chaotic impact of future disasters being planned by the perpetrator. The investigation is interwoven with several relationship situations that affect the final outcome.

*Forgive Us Our Trespasses (The Lord's Prayer Mystery Series, Volume III)*
RADMAR Publishing
ISBN 978-0-9829160-1-8 (paperback)
ISBN 978-1-4657-3739-7 (Smashwords eBook)
ASIN B005SULQ6Y (Kindle Edition eBook)

Arthur Blake, Pastor of Parkville United Methodist Church, tries to assist his father to resolve his trauma after learning that his best friend, recently killed in a car accident, may have been an imposter with a heinous background. The investigation reveals that the presumed accident was but one link in a chain of murders. Blake works to determine the true identity of his father's friend, while also discovering the man's past activities and affiliations. Arthur works to solve the murders in conjunction with his colleagues at ABC Consultants. He also draws on assistance from associates at a covert government agency with which he has worked before. The coordinated effort to solve the puzzle examines incidents that span the period between World War II and the present in order to defuse the personal, national, and international dangers resulting from them.

*Thy Will Be Done (The Lord's Prayer Mystery Series, Volume IV)*
RADMAR Publishing
ISBN 978-0-9829160-2-5 (paperback)
ISBN 978-1-3013-4293-8 (Smashwords eBook)
ASIN B009JU6EZM (Kindle Edition eBook)

The sudden death of a young woman attending Parkville United Methodist Church infuriates her brother and leads to congregational outrage over his outburst and subsequent murder. The investigation of that slaying by Pastor Arthur Blake and his associates leads to revelations of a previously undetected criminal organization operating in the area. Unraveling the mystery and scope of this group entangles Arthur and his associated investigators in a web of conspiracies extending from Illinois to both U.S. coasts and through Mexico to Guatemala.

*Deliver Us from Evil (The Lord's Prayer Mystery Series, Volume V)*
RADMAR Publishing
ISBN 978-0-9829160-3-2 (paperback)
ASIN B00EBDUXFY (Kindle Edition eBook)

Arthur and Irma's wedding day has finally arrived, but an unexpected interruption leads to their need to investigate a possible murder committed by someone close to them. With the aid of friends and federal agents Penny and Joe Gonzalez, they follow a series of clues, crisscrossing the United States to learn more about the murder, related subsequent events, and the significance of a rare object brought home by a veteran of the Iraq War. A second murder close to Pastor Arthur Blake's church involves them in a new investigation, assisting Parkville Police Chief Bobby Andrews. Are these murders and the tracking of that strange object connected? Will marriage deteriorate or improve the relationship between Arthur and Irma? Character flaws in many relationships color the outcome.

*Overcoming: An Anthology by the Writers of OCWW*
Edited and with an Introduction by Richard Davidson
RADMAR Publishing
ISBN 978-9829160-4-9 (paperback)
ASIN B00E80NN4I (Kindle Edition eBook)

This anthology covers many aspects of overcoming life's problems, obstacles, and challenging developments. The contributing writers have used fiction, non-fiction, memoir, poetry, historical chronicle, and drama to highlight our continuing need to overcome our problems, rather than dwell on them. The reader will learn from many talented writers the skills needed to respond constructively, energetically, and sometimes humorously to whatever obstacle bars one's path. Apply their lessons to your own needs and to those of others you cherish.

*Implications: An Arthur Blake Mystery Novel (Imp Mysteries, Volume 1)*
RADMAR Publishing
ISBN 978-0-9829160-6-3 (paperback)
ASIN B00LY9IBWK (Kindle Edition eBook)

Bishop Howard Chandler has assigned Pastor Arthur Blake to investigate the burning of a church in the small city of Amboy, Illinois. He learns from that church's pastor that she had to overcome past improprieties by former members. During the investigation of the fire's cause, Arthur and the other state fire investigators uncover disturbing aspects of the ninety-year-old church's design and history. Arthur calls on his federal associates for assistance, as the investigation of a local church fire expands to seeking solutions to related crimes occurring from the present to recent years and back to the Prohibition Era. Progress in the investigation intertwines with new developments in Arthur's family life.

*Impulses: An Arthur Blake Mystery Novel (Imp Mysteries, Volume 2)*
RADMAR Publishing
ISBN 978-0-9829160-8-7 (paperback)
ASIN B012LFQXYI (Kindle Edition eBook)

Several disturbing dreams cause Arthur Blake to wonder whether he is trying to do too much for the many people who seek his services. These qualms are complicated by Bishop Howard Chandler's suggestion that Arthur temporarily set aside his official duties and take an extended sabbatical leave. His resulting internal debates about career moves are set aside when the pastor who replaced him at the Parkville church dies in an apparent suicide possibly linked to several deaths at the Parkville Rehabilitation Home. The bishop assigns Arthur to determine the circumstances behind the new pastor's death, while Arthur and Irma, his wife and constant investigative partner, also study a mysterious shipment at his father's antiques shop. The sudden disappearance of a young associate provides another mystery and leads to questions of life after death and reincarnation. Events that initially appear simple become increasingly complex as the true natures of many people come into question.

*Impostor: A Genealogical Mystery (Imp Mysteries, Volume 3)*
RADMAR Publishing
ISBN 978-0-9829160-9-4

When Debbie Danforth discovers a flaw in the genealogy of her live-in boyfriend, Jeremy Hadley, he and his family try to discredit her findings, but eventually admit they must be true. Jeremy and Debbie run a private detective business, the Sandley Agency and commit their skills and resources to learning about the impostor Debbie has discovered in the Hadley ancestry. They are assisted in this effort by Penny and Joe Gonzalez, principals in a covert federal agency, with whom Jeremy has previously worked as a consultant. Their joint investigation uncovers both unique details concerning the mysterious Hadley impostor and little-known facts about events leading up to World War II in both Britain and the United States. Was the person who masqueraded as a Hadley a villain or a hero? Did other Hadleys know he was a fraudulent member of their family? Did his actions assist or impede the British and the Americans as they faced the growing menace in prewar Europe?

Learn more about the writings, humor, and random thoughts of Richard Davidson at: radmarinc.com davidsonbookshelf.com betterlifedecisions.blogspot.com and at the Independent Mystery Publishing Society (IMPS) https://www.mysteryimps.com Richard Davidson's author page on Amazon is located at https://www.amazon.com/author/richarddavidson Follow and *Like* Richard Davidson, Author on Facebook at https://www.facebook.com/richarddavidsonauthor?ref=hl Follow him on Twitter @mysteryimp

www.ingramcontent.com/pod-product-compliance
Lightning Source LLC
Chambersburg PA
CBHW051242260626
47162CB00002B/555